NOLA

STREET TALES

COST TO BE THE BOSS

THE FINALE

A Novel by

E. Nigma

To submit a manuscript for our review,

email us at

submissions@majorkeypublishing.com

Synopsis

Almost two months after the war with Dre ended, Sharice is offered a chance to get what she's always wanted, which is the title of boss in the Faction Organization once again by accepting a job to take over the Houston drug trade. To achieve this rank, she's going to need to get her team together, which is easier said than done.

Her longtime friend, Connie, is just getting back on her feet after her hospital stay. Bull has been MIA still struggling with his emotions after being ordered to kill his best friend. Michelle and James continue their undercover affair with each other, which is starting to cause problems with Michelle's boyfriend, Theo. Lastly, Sharice's old flame, Jerome, is off doing his own thing with little contact with her since they decided to split with each other.

Sharice also will have her hands full with Rock, the dealer who runs most of the Houston drug that has been battling the Faction crew for the past couple of months and winning. Unlike any enemy she's faced before, Rock and his crew are just as calculating and intelligent as Sharice, making this her most challenging foe to date.

With the FBI receiving an increased budget to deal with her crew, and a Houston drug organization not backing down, Sharice will have to pull out all the stops to outsmart her opponents to be able to claim the boss status she's wanted for quite some time. There is a cost to be the boss, and Sharice will pay whatever it takes to defeat her enemies to come out on top.

Acknowledgment/Dedications – N/A

Author Notes – N/A

Contact/Social Media Info

Facebook   - www.enigmakidd.com
IG   -   enigmakidd
Snapchat   -   ericnigma
Twitter   -   @NigmaEric
Email - enigmakidd@gmail.com

Chapter 1

Road to Recovery

It's just after midnight at an all-night fast-food establishment in one of Houston's notorious neighborhoods, Sunnyside. There are a good bit of customers taking advantage of the late-night hours as this chicken spot is one of the best in the city. The parking lot is filled with cars, some that are decked out with rims, exotic paint jobs, and expensive sound systems that shook the ground with the loud bass sounds. As the almost party atmosphere went on at the local shop, Jose and Emmanuel make their way through the crowd with their food in their hands and take a seat at an unoccupied bench in the middle of the seating area. Jose looked around the area and chuckles before taking a sip of his drink.

"It's off the chain over here, holmes," Jose said. "I mean, look at these bitches out here. Reminds me of back home."

"Fuck that," Emmanuel responded, waving off his friend. "Don't ever compare these hoes to Miami hoes. This piece of shit city doesn't have nothing on home. You're just trippin' because you ain't got shit since you been here."

Jose looked at his friend, almost like he was offended with that statement.

"The fuck you talkin' about? I've been through several hoes since I've been down here," he responded.

"Bullshit! We've been down here for a month and a half now, and I ain't seen you with one bitch so far," Emmanuel replied before taking a bite of his chicken. "You know good and damn well that these hoes don't have shit on back home. Now that I think about it, you wasn't gettin' shit there either!"

Emmanuel chuckled as Jose waved him off once again.

"Get the fuck outta here with all that," he rebuked

before changing the subject. "Man, I'm sick of being out here for real. How long we gotta stay out here, you think?"

"Until the job is done," Emmanuel answered. "That vato Rock is makin' this shit harder than it needs to be. If we could get a lead on his ass and drop him, we'd be home tomorrow."

"What are you talkin' about?" Jose questioned. "We know he's out in the Fifth Ward. Knowing where he is ain't the issue. Getting there unnoticed is. Puto never leaves the block. I'm just sayin', how long are they gonna make us wait for this shit? They should swap us out, like the military and shit."

Emmanuel burst into laughter as Jose started digging into his meal.

"Nigga, is you high?" He teased, poking fun at his friend. "This is the Faction life, holmes. This ain't no diplomatic bullshit. We're not stationed overseas and shit. Rico and them want us to take care of this shit. If it takes us another ten minutes, or ten years, we're here 'til the shit is done. They paid us top money, and they expect results not no 'we should swap out' bullshit. The fuck is the matter with you?"

Jose didn't respond as he took several more bites of his food. Emmanuel sipped his drink before turning his attention back to his friend.

"You know what I think? I think you need some cono," he responded, smirking. "I'm just sayin', you haven't been in shit since you been down here. Why don't I hook you up with Angie? She's been lookin' for someone to smash. She likes cocaine boys. She's not a bad piece of ass, and cute too. Let me set that up for you."

"Please," a disgusted Jose responded. "I wouldn't fuck that puta with your dick. As many niggas that then ran through her. Stop it."

"I'm just lookin' out for you. You gettin' all homesick, and shit, and you said these women out here tonight are the shit," Emmanuel reminded his friend. "Angie will take care of you. Get all that frustration out of that polla of yours."

"Fuck you," Jose responded with a chuckle before continuing to eat his meal.

Emmanuel chuckled himself when out of the blue, two

women walked over and approached the two friends. Jose looked up and was surprised by their beauty as one of the females was wearing a halter top with her breasts slightly peeking out from her v-neck top. She's also wearing some booty shorts with fashionable heels. The other female was dressed similarly, the only difference, outside of color and designer is she's wearing Vans shoes.

"Hey, boo. You mind if we sit with y'all?" One of the ladies asked.

Emmanuel chuckled as he nodded his head. He checked out the one that sat next to him and is instantly attracted to her. She smiles back at him behind her dark black bob hair.

"Thanks. It's packed like a bitch out here tonight," one of the females responded. "These heels got my feet hurtin' like a mug out here."

"I told your ass you was doin' too much," the other female said as she flirtingly runs her fingers through her mahogany streaked hair. "Y'all don't mind her. She out here tryin' to look like she's livin' her best life and shit, and now her feet hurt."

"Oh, it's no problem at all," Emmanuel reassured with a flirty smirk. "So who y'all here with?"

"We're here with us," the bob haired female responded. "We're waiting to get our order and bounce to a party goin' down tonight."

"Is that a fact?" Emmanuel replied as he got a little closer to the female next to him. "Why don't you skip the party and hang with me and my man here, Ms…?"

"Rhianna," the bob haired female said, smirking. "And why would we blow off a party for some guys we met at a chicken shack?"

"Because me and my man here can show you a good time," Emmanuel answered before turning to his friend. "Ain't that right, Jose?"

Jose nodded his head but was speechless, looking into the brown eyes of the mahogany haired female.

"Hey, Jose. I'm Peaches," she said, knowing she had his full attention. "So you gonna let your friend speak for you? You tryin' to make a friend tonight?"

"I don't know, Peaches. I mean, are you as sweet as your name sounds?" Jose replied, causing her to giggle.

"I don't know. I kinda like this one," Peaches said to Rhianna. "He looks like he could use a friend for the night."

"What about the party though?" questioned Rhianna.

"Girl, you know that shit gonna be goin' all night. We have some time," Peaches said with a smile. "So what y'all lookin' to get into tonight? I mean, don't be wastin' our time."

"Never that," Emmanuel said with a chuckle. "After y'all get your order, why not head back to our crib so we can get to know each other a little better?"

Before Peaches or Rhianna could respond, blood suddenly splattered everywhere. Jose had been shot in the head by a masked figure, who had slowly made his way behind him. Emmanuel was terrified as he quickly reached into his belt strap, trying to pull his gun out. He's unable to as the masked gunman fired a shot into his head as well splattering more blood on both Peaches and Rhianna, who are terrified. The crowd began to scatter with all the commotion going on as Peaches turned to the masked gunman with anger in her eyes.

"What the fuck?!" She screamed as she tried to wipe the blood from her face. "You were supposed to wait for us to pick up our order before ridin'!"

"Girl, shut the fuck up and get in the car," the masked gunman responded as a getaway vehicle pulled up to the curb.

"This is some bullshit, Double R," Peaches said as she and Rhianna quickly rose and ran over to the car.

Double R looked around the area and checked his victims once more before running over to the getaway car as well. After he was in, the car burned rubber and quickly made its way out of the area and down the block.

A few days later, in New Orleans, Connie and Sharice exited their vehicle in front of a hole in the wall restaurant. Sharice looked around confused before turning her attention back toward her friend.

"What the fuck is this, Connie?" She asked before looking towards the restaurant. "I've been in the east plenty of times, but I don't remember this place."

"You gotta have an open mind going to a place like

this," Connie teased with a sinister grin. "Besides, you said I can pick where we ate at."

"Yeah, but I was talkin' about a nice place or somethin'. Where the fuck you got me going?" Sharice inquired, causing Connie to shrug.

"You'll see. Come on, I think you'll like it," Connie responded as she leads the way.

Sharice frowned but followed her friend. They are about to enter the restaurant when Sharice's cell phone suddenly rang. She motioned Connie to wait as she picked up the line.

"Yeah... what? Why are you calling me with that? Get with Kristy, she'll take care of it... yeah... just call her, okay?" Sharice said before hanging up the line. "I swear to god, them hoes are gonna drive me insane!"

"Cathouse again?" Connie asked as she approached her friend.

"Yeah. So, some dumb bitch ran outta condoms and decided to steal some from one of the other girls. One thing led to another, and... you know what? Fuck it. I don't wanna even talk about it," Sharice responded as she

15

grabbed her head in frustration. "Sick of dealin' with hoes and cathouses. Mike is just doin' this shit to punish me for that whole Dre fiasco."

"It's been over a month with that shit. When's he gonna let it go?" Connie replied.

"You know good and well that nigga carries a grudge," Sharice pointed out before putting her cell phone in her purse. "He's more of a bitch than the hoes at the house."

Connie laughed as Sharice managed a smirk herself.

"I'll be glad when I can hand that shit off to somebody else. Fuckin' Money and his hurt feelings!" Sharice said before looking towards her friend once again. "My bad, I don't wanna bring this shit out today. I know I've been promisin' you a lunch since you got out of the hospital. So let's just get some food and forget about all these raggedy as hoes."

Connie smiled as she led Sharice into the restaurant. Sharice was stunned when she walked in and noticed naked Asian women lying on the tables in the restaurants as the customers eat their Chinese delicacies off of their bodies. Sharice quickly turned to Connie, who burst into laughter.

"Seriously, Connie?" Sharice asked as her friend continued laughing at her.

"Aye, my bad," Connie responded, still chuckling. "I mean, I didn't know we was gonna have that conversation, for real. Hey, you said I pick where I wanted to eat. This place is cool, for real."

Sharice shook her head as Connie walked over to the host.

"Peng, what's up, my dude?" She said as she walked over to an elated Peng.

"Connie! My dear, where have you've been? We've missed you," he said in a strong Asian accent as the two shared a hug.

"Hey, I've been away for a minute, but I'm back now, baby," she replied. "All I've been thinking about is gettin' some raw fish from this spot, ya dig."

"We'll have your usual table set up in just a minute," Peng said before scurrying off.

Sharice looked at her friend with her arms folded in disbelief as Connie shrugged.

"Don't knock it until you try it," Connie pointed out to her friend. "They have some of the best sushi in town. They got good reviews and shit. Trust me."

Sharice rolled her eyes as Peng quickly rejoined them with a smile on his face a few moments later.

"Ladies, right this way," he said before leading them to their table. "I've had them prepare some of your favorites, Ms. Connie. I hope you don't mind."

"Not at all, Peng," Connie responded smirking.

As they arrive at their private booth, Sharice was still uncomfortable as an assortment of sushi was on top of a female Asian worker already lying upon their table. Connie quickly took a seat as she licked her lips in anticipation of her meal and the sexy female that graced their table.

"If there's anything I can get you, please let me know," Peng said as Sharice stopped him from leaving.

"Yeah, check this out, can I get a plate with the food on it?" Sharice asked.

"There are plates on the table," a confused Peng responded.

"No, see, I want some of that on a plate," Sharice tried to explain. "I don't want my food on top of anyone. Just a plate with the same shit from the back."

Peng looked at Sharice strangely before nodding his head and making his way back to the kitchen. Sharice took a seat in the booth and watched her friend chowing down on the sushi she's plucked off the female's body.

"This is some good shit, you need to try this for real," Connie said with a mouth full of food.

Sharice cringed. The atmosphere was clearly making her uncomfortable. She distanced herself as far as she could from the table because she was just across from the female's feet. She shook her head at her friend as Connie finally noticed her friend's mood.

"What's wrong?" She asked, licking her fingers.

"What's wrong is, this is the last time I'm lettin' your ass pick the venue," Sharice quipped. "What the fuck would make you think I'd be okay with this? I mean, seriously, Connie."

"Aye, you're the one always talkin' about you need to try new shit," Connie pointed out. "I'm just sayin', this is something new. You're in one of the best sushi joints in the city with a beautiful atmosphere and shit. You need to relax and enjoy your surroundings."

"There's ass crack on the table," Sharice pointed out before looking at the female. "No offense, ma'am."

"She's not gonna respond. They're trained to lay in silence. It's an Eastern Philosophy thing," Connie responded, causing Sharice to chuckle.

"Bitch, since when are you into Eastern Philosophy?" Sharice responded, smirking.

"Shit, I got all into it when I was up in the hospital," Connie replied, causing the smirk to disappear from her friend's face. "I mean, there wasn't shit else to do, so I started readin' different shit. Maybe it was me feenin' for this shit that got me interested, I don't know."

Sharice nodded her head. Thinking about her friend sitting in the hospital still bothered her. All the days she spent by her friend's side, hoping and praying that she recovered, made her feel like a fraud at times. She's still battling with her feelings because she hasn't forgotten what Connie did to Lavina. She'd been avoiding this lunch meeting for the last couple of weeks because she didn't know how to feel. Before the shooting occurred, she was all but done with her longtime friend. After Connie took a bullet for her, however, things changed. She felt alone all those days that her friend was in the hospital. Nobody understood her life like Connie did, and knowing she almost died hurt Sharice in a way that nothing could. Still, this was the friend who hurt her with her actions as well. She made a promise to kill whoever was responsible for Lavina's death to her sister. A promise she could no longer keep.

As Sharice sighed, Peng returned with an assortment of sushi on a plate as Sharice requested. Sharice placed the plate on her lap, still keeping her distance from the table. Connie looked over and began laughing at her friend.

"Girl, you doin' too much right now," Connie said as Sharice took a bite of her food.

"Look, you do you. Don't worry about what I'm doin' over here," Sharice responded with a slight grin.

After Sharice took a few bites of her meal, Connie grabbed a napkin, wiped her face, and turned to her friend.

"So, I think it's time for me to get back in," Connie said to a confused Sharice.

"Get back in? What are you talkin' about?" Sharice asked.

"You know what I mean. I want back in the game," Connie answered. "I've been sittin' on the sidelines for a minute now. Injury aside, I'm feelin' good. I'm ready to hit the streets again."

Sharice nodded her head, bringing attention to the female on the table, which Connie waved off.

"I ain't said nothing real," Connie responded, knowing what her friend was trying to say. "I'm just sayin', I've been in-house long enough. I want back in. I'm ready."

Sharice took a few bites of her food as she pondered her friend's request.

"Connie, there's a place and time to discuss shit like that, and this ain't it," she responded, letting her friend down. "You're just gettin' back on your feet. The doctor said take it slow. No need for you to jump back in and risk hurtin' yourself."

"But I feel fine. Ain't no reason I can't-"

"I said not here," a stern Sharice said, cutting off her friend.

Connie sighed, disappointed by her friend's decision. Sharice noticed her friend's mood and took a deep breath before responding.

"Look, I'll give it some thought, okay?" Sharice said, changing Connie's mood. "But not here. We'll talk. Cool?"

"For sure," Connie responded with a smile. "So, since we can't talk about that, let's talk about somethin' else. What's up with you and Jerome?"

Sharice rolled her eyes as Connie once again touched on a subject she didn't want to discuss.

"There's nothin' up with us. We decided to take a break. I had shit I wanted to do, and our thing just wasn't gonna work," Sharice admitted. "It's for the best right now."

"So what I'm hearin' is you not gettin' no dick," Connie responded smirking.

"I just told you about how I'm tryin' to do my thing, and the only thing you took from that is I'm not gettin' any dick?" Sharice asked, confused.

"Well, are you?"

Sharice didn't respond as she dug into her food once again, confirming Connie's beliefs.

"I take that as a no," Connie replied.

"Girl, fuck you," Sharice replied with a smile. "Just eat your shit off this bitch so we can get outta here. I think I'm gonna need a doctor's appointment after eating in here."

"I'm just sayin' y'all always was good together. I don't see the problem," Connie continued trying to stay on the subject. "It's cool to have somebody like that, you know. Fuck, I had a girl I was tight with. I get shot up and shit, and I ain't heard from her since. Shit probably scared her off or somethin'."

Sharice nodded her head, knowing Connie was referring to Rose. She didn't have the heart to tell her friend that she suspected Rose was undercover law enforcement. She tried to keep a positive vibe around Connie to keep her spirits up after her hospital release and didn't think bringing her down with that news was necessary.

"Well, I'm sure there have been many other girls since you've been out," Sharice remarked.

"Oh, you know that," Connie responded with a giggle. "Still, ain't none of them ol' girl. That's why I'm sayin' if you got somebody out there you into, you need to make that shit work. Me and Rose wasn't even together like that, but somethin' about her made me open up and shit. Pussy is pussy, but to have someone you can talk to about shit... there ain't nothin' better than that."

Sharice nodded her head, surprised that Connie's newfound outlook on relationships was what it was. It did give her some things to think about regarding her and Jerome's relationship.

In a popular Miami night club, the building was filled from wall to wall with music blasting, causing the dance floor crowd to groove with the flow. In the back corner of the club was the VIP section, where Rico and several of his associates were lounging and enjoying themselves, celebrating one of his crew's birthday. While Rico's crew were enjoying themselves flirting with women and guzzling alcohol, Rico's sitting quietly enjoying a drink alone. The Houston project wasn't going as planned and was taking a lot longer than he anticipated. He wasn't in the mood to celebrate. While he's processing his next move for his Houston crew in his head, he's distracted by Agent Flores, who's undercover as a waitress in the club. She's wearing a tight skirt and a revealing top with her hair flowing. Her legs caught the eyes of the Faction boss as she walked over with a bottle of champagne.

"Hey, do you want me to top you off?" She asked, much to the pleasure of Rico.

"Sure, why not," Rico responded as he held out his glass for the undercover Fed to fill. "You must be new. I haven't seen you around here before."

"Yeah, just started last week," Flores responded.

Rico nodded his head as he took a sip of his drink. Flores was about to walk off when Rico reached out his hand and gently pulled her back.

"You look like you've had a busy night. Why don't you stay a little while? Kick your feet up," he said, motioning her to take a seat.

"Thanks, but I gotta get back," Flores answered. "I don't wanna get fired on my first week, you know."

"Well, chica, I don't think that will be a problem," Rico responded smirking. "I'm the owner of this establishment, and if I feel one of my employees needs a break, it's my duty to make sure they get that break."

Flores chuckled as she looked around as if she's considering his proposal. After a few moments, she took a seat next to him, much to his excitement.

"Would you like a taste?" He asked, offering her some of his champagne.

"No thanks, not while I'm working. Break or not," Flores said with a smile.

Rico took her in, watching her every moment. She slowly crossed her legs, knowing she had his attention, trying to work over her target.

"By the way, I didn't catch your name," Rico said.

"I thought you were the boss," Flores fired back. "Shouldn't you know my name?"

"Well, I don't complicate my life with those minor details," Rico responded as he leaned back. "Do I have to get Juan to show me your W4?"

Flores smiled, getting a little comfortable in her chair as well.

"Maria," Flores responded.

"Ah, Maria," Rico repeated. "Such a typical Latina name. Please don't tell me your last name is Smith or something like that."

"It's Juarez," Flores, rather Maria, responded. "Maria Juarez."

"Ah, Ms. Juarez," a flirtatious Rico responded, smirking. "Allow me to introduce myself. I am Ricardo Hernandez, but my friends call me Rico."

"Well, hello, Mr. Ricardo," Maria responded, flirting with her target.

"I said my friends call me Rico," he pointed out. "So you're saying you don't wanna be my friend?"

"I just met you like five seconds ago," Maria replied with a chuckle. "Let's see where the conversation goes, then we'll talk, Ricardo."

Rico chuckled as he moved in a little closer to Maria. The two were having a conversation when a crew member who was in charge of security quickly made his way from the front of the club and into the VIP area. He whispered in Rico's ear, alerting him of a call he's received. Rico's mood changed as he turned back towards Maria.

"Excuse me, Chica. I'll be right back," he said, rising from the booth and walking off with the crew member.

The two entered into a hidden back office located next to the VIP area. After the door was closed and secured, the crew member handed Rico the phone.

"Yeah, it's me," Rico answered.

He frowned as he's informed of Emmanuel and Jose's deaths in Houston. After a few moments, he hung up the line and tossed the phone across the room.

"Son of a bitch!" He yelled as he tried to get himself together.

"Boss, you alright?" His henchman asked.

Rico took a deep breath, thinking for a few moments in silence.

"I'm fine," he responded, reassuring his crew member. "Have them bring my car around. I'm done for the night."

"Sure thing, boss. What about Enrique? I mean, they

haven't even brought out the cake yet," the crew member pointed out.

"Enrique will understand. No need to ruin the party with more disparaging news," Rico replied.

The henchman nodded his head and was about to walk off when he suddenly turned back around.

"What about the chica?" He asked.

"What chica?"

"The one you were entertaining?" The henchman responded.

Rico thought for a moment but was still angry with the news he just heard.

"Tell her to get back to work," Rico responded.

The crewmember nodded his head and was about to exit the room when Rico has a change of heart.

"Wait," he said as he met the crewmember at the door.

He peeked out from the door and admired Maria's beauty from a distance once more. After a few moments of leering, he turned to his attention to the crew member.

"Apologize to her. Tell her I had to leave with pressing business. Ask her... ask her would she like to meet for dinner this Saturday. No pressure. If she accepts, tell her we'll be in touch," Rico instructed his henchman.

He nodded and walked off to carry out his boss' orders. Rico watched as the crewmember approached Maria and gave her the news. After a few moments, she smiled and nodded her head as she rose and walked off to tend to her waitressing duties. Rico leered at her for a few moments longer before he walked out of the office and headed out of the club, waiting for his car.

Later that night, Agent Flores walked into her apartment for the night and quickly began to remove her Maria persona from her body. She kicked off her heels and removed her jewelry. She took a seat on her couch and grabbed her feet one by one, which are sore from working the club all night. She took a deep breath, trying to relax when her cell phone suddenly rings. She walked over to her purse that she left by the door on the foyer area and pulled out her phone before taking a seat on the couch once again.

"Hello?" She said as she answered.

"It's me," Agent Daniels said. "Is it safe to talk?"

"Hey. Yeah, I'm just getting in," Flores responded as she kicked back onto the couch.

"How did it go tonight?" Daniels asked.

"Went pretty well. Although I don't know how long I can take these late nights working on my feet in heels," Flores responded, grabbing her head with frustration. "Tips are good though, so I guess there's a silver lining in everything."

"Anything to report?"

"No, not really," Flores said. "Well, other than the fact that I met with Rico, and he invited me on a date this weekend."

Flores giggled as Daniels chuckled himself.

"You are a piece of work, you know that?" Daniels responded. "Not even a week and you're already at the top level. How'd you pull that off?"

"Enrique Morales had a birthday party at the club tonight," Flores explained. "I didn't know that the big boss man would show up, but when he did, I made my move. It didn't take much. I was dressed for Enrique and ended up with Rico, so we're a lot further along than we had planned."

"True, but be careful," Daniels warned. "We monitored Sharice and Connie's meeting for lunch earlier today. Connie might be returning to the streets soon. If she heads to Miami, we may have to pull you."

"Relax, I got this," Flores responded, rolling her eyes. "The only people who've seen me is Connie, Sharice, and Money. Money is under our control, and Connie and Sharice have never been to Miami from what we know. So I'll be fine."

"I've been in this game a lot longer than you, Flores," Daniels warns. "Whatever can go wrong, will go wrong. Just... play this one safe, please. Rico may not be as volatile as Connie, but he's just as dangerous. He's a boss, and has many buttons he can press at any time."

"Okay, mom. I'll be on my best behavior," Flores answered with a smile. "So Connie's back in the game? It's a shame, I would have liked to have been there for that."

"Just more for us to do. Actually, it'll be fun to see how

things pan out between her and the new power on the street, Michelle," Daniels responded with a chuckle.

"Michelle, huh? Cutie pie moving on up, I see," Flores replied. "I don't know, I think my girl Connie can take her."

"A hundred bucks says Michelle comes out on top," Daniels fired back. "She's smart, cool, and calculating. One thing she's not is a hothead, unlike your old friend."

"Never underestimate Connie. She's smarter than she looks," Flores replied with a chuckle. "Anyway, let me go get some rest. I need a nice soak right now. I'll keep you posted."

Flores sighed as she hung up the phone, completely exhausted. She took a deep breath before rising from the couch and heading into the bathroom.

In New Orleans, in an uptown apartment, Michelle and James are in the bedroom having sex. James was stroking Michelle, trying to break her, but suddenly stopped mid-stroke and looked around the room, confusing Michelle.

"Are you serious right now?" Michelle asked with a

hint of attitude.

"Quiet! I thought I heard something," James whispered, continuing to look around the room.

"Nigga, you ain't slick," Michelle responded, smirking. "Your ass was about to bust, so you tryin' to slow shit down. I'm hip to your game, on the real."

"No, I thought I did hear some shit," James replied before he started working Michelle once again.

The mood was lost, however, as Michelle pushed James off to the side.

"What?" He asked, confused.

"I don't like that stop and go shit," Michelle responded. "Either you gonna do it, or you not. See, that's why I didn't wanna do this shit!"

"Get the fuck outta here with all that! You was wantin' to do this shit too, don't act like it was all me," James pointed out.

The two continue to argue back and forth when the bedroom door opened suddenly. Duke Jones, a hustler in the area, walked in, stunned to see both Michelle and James in his bed arguing with each other.

"What the fuck is this?!" He yelled, grabbing both of their attention. "Who the fuck are you? And why are y'all in my crib?"

Michelle smiled as she shook her head. Before Duke can question them again, a puff of smoke blast through the covers as a bullet hits him in his neck, causing him to fall over. Michelle quickly jumped out of bed to reveal she's holding a gun equipped with a silencer. She walked over towards Duke's fallen body and watched as he gasped for air, spitting up blood. She fired a second shot into his head, putting him out of his misery. She tiptoed around the area, making sure not to touch any blood that has splattered. After a few moments, she turned and looked towards James, who was pulling up his pants.

"He's all yours," she said as she started getting dressed as well.

"Hell naw! The deal was if you let me hit it, I'd clean up the mess afterward," James responded. "I ain't finished, for real."

"Baby, I lived up to my promise. I let you hit it," Michelle said, smirking. "As far as you not finishin' up, those are the breaks in life. Women have been livin' like that for years. Deal with it, champ."

Michelle walked out of the bedroom as a frustrated James sighed, looking at the work ahead of him.

"Don't forget the sheets!" Michelle yelled out from the living room.

James grabbed his head, frustrated before getting to work disposing of the body.

Chapter 2

City of Dreams

Just after midnight, Sharice was in her office at Club Exotica looking over several documents at her desk when her cell phone suddenly rang. Before she could answer, it stopped ringing. She took a look at the caller id and wrote down the number before going into her desk drawer and pulling out her burner phone. She cut the phone on, and once it's loaded, she returned the call.

"Hey, it's me," John answered on the other line.

"Hey. Kinda figured it was you, Johnny baby," Sharice responded as she leaned back in her chair. "How're things going out in Atlanta?"

"Atlanta is doin' just fine, hon," John responded. "The

reason I'm callin' you though is not about Atlanta. It's something in New York I need your assistance on."

"New York? What's in New York?" Sharice asked.

"I'll fill you in on the way," John responded. "There's a plane leaving out around one-thirty. Should only take a few days. I cleared it with Mike."

"Whoa, wait a minute. Back up. You mean one-thirty as in the next hour?" A confused Sharice responded. "Shit, John, I gotta pack and all kinds of shit. I can't just up and bounce like that."

"Reese, please. I really need you for this thing. The trip and everything is all paid for. That includes wardrobe and hotel expenses—all on me," John pleaded.

Sharice thought for a moment as a smirk enters her face.

"All expenses, huh?" She replied. "You know that can cost you, right? Giving a girl like me an all-expenses paid trip? That can slip into six-figure territory fast and in a hurry."

"Like I said, whatever you need is on me," John reiterated.

After a few moments, Sharice checked her watch once more.

"Okay, I'm in," she responded.

"Great. The ticket will be waiting in your name at the terminal," John responded before hanging up the line.

Sharice sighed as she picked up her normal phone and called Michelle.

"Hey. Bring the car around. I need you and Connie to take a ride with me," she instructed as she locked away the papers on her desk.

Ten minutes later, Sharice was riding in the back seat of Michelle's car with Connie sitting on the passenger's side. Sharice was silently thinking about her next words, which she knew was going to cause an uproar.

"So, that nigga didn't say anythin' else on why you going to New York?" Connie asked.

"No, but it sounded pretty urgent," Sharice responded. "He said I'm gonna be out there for a few days. So that things won't fall apart while I'm out there, I'm gonna need y'all to keep things in order. Connie, since you're back on your feet and shit, I want you to take lead on things out here."

A big smile entered Connie's face, but Michelle was stunned by Sharice's decision.

"Connie? Are you fuckin' serious?" A disgruntled Michelle asked. "I just did that thing for you yesterday. I've been bustin' my ass gettin' shit together on those streets, and you're gonna put Connie in charge?"

"You heard what she said," Connie fired back. "So respect the title. I've been in this game for a minute, just in case you forgot!"

"I thought you get points for staying outta the hospital," Michelle quipped, enraging Connie.

The two went back and forth with each other as Sharice clutched her head in frustration. After a few more insults are thrown around, Sharice sighed before responding.

"That's enough!" She yelled, causing both of her subordinates to quiet down. "I'm sick and tired of actin' like I'm running a fuckin' daycare with you two! Now, Michelle, Connie is in charge while I'm gone! I don't wanna hear shit about it! She's in fuckin' charge! Are we clear?!"

A visually frustrated Michelle nodded her head as she continued to navigate the car in silence.

"Now look, we need to hold strong right now," Sharice continued. "I'm already down Bull for God knows how long. I don't need my other top people actin' like they're married and shit. Y'all clear on that?"

Both Connie and Michelle nodded their heads. Sharice sighed and calmed herself down as the rest of the ride remained silent between the friends.

Fifteen minutes later, Sharice and her crew pulled up to the airport terminal. Sharice exited the vehicle but motioned Connie to exit as well before turning her attention to Michelle.

"Hey, loop back around and pick her up," she instructed.

Michelle nodded her head as she pulled off, leaving Sharice and Connie alone.

"Connie, whatever issues you have with Chelle better be fixed by the time I get back," Sharice said, surprising her friend.

"Whatever issues I have? Reese, the shit ain't on me," Connie quipped as the two began walking into the airport. "That bitch has been tryin' to replace me ever since I was laid up. I've been then told you that. She always actin' like-"

"I fuckin' mean it, Connie!" Sharice snapped, interrupting her friend. "People are gonna be watching on this one. If you fuck this up, there isn't gonna be any second chances. Show Mike you are capable of runnin' shit. I can't keep coverin' your ass with him. It's time you grow up and handle shit, on the real."

Connie wanted to respond, but she knew Sharice was right. She promised herself after the shooting that she would be more like Sharice and less of a hothead. She also knew that Sharice hasn't fully forgiven her for Lavina's death, and wanted to work to regain the trust of her longtime friend.

"You're right, you're right," Connie responded. "I got you, Reese. I won't let you down."

Sharice nodded her head as the two friends embraced for a moment. Sharice took one last look at her friend before she headed over to airport security. Connie smiled with excitement as she made her way out towards the terminal entrance. Just as she walked out, Michelle pulled back up to the curb. Connie hopped into the passenger side as the car pulled off.

"Look, I know me and you don't see eye to eye on shit, but we need to put that behind us, so we can handle things," Connie said, confusing her rival. "With Reese being out of town, niggas are gonna look to fuck with us. We need a unified approach or some shit."

Michelle rolled her eyes, unimpressed with Connie's proposal.

"Fine," she struggled to say while keeping her eyes on the road.

"Fine? What does that mean?" Connie questioned, looking for a more definitive answer.

"It means fine, fuck! What else you want me to say?" Michelle quipped.

Connie smirked as she leaned back in her seat. In her eyes, she was the current empress of the city. This was her time to shine, and she was going to take every advantage.

Hours later, after arriving in New York, Sharice was in a taxicab being escorted to her hotel. She felt like a child looking at the big city lights. It was always a dream of hers to experience New York City, but she could never find the time. Attending New Year's Eve in Times Square was one of the many experiences that were on her personal bucket list that she was never able to accomplish. She had a big smile on her face as she recognized several landmarks on her drive to her hotel, almost forgetting she was there for business. As her cab made it to her hotel, she was impressed because it was right in the Times Square area. She exited the cab and took in the scenery for a few moments before walking into the hotel. In her room, she was let down slightly cause the room was smaller than she expected. She perked up when she noticed several items on the bed, including a card. She took a seat on the bed and opened the card. In it was a handwritten message from John.

Whatever you need. No limit

The note was accompanied with a credit card. Sharice

chuckled to herself as she looked at the credit card, which happened to be a black card.

"John, you really know how to treat a girl," she said to herself as she walked over to the window and opened the curtains to see the full view of the city.

She screamed to herself before falling into the bed, kicking her legs in the air. She calmed down after a few moments and peered out towards the window once again, still stunned to be in the big city.

The next morning, Sharice was in the bathroom wearing a robe and getting ready when there was a knock at her room's door. She walked over and checked the peephole before letting John walk into the room.

"Johnny, baby," she said before kissing the Faction boss on the cheek. "How's it going?"

"How you doing, hun?" John replied as he checked around and noticed a bed full of shopping bags. "Damn, you didn't waste any time, I see."

Sharice giggled as she walked over towards the bed and took a seat, moving several bags to the side.

"I haven't slept since I got there. I'm gonna be real with

you, John, and no disrespect, but you're a fuckin' fool to move to ATL from here. I mean, oh my God!" An excited Sharice said, smirking. "Then you got the nerve to give me a card talkin' bout no limit? Are you fuckin' insane? I did this in a few hours, but I ain't done. I'm just letting you know."

John laughed as he took a seat at the desk area.

"You'll have plenty of time for that, but first, business," he responded.

Sharice took a deep breath and nodded her head.

"Alright, business it is," she answered. "So you gonna let me in on why I'm here and why you're showering such gifts upon my feet?"

John nodded his head as he took a few moments to gather his thoughts.

"Twenty years ago, I left Jersey due to a war between the families," he began. "I came to Atlanta to hide out until things were settled, so to speak."

"Yeah, I know. You've told me that before," Sharice pointed out.

"Yeah, but here's the part I didn't tell you. After the

47

war was over, the actin' boss at the time, Mr. Gigante, called for me to come back home and be his underboss," John continued with a smile. "We grew up together in this thing, and when everything was said and done, he was the new man in charge in Jersey. The thing is, I had already set some things in motion out in Atlanta. Wasn't much of a presence of our thing out there at the time, and once me and a few of my crew set things up, I was makin' money like you wouldn't believe."

Sharice nodded her head as the Faction boss continued with his story.

"Some of my crew went back, but I didn't. Told the ol' man that I was good where I'm at. Plus, my cousin, Massimo, was next in line for a bump," he explained. "At the time, I didn't think of myself as a lifer in this business. My cousin was the one who got me into this thing. When we was kids, he always looked up to the crews tryin' to make a name for himself. He was a bit of a hothead though at a time when a lot of the crews back then was tryin' to stay under the radar, not be a part of the news."

Sharice nodded her head once again. She could relate

to how difficult it can be dealing with a hothead, thinking of Connie.

"Guys like Gotti gettin' news coverage was the exception, but it was what it was," John said, thinking about the way the old days were. "Anyway, Massimo finally got his shit together and was a good earner at the time, but they were gonna pass him up for me. I knew how much this life meant to him, so when you add that onto the fact that I was sittin' on a gold mine in Atlanta, coming back home wasn't an option for me. He's always wanted that position out here, so I took a pass, and suggested to the ol' man that he reach out to my cousin for the bump up."

"So I guess your cousin was happy as shit to get the bump," Sharice responded as she got a little more comfortable on the bed.

"Well, yes and no," John responded. "You see, there's a certain collection of wise guys out here who felt I betrayed our thing by bringin' it out there and associatin' with the Blacks and the Hispanics. I mean, we can do business with other races, but this thing of ours was exactly that- ours. Cause of that, me and the folks who stayed out in Atlanta aren't well liked. Mr. Gigante didn't care because he got a piece of my action, and he knew if he needed a favor, I was there for him. I was always under his protection, and it didn't matter what nobody said, because to him, I was part of the family."

John had a smirk on his face as he thought about his past relationship with his old boss. The smile slowly started to fade as his new reality filled his mind.

"About a year ago, Mr. Gigante got pinched by some sweepin' FBI bullshit case. Some rat gave them everythin'. He was still runnin' the family while waitin' for trial, but a few months ago, he died on the inside. Fuckin' cancer," John said. Sharice could tell that his former boss' death weighed heavy on him. "My cousin, who wasn't part of the sting operation, was bumped up to Boss. He now is the King of Jersey."

"Okay, that's what you wanted for him, right?" Sharice asked.

"Yeah, I'm proud of him. He wanted it, and he got it," John chimed in. "The thing is, he's still hurt over this bullshit of me not comin' back all those years ago. I don't have the protection I once had. I did a lot of business on the New York docks because of Mr. Gigante's blessing. With him being out of the picture now, Massimo is the one who makes the decisions. I have to cut a deal with him if I want to continue to do business down here."

Sharice thought for a minute because she's slightly confused.

"I'm not understandin' here, John," she responded. "I mean, he's your cousin, right? I know he feels a certain way about shit, but you're still blood. And even if he did act like an asshole and deny you, you could just bring what you need in on Miami's docks or mine. I don't see what the big deal is."

"The people I work with overseas only ships to the east coast," John responded. "If I can't work out a deal with Massimo, I'm probably going to have to move my operation to Philly. I got a guy out there, but he's a greedy prick who's gonna cut into my bottom line."

"What about the other bosses?" Sharice asked. "I know I'm not caught up on my mafia history, but aren't there five bosses in New York that you could do business with?"

"Not without Jersey's blessing," John responded. "I'm not a part of their crew or associated with anyone out in New York. I know some guys, sure, but for what I'm askin', I need the blessing from my old crew. They aren't gonna deal with someone like me, who many believe I betrayed them. Besides, I'm from Jersey. Most of them look down at us anyway."

"Okay, I get that, but why do you need me for this?" Sharice inquired. "I mean, you could have bought Frankie out here with you. I'm sure the Italians out here would feel more comfortable around him than me."

John sighed as he rose and walked over to the window. He took a look down at the city he spent a lot of time at as a kid.

"Being a boss isn't that much different as being a captain of a crew," he said, turning his attention back towards Sharice. "You got a lot of people lookin' at you, and if you're an effective leader, they'll follow you through the gates of hell. If you're not an effective leader, or you show a hint of weakness, your crew may lose respect for you, or get ideas of their own about leadership."

Sharice pondered John's words as she got up from the bed as well.

"So, you don't wanna look weak in front of your crew?" Sharice asked, causing John to smile.

"Look, I don't know how these negotiations are gonna turn out," John admitted. "I'm not the type of person who kisses ass, but there's a chance I'm not gonna look like my normal self through all this. Having you there may be a problem for them because they'll underestimate you. Me? I know who you are and how you think. I could use that to my advantage."

John's eyes worked their way down Sharice's body as a smirk entered his face.

"Besides, someone like you may throw them off their game," he responded, causing Sharice to giggle.

"Really? You wanna go there, John?" She playfully responded. "I got you, you know that. I just find it crazy that you don't mind me seeing you at your weakest."

John walked up to her as the two are in each other's space. He leered at her once again as flirtatious Sharice batted her eyes while checking him out as well.

"Well, if anyone has to see me at my weakest, I'm glad it's you," he responded before backing away.

Sharice laughed as she took a seat back on the edge of the bed. She slightly opened her robe to reveal her undergarments that catch John's eye.

"So, you want me to pose in some of my new outfits for you?" She asked, still flirting with the boss. "I can always use an extra set of eyes."

"As much as I would love to, my hard-on would disappear once I find out how much I paid for this shit," John joked, causing Sharice to burst into laughter once more. "Besides, we don't have time. I got a sit down with Massimo at noon. I wanna get there early and check out the lay of the land. So get together, hun. We'll grab breakfast and head out."

Sharice sighed but does as she's told.

"Your loss," she said as she dropped her robe.

A stunned John admired her perfect body wearing nothing but her bra and panties as she walked towards the bathroom. Just before she entered, she looked back at him and winked. After she entered the bathroom, John shook his head, smirking.

Back in New Orleans, just before noon, Connie walked into Sharice's office in the club and smiled, taking in the atmosphere. She strutted over to Sharice's desk, took a seat in her friend's chair, and kicked her feet on top of the desk, feeling the power of being in charge. She leaned in the chair comfortably before reaching out to the desk drawer and pulling out a cigar Sharice had stashed. She went into her pocket and lit the cigar before taking several puffs. As she's getting acclimated to her new role, she's surprised when her friend Tracy walked into the office. Both women were stunned to see each other.

"Trace, what the fuck are you doin' here?" Connie asked.

"I was just about to ask you the same thing," Tracy responded as a smirk grew on her face. "You're a little comfortable, I see."

"Hell yeah! Didn't Sharice tell you? I'm runnin' things while she's out of town," Connie responded before taking several puffs of the cigar.

"Shit, I didn't even know the girl was out of town," Tracy responded before sitting across from her longtime friend. "How long is she gonna be gone?"

"She said a few days, but who knows," Connie answered, sitting upright in the chair. "Anyway, what you doin' in here so early? Didn't you just get off like a few hours ago?"

"No, yesterday was my off day. I like to come in a little earlier when I'm off the day before. Make sure we're stocked with the good shit, paperwork is done, things like that," Tracy responded. "Why are you here so early?"

"I gotta meeting with the crew," Connie responded. "I wanna make sure we're on the same page. This shit is kinda important to me."

Tracy shook her head with a smirk when the door suddenly opens. Michelle and James both enter the office. Michelle has an attitude as she made her way towards the desk. Connie has an arrogant smile on her face as she turns to Tracy.

"You mind givin' me and the crew a moment?" She asked.

Tracy chuckled as she got up.

"Alright, I'm downstairs if you need me," she replied before walking out of the office.

As soon as the door closed, Connie turned her attention to James and an irritated Michelle.

"What the fuck, Connie?! Why are we here?" Michelle asked.

"Have a seat," Connie responded.

"I don't want to have a fuckin' seat!" Michelle fired back. "I ask you again, what the fuck is going on?"

Connie frowned before continuing.

"So, check this out, I checked out my girl's books last night, and notice we have some folks behind on payments," she said, causing Michelle to chuckle.

"Let me get this straight, you've been looking over the books for less than a day, and you were able to put that together," she responded, smiling. "Are you serious right now?"

"Yeah, I did," Connie responded proudly of herself. "Now, what I wanna do is get the crew caught up. Sort of a return home present for Sharice."

Michelle shook her head, chuckling, which bothered Connie.

"What the fuck is so damn funny?" Connie quipped.

Michelle sighed before responding.

"Those people that you so-called found on the books short all have passes by Sharice," she explained. "They have an arrangement for one reason or the other. Basically, you just spent time lookin' over shit that was already agreed on. It was a nice job though picking up on it. I'm sure Sharice would be proud."

An embarrassed Connie frowned as James stood silently in the room, trying to contain his laughter. She didn't appreciate Michelle's sarcastic response and notices a smile on her face. Connie rose and approached Michelle, meeting her face to face.

"You think you're so fuckin' funny, don't you?" She asked.

"Are we done?" Michelle questioned, not falling for Connie's intimidation.

"Excuse me?"

"Some of us have collections to make. So can we go,

or is there some other bullshit you want us to waste time doin'?" Michelle fired back, further enraging Connie.

The two stood toe to toe as Michelle grew tired of Connie's games.

"Let's get outta here, James," she said, backing down and heading towards the door.

"James, hold up," Connie said before he and Michelle were able to make it out of the office. "Take the day off. You deserve it."

"What the fuck? We gotta make our collections, and you then already fucked up our schedule with this bullshit meeting," Michelle responded.

"Don't sweat it, baby girl. We're still gonna make your pickups like normal," a smug Connie responded, confusing Michelle.

"Hold up. What do you mean we?" She asked.

"I'm gonna ride with you," Connie explained, frustrating Michelle.

"Nah, that ain't a good idea," she replied. "Me and James got our thing goin' that works for us. Besides, ain't you like five minutes out of the hospital? You need to take it easy, for real."

Connie motioned James out of the room as she approached Michelle once again.

"After you," Connie motioned.

Michelle grabbed her head in frustration before finally making her way out of the office, followed closely by Connie.

Back in New York, Sharice and John were at the docks waiting for John's cousin to arrive. Sharice was leaning on their rental car, getting frustrated as she checked the time on her phone.

"I think they played us," she said, looking at John. "They were supposed to have been here over an hour ago. I think they fucked us, John."

"Patience, hun," John responded. "It's a power move. They're tryin' to see how desperate we are."

"And are we really this desperate?" Sharice inquired.

"Yes, we are," John responded, shaking his head. "Better to be in bed with the devil, you know."

Sharice shook her head in frustration, looking around

the area once more. Ten minutes later, John tapped Sharice on her shoulder and pointed out the approaching car making its way towards them. She quickly straightened out her skirt as the car stopped right across from them. Massimo and two crew members exited their car and approached them. All three men were wearing high-end Italian Suits to show their wealth, or at least the appearance of wealth. Massimo was a lot shorter than Sharice imagined him. John's stories made him seem like he was bigger than life, but he wasn't much of a threat in her eyes. He was balding with an unmissable mole on the side of his face. Sharice tried not to stare as he sized both her and John up.

"John, it's been a long time," he said in his heavy New Jersey accent, finally breaking the silence.

"That it has," John responded.

He moved in to hug his cousin, only to be rejected. John backed away as Massimo checks out Sharice once more.

"Well, I can tell by the company you're keeping ain't much changed, huh?" He replied with a chuckle.

John sighed as he ignored his cousin's remarks.

"Look at you. Head of the family now just like you always said you'd be," John said, trying to change the subject.

"Hey, take it easy, John," Massimo responded, waving him off. "I don't know what you're talkin' about."

"Oh, I get it," John responded as he started to unbutton his shirt.

He opened up his button-down and raised his t-shirt to let Massimo and the others see that he wasn't wired. Massimo ignores John as he walked up to Sharice.

"The broad too," he said, offending her.

"What? You've got to be kiddin'?" Sharice replied before looking towards John. "John, is he serious right now?"

John nodded his head as a frustrated Sharice begins unbuttoning her top.

"Unfuckin' believable," Sharice replied. "All the way to New York for this shit!"

Sharice opened her top, which revealed her bra. Massimo chuckled and looked towards John.

"The bra too," he said, which infuriated Sharice.

"Go fuck yourself!" She exclaimed.

"Whoa! You suck John's dick with that mouth?" Massimo responded, smirking.

Sharice was about to respond when John intervened.

"Sharice, please?" He pleaded with her.

After a few moments, Sharice frowned before she removed her bra, satisfying Massimo's request.

"Well, I don't think that even the Feds found a way to wire those yet, am I right?" he said, looking at his crew, causing them to laugh.

"Fuckin' bastard," Sharice whispered to herself as she and John buttoned up their shirts.

"So, you're not wired. Why the fuck are you here?" Massimo asked as he approached his cousin.

"Well, I wanted to talk in private if we could," John requested.

"In private? For what? We're all friends here, are we not?" Massimo said with a smile on his face. "Let's skip the pleasantries and get to the fuckin' point cause I got somewhere to be."

John thought for a moment before nodding his head with understanding.

"To business then. I had an arrangement with Mr. Gigante to run shipments through the docks out here. He cleared it with the families to allow me to do business on the docks. I'm down here asking as a favor to me, that you do right and honor that agreement. Your taste would be the same that Mr. Gigante got," John explained.

Massimo chuckled to himself before looking at his guys.

"You hearin' this guy?" He said before turning his attention back towards his cousin. "You gotta lot of nerve coming back this way."

"I thought we were past all that?"

"Past all that? Listen to this guy," Massimo responded with a chuckle. "What are you, outta your fuckin' mind? We don't deal with your kind out here."

"Massimo, we're family. Why you gotta do this?"

"You jumped ship remember?" Massimo reminded his cousin. "You tucked your tail and ran while the real men took care of business. Then instead of comin' back like you were told, you stayed down south and brought this thing of ours to the spics and the niggers."

Massimo looked towards Sharice, smiling.

"No offense, hun," he said before turning his attention back towards his cousin. "Who the fuck is this broad anyway? You're bangin' a shine now?"

"You know what, you need to slow your roll you guinea muthafucka!" Sharice fired back, having heard enough of Massimo's insults. "John is down here tryin' to put money in your fuckin' pockets, and you're being real disrespectful. You need to quit actin' like-"

"Sharice, that's enough!" John exclaimed.

Sharice had never seen John so passive. She became frustrated but backs down as she's told. Massimo laughed as he watched Sharice fall back.

"You better tell your homegirl here to chill," he responded before thinking for a moment. "Thirty-five percent."

"Get the fuck outta here. What are you tryin' to rob me now?" John fired back showing his first hint of aggression. "I come here lookin' for a favor, and you spit in my face?"

"What, you think I'm stupid? I know why you're here," Massimo said he got in his cousin's face. "You're here because you know none of the five families would give you the time of day. Gigante always did think your shit didn't stink, and it made him look weak. I'm not gonna be the next one havin' New York lookin' down on me on account of your bullshit! You wanna do business, it's gonna cost you. Take it or leave it!"

John remained silent as he considered his options. After a few moments, he looked towards Sharice, who was shaking her head, trying to advise him to refuse the offer.

"Let me think it over," John responded, stunning Sharice.

"Think it over? John, you can't possibly be entertaining this bullshit!" She exclaimed.

"Oh, here she goes again," Massimo responded with a chuckle.

Before Sharice can respond, John held her back, motioning her to back down. Sharice threw her hands up in the air in disbelief before walking over to the passenger side of their car.

"You have 'til tomorrow to make a decision, or the price goes up," Massimo said before he and his crew walked back to their car.

As Massimo and his crew pulled off, Sharice once again showed her disappointment to her boss.

"John, all due respect, but what the fuck was that?" she asked. "I ain't never seen you back down like that to anybody."

John looked towards her, almost like he was offended. After a brief stare down, he shook his head, realizing she was right.

"I assume you got some more shoppin' to do, so take the car," he said. "We'll need to talk to some guys out in Philadelphia in a couple of days. I'm gonna catch a cab."

"John, wait! John!" Sharice yelled as John made his way towards the main road.

Her words fall on deaf ears as John walked, pondering his next move. Sharice looked on, regretting calling him out but knew that wasn't the John she knew. The John she knew would have broken Massimo's nose at the first sign of disrespect. She understood that they're family, but didn't agree with John cutting him so much slack. After a few moments, she got into the driver's side of the car and pulled off.

Back in New Orleans, Michelle was driving down the street with Connie on the passenger side, counting the money from their previous pick up that evening. Both women were silent and avoiding eye contact as Connie nodded her head with the count before putting it into a bookbag. Michelle was annoyed with her passenger as Connie relaxed in her seat.

"So, who's next?" She asked, a frustrated Michelle.

"We're heading uptown now. A dude named Sambo has been puttin' in work in both our territories in the past month," Michelle explained, piquing Connie's interest.

"Really? Never heard of him," she responded.

"Well, you weren't around the past month, remember?" Michelle pointed out. "Shit did continue while you were out."

Connie frowned, not liking the attitude Michelle was giving her. She's trying to abide by Sharice's words about making things right between her and Michelle, but she felt Michelle was trying to push her buttons. Michelle, on the other hand, felt betrayed. With all of the work she put in while Connie was out counted for nothing. She felt she should have been left in charge. After a few moments, Connie decided to question her once again.

"Are we gonna have issues with this Sambo nigga?" She asked.

"I'm sure he won't have the money," Michelle responded, confusing Connie.

"What do you mean, he's not gonna have it?"

"I mean, he's not gonna have the shit," Michelle responded with an attitude. "Look, he has this fetish thing where he likes chicks to whip his ass or somethin'. I don't understand the shit, but normally I go and collect, he says he didn't have it, I fuck him up, and he gets me the money the next day or so. The nigga does this shit all the time, so it ain't nothing."

"And you settle for that shit?" Connie inquired.

"I mean, it's nothing. Kinda fun if I'm being real," Michelle answered with a slight grin.

"Oh, so I see you like a little kink yourself," Connie pointed out, picking up on Michelle's slight grin.

Michelle's mood changed as she looked at Connie.

"See, this is why I didn't wanna do this shit with you!" She fired back.

"What?"

"Fuck it, I'm just gonna be real with you," Michelle said as a confused Connie waited for her words. "I know Sharice is your girl and all, so I keep my mouth closed, but females like you are what's wrong with the game!"

"Females like me?"

"Yeah. What do y'all call y'all selves now, pugs, butch, whatever the fuck. Lesbians!" Michelle fired back, which angered Connie.

"So you gotta problem with me cause I'm gay?" Connie asked.

Michelle slightly nodded her head while keeping her eyes on the road as Connie shook her head in disbelief.

"Ain't that some shit," Connie said.

"Hey, you asked, I told," Michelle responded as she parked the car on the curb.

"So, what is it then, huh? What is it that you hate about us?" Connie inquired. "Did one of us do you dirty?"

Michelle didn't respond as she looked around the area. After a few moments, she turned to Connie, who was still waiting an answer.

"We're here," she said before opening her car door.

Before Michelle could exit the vehicle, Connie grabbed her by her arm and stopped her from leaving.

"Hold up, you didn't answer my question," Connie said, still interrogating her associate.

"Look, we got shit to do! We don't have time for all this," Michelle quipped.

After a few moments, Connie nodded her head and released Michelle's arm.

"Aight, let's do this. But this shit ain't over," Connie responded.

Michelle ignored her faux leader and exited the car, followed closely by Connie. The two made their way up to Sambo, who was sitting on a street stoop looking over a corner he operated. Connie was stunned to see the tall, lanky Sambo stretched out on the stoop. *He had to be at least six-nine or six-ten,* she thought. She couldn't believe someone like him was into what he was into. He noticed Michelle approaching and smiled as he stood up to greet his visitors.

"Chelly, what's up? I was just about to call you," He said as he approached the two.

Michelle was disgusted as she saw the sweat flowing down his dark skin.

"For fuck's sake, Sambo, get a towel or something," she said. "That shit reeks, for real."

Sambo chuckled as he scratched his braided hair.

"My bad. It's hotter than a bitch out here," he responded. "You know how it is though, gotta keep niggas on point, you know. No time for the fresh and clean thing."

Michelle rolled her eyes as she became impatient with him.

"You got my money, or not?" She asked.

"Just one second," Sambo said as he took a look at Connie. "Who is this lovely thing you brought down here today?"

Michelle was confused, wondering why Sambo would

consider Connie a lovely thing. Connie smirked as she stepped forward.

"I'm Connie," she said, introducing herself.

"Hold up. You're *the* Connie?" Sambo asked like he was a fan.

"In the flesh."

"Damn, your name rings out shorty," he responded, smirking.

Connie chuckled and was about to respond when Michelle cut her off.

"Look, nigga, you can suck her cooch on your own time. I got shit to do!" Michelle quipped. "Do you have my money or not?"

Sambo laughed as he went into his back pocket and handed Michelle an envelope. She snatched the envelope from his hand and started counting the cash inside. Connie looked over and noticed Sambo smiling at her. She cringed, thinking about what was on his mind as he licked his lips towards her. After a few moments, Michelle sighed as she looked towards Sambo.

"Why do you always do this?" She asked before

putting the envelope in her pocket. "This shit is short, and you fuckin' knew it!"

"My bad, boss lady. Looks like you're gonna have to teach me a lesson," a flirtatious Sambo responded.

Michelle sighed as she pulled out her gun. She's about to strike Sambo when Connie stopped her.

"Yo, I got this," she said, surprising Sambo.

"Connie, you don't have to do this. I got-"

"I said I'll handle it!" Connie exclaimed. Michelle gave her a look before backing down.

"Fine. He's all yours."

Connie reached for her gun and swung it, forcefully hitting Sambo in the cheek, sending him backward. She delivered several more blows to his chest and stomach until Sambo finally fell to the ground. She towered over Sambo and continued to strike him with her gun for several moments before suddenly slowing down. She was out of breath since her energy was still not where it used to be, much to Michelle's delight as a slight grin crept across her face. An exhausted Connie dropped to a knee. She continued to breathe heavily before Michelle walked over and looked down at Sambo.

"I'll be back in two days, Sambo. You better have my money then," she said before reaching out her hand to Connie, offering assistance.

Connie batted her hand away and got back onto her feet on her own. The two females made their way back to Michelle's car and jumped in. Connie was still struggling to breathe and noticed a smile on Michelle's face as she started the car.

"What the fuck are you smilin' for?" Connie asked as Michelle pulled off from the curb.

"Nothing."

"Don't give me that nothin' shit! Stop fuckin' with me!" Connie exclaimed, seeking answers. "What's so fuckin' funny?"

"I don't know. I mean, I just find it funny that the great Connie is strugglin' with collections. Just seems odd to me, wouldn't you agree?" Michelle mocked as she continued to drive down the road.

Connie grunted as she sat silently, much to Michelle's satisfaction, who continued to drive down the road with a smile on her face.

Sharice was in her hotel room, trying on an outfit she recently purchased with two different styles of heels on trying to get the perfect look as she admired herself in the mirror. As she posed, trying to get a feel for her look, there's a knock suddenly at her door. She walked over, looked in the peephole and opened the door for John. He's blown away by her new dress, which is a strapless style cut.

"Well, what did I walk into here?" John asked as he walked in and kissed Sharice on the cheek.

"Hey, just tryin' on a fit that you purchased," Sharice answered as John made his way into the room. "You like?"

John checked her out once more and nodded his head with approval.

"You look nice, hun," he said before noticing her shoes. "You realize you got on two different shoed there, right?"

"Yeah, I was checkin' to see which one goes better with this fit? Any thoughts?" Sharice replied as she posed.

John chuckled to himself as he leered at her once more.

"You could be barefoot for all I care," John responded, causing Sharice to laugh.

He noticed several high-end luggage bags in the room as well before he took a seat at the computer desk.

"See you got you some luggage," he said, pointing out the bags.

"Yeah. I mean, how else was I gonna get all this shit home," Sharice responded before taking a seat at the edge of her bed. "I hope that's not a problem."

"No, you're fine, hun. You're fine," John responded before going into the reason for his visit. "I talked to my guy out in Philly. He can meet with us tomorrow night. We can catch the train around three. If we finish early, we can get on the train back. If not, we may need to get a room."

Sharice sighed as she took a look at her boss.

"Come on, John. Are you giving up here?" She inquired. "I mean, what I saw today was bullshit, John. I know you see it."

"What are you gonna do, huh?" John asked. "He's my cousin, Reese. Some things you gotta let play out."

Sharice shook her head in disagreement.

"It ain't right," Sharice responded. "I'm just sayin', you should go back and-"

"It's not happening," an irritated John responded as he rose. "Just make sure you're packed up for tomorrow."

John quickly walked out of the room, leaving Sharice hanging. She thought to herself for a few moments before grabbing her cell phone and pulling up her Uber app. After hesitating initially, she placed her request to have someone pick her up outside of her hotel. She quickly got dressed in something a little more casual before hustling downstairs to meet her ride.

Later that night, Connie's sitting in her SUV, looking at Sambo and his crew on the uptown corner. After a few moments, she took out a vile of cocaine and quickly sniffed it, trying to get her attitude right. She pulled out her gun and finally made her way out of the vehicle and down the block, heading towards Sambo. As she approached, Sambo noticed her and smiled.

"Well, if it isn't the infamous Connie," he said,

approaching her. "What brings you out this way, baby girl?"

"I'm here to get my money," Connie responded as she keeps her eye on Sambo's crew.

"I thought we cleared that shit up earlier," Sambo responded. "I'll get y'all the rest in a couple of days, ya heard me."

Connie turned her attention to Sambo with a fierce look on her face.

"I ain't Michelle, nigga," she fired back. "I don't play this bullshit game y'all do. So I'm gonna need you to get off your ass and get my shit now!"

Sambo chuckled as he turned and looked at his crew, who were equally amused.

"And if I don't?" Sambo asked, testing Connie.

"Like I said, I ain't Michelle," Connie warned before pointing her gun towards Sambo. "I'm a different type of bitch. So, like I said, get me my shit!"

Sambo still didn't take Connie seriously but changed his mind once he noticed the look in her eyes. His crew looked on as well as things became tense.

"What the fuck? Are you crazy?" Sambo fired back. "Pointin' a gun at me? Them braids must be wrapped too tight or some shit! You then lost your fuckin' mind!"

Connie became impatient.

"My money, yes or no?" She asked, giving Sambo one final chance.

Sambo walked up to Connie with his chest pressed firmly against her gun nozzle.

"No! Now get the fuck up outta here," he responded, staring down Connie.

Connie didn't hesitate as she pulled the trigger blasting Sambo in the chest, much to the surprise of his crew members. He was on the ground coughing up blood when Connie decided to end his life with a shot to the head. The rest of the crew was frozen in place as she looked towards them, her gun still drawn.

"Let that shit ring out!" She yelled to make sure she got her point across. "Connie is back on the block, and if any of you muthafuckas got a problem with that, we can handle up now, ya heard me!"

Sambo's crew didn't respond since they were all

nervous, not wanting to be the next victim. After a few moments, she smiled at them and cautiously backed away from the corner and into her SUV. An evil smile filled her face as she raced down the block. For the first time since her shooting a month and a half ago, she felt like her old self.

At a restaurant in the heart of New Jersey, Massimo and crew members were all dining with each other, laughing, joking, and enjoying the atmosphere. It's a typical mob-owned restaurant that Massimo and his family hung out at almost daily. There were other non-mobster customers there, but for the most part, it was filled with made men. Massimo and his crew were in the VIP area, which was closed off from the rest of the restaurant. They did a lot of dealings there, so they made sure the place was swept for bugs daily. Everyone was having a good time when Massimo noticed Sharice walking in their area. A crew member stopped her from advancing as Sharice looked over towards John's cousin.

"I'm just here to talk, Massimo. I'm not here to

bullshit," she said with her hands raised.

After a few moments, Massimo waved her over. He offered her a seat and smiled, admiring her beauty from afar.

"Can I get you anything?" He asked.

"No, I'm good," Sharice responded as Massimo got comfortable.

"So I see you're a resourceful broad, not just some run of the mill mulignan," he responded.

"I don't know if I should take that as a compliment or an insult," Sharice responded, causing Massimo to chuckle.

"Maybe it's one and the same," he responded before taking a quick sip of his drink. "So, not to be rude or nothin', but what the fuck do you want?"

"I was hoping we could talk," Sharice replied.

"We're talkin' right now."

"I meant talk privately if you don't mind."

"Are you kiddin'? I don't do business with your kind," Massimo replied.

Sharice smiled as she attempted to charm him.

"Come on, you're the big man around here. You're not afraid to meet with little old me, are you?" She said, smirking. "I won't bite, I promise."

Massimo thought for a moment as he checked her out once more. He didn't feel as if she was a threat to him, and decided to take her up on her offer.

"Alright. Let's walk," he said as he rose from the table.

He and Sharice made their way out of the restaurant and slowly began walking the block.

"So, I'm here. What do you want?" Massimo said.

"I wanna see what's the big deal with you and your cousin," Sharice answered. "Why do you resent him so much?"

"Resent him?"

"Hatred, or whatever it is you wanna call it. What's the beef?" Sharice clarified.

Massimo didn't respond initially as he looked around the area.

"Everything you see around here used to be owned by your people," he said, confusing Sharice.

"My people?"

"Yeah, the mooleys used to own this area. This neighborhood was turning to shit until us Italians took it over and ran all the trash outta here," he responded, upsetting Sharice.

"So you just hate all niggas now? Is that it?" Sharice inquired with an attitude.

"Yeah, I guess you could say that," Massimo responded with a chuckle.

Sharice rolled her eyes as the two continued to make their way down the block.

"Look, no disrespect, but what the fuck does that have to do with anything?" Sharice asked.

"Your friend, my fuckin' cousin John, always had a thing for you blacks," Massimo pointed out. "He thought doin' business with your kind wasn't any different than doin' business with his own."

"I assume you didn't feel the same way?"

"Don't get me wrong, your people have a good thing goin' on movin' drugs and shit like that, but this is our thing. John broke the rules when he brought our thing to your kind and the spics," Massimo explained.

The two stopped at the corner as Sharice shook her head, smirking.

"This thing of yours, huh?" She said, chuckling to herself. "I hate to burst your bubble, but this thing of yours is no longer an Italian thing. Shit, the Godfather alone killed that shit. Nah, there's somethin' else behind your bullshit."

"Whoa, take it easy. We're in my neck of the woods, remember?" Massimo fired back.

Sharice nodded her head and backed down as Massimo thought for a few moments.

"This shit should have been ours, me and John's," he said, calming down a bit. "Back in the day, this is what we always wanted."

"Yeah, I heard all this before," Sharice pointed out. "John didn't come back because he wanted you to be the next king, and so-"

"The fuck you talkin' about?" Massimo replied, cutting Sharice off.

"What?"

"You said John didn't come back, because of what?"

"Because he wanted you to be the man out here, from what he told me," Sharice replied.

Massimo was quiet for a moment before shaking his head in denial.

"Bullshit," he replied. "You're just makin' that shit up tryin' to hustle me."

"Hustle you? Why would I… you know what? Fuck this. I came out here tryin' to reason with you, and you treatin' me like I'm some fuckin' con artist," Sharice fired back.

She was about to walk off when Massimo called her back.

"Hey!" He said, catching up with her.

Sharice stopped in her tracks and sighed as Massimo approached her.

"Let me get this straight. You sayin' John didn't come back 'cause he wanted me to get the top spot?" He inquired.

"Yeah, from what he told me," Sharice answered. "He said he had a nice thing going on in Atlanta, but your boss wanted him to be his underboss or somethin' after that mob war way back when. I don't remember the details, but he said he was cool doin' what he was doin', and suggested they give you the bump. That's why I'm trippin' on how you could do him dirty like you're doin'."

Massimo tried to read Sharice to see if her story was genuine or not. He never knew the reason John stayed in Atlanta.

"Why am I just now hearin' this shit," Massimo asked. "I mean, you gotta see the timing of all this from my eyes."

"Massimo, let's be real, would you have listened if John did tell you this?" She asked. "Seems to me you and your cousin need some face time, but I'm not here for that, I'm here for business. Now we all know you get your cut on those docks. I'm here to make you an offer you can't refuse."

Massimo looked at Sharice, strangely causing her to burst into laughter.

"I'm sorry, I couldn't help myself," she said as Massimo smirked as well.

"Cute," he replied. "So, what do you got for me?"

"Eight percent of the cut," Sharice responded which

Massimo quickly rejected.

"Get the fuck outta here with that," he fired back. "Gigante got fifteen of the cut. You're tryin' to lowball me?"

"No, I'm not, you didn't let me finish," Sharice responded as Massimo backed down. "I know you guys got a lot of shit movin' from overseas too, specifically shit in the Gulf. What I'm proposing is that you give John the eight percent deal here, and I'll reciprocate with an eight percent rate down in New Orleans. I'm no fool. I know your mafia's, or whatever it's called now, reach is long. I'm sure you got a dock deal in Savannah, maybe? Port Author? Jacksonville? You can't tell me you're not doin' some shit down south."

Massimo chuckled to himself, not willing to reveal what he has going on.

"See, that smile there says it all," Sharice remarked. "You ain't slick. Either way, I know you not gettin' a rate like eight percent from them other spots. Plus, I can offer you other accommodations for you whenever you're in my neck of the woods that them other folks can't."

"Accommodations? Like what?" A curious Massimo asked.

"I'm very friendly with the casino down there," Sharice responded. "You and your crew ever make it down to New Orleans, I can steer you to some high stakes games, or get you some trim at one of our houses. Y'all still call it that, right? And I'm not talkin' bout no raggedy bitches, I'm talkin' high class and clean."

Massimo nodded his head, impressed at Sharice's offer. He thought for several moments before agreeing to her proposal.

"I see why John keeps you around now," he said as the two shook hands. "Maybe black lives do matter."

Sharice shook her head and giggled as she looked around the area.

"Glad we could settle this," Sharice responded. "So, you'll hit your cousin up and make it official?"

"Sure thing, hun," Massimo answered. "You need a ride somewhere tonight? I can get one of the boys to make sure you're home safe."

"Nah, I'm good. Thanks for the offer though," Sharice

responded before walking off.

Massimo smiled as he watched her from the back, licking his lips before heading back into the restaurant.

Back in New Orleans, Michelle was in her apartment kitchen cooking dinner, wearing nothing but an oversized shirt. As she worked the spatula over a pot on the stove, her boyfriend, Theo, walked into the kitchen and was immediately turned on by her appearance. Unlike James who was a pretty boy, Theo was more down to earth. He wasn't overly attractive and didn't have much weight to him. He's more of a nerd compared to what she normally deals with, but she loved him, nonetheless. He walked up behind her and began fondling her breasts, causing her to giggle.

"Alright, keep playing," she said with a smile. "We'll never eat if you keep playing around."

"Well, maybe we can skip the meal and just get right to it," a sly Theo responded as he continued to stroke her breasts.

"Hell nah!" Michelle responded as she removed his

hands from her. "I then spent all this time fixin' this shit. We gonna eat. After dinner, then you can have dessert."

Theo ignored her as he began fondling her once more. This time, he started stroking on her womanhood, exciting Michelle.

"How about an appetizer to help me along?" Theo responded as Michelle turned and faced her love.

She smiled before kissing him. As the two began to get hot and heavy with each other, her cell phone rang, spoiling the mood. Michelle grabbed her phone and checked out the caller id before pulling away from her love.

"It's work calling. Give me a second," she said as she before she turned off the fire on the food and hurried into the living room before answering. "Yeah, it's me... no, go ahead, it's cool."

Michelle's face dropped as she became visually frustrated after hearing the news of Sambo's death from one of her street connections.

"When did this happen?" She asked, seeking answers. "Alright... no, don't sweat it. I'll take care of it... thanks."

Michelle shook her head in frustration.

"That fuckin' bitch!" She exclaimed, catching the attention of Theo.

He made his way into the living room with a look of concern in his eyes.

"Shelly, is everything alright?" He asked.

The frustrated Michelle didn't respond, remaining silent as she processed in her head what she just heard.

The next day, Sharice was in her hotel trying on another outfit she's just purchased when there was a knock on her door. She walked over and opened the door for John, who was once again blown away with her appearance.

"It's like walking into a beauty pageant every time I come here," John joked as he and Sharice share a quick hug and cheek kiss.

"I mean the shopping here is crazy, John. I can't get none of this shit back home, for real," she said as she walked back over towards the mirror. "What's up? Everything good?"

"Yeah, things are great, thanks to you," John

responded. "I got word that you met with my cousin. He called me this morning and told me about the deal you negotiated."

Sharice sighed as she turned and faced John.

"Look, I know I may have overstepped," Sharice responded. "But he was pissin' me off. I love you too much to let some asshole dog you out like that. I wanted to get to the bottom line, and we got to talkin', and a deal was hammered out. I hope I didn't disrespect you in any way."

A smile slowly grew on John's face as he kissed her on the cheek once more.

"You did good," he said as Sharice smiled as well.

"So things good between you two now?" She asked.

"No. I mean, I can't do the whole public thing with him and whatnot. Still too many wise guys upset over that whole situation," John explained. "But with his blessin', I'm able to conduct my business. He told me we can catch up in New Orleans sometime. Said the night was on you."

Sharice laughed as she nodded her head.

"Cool. Just let me know when, and I got y'all," she responded.

John looked around the room and noticed several new shopping bags he hadn't seen on their last visit.

"I assume all this is on me too?" he asked.

Sharice was a little embarrassed but slowly nodded her head.

"If I went overboard, I'll pay you back. I promise," she said.

"Pay me back? After what you did for me? Hit the stores again. You deserve it," John said, exciting Sharice.

"You really should look at how much I spent before agreeing to that," Sharice said, smirking.

Before John can respond, he received a call on his cell phone. He checked the number and sent it to voice mail.

"Look, I gotta take this. You wanna do dinner tonight?" He asked.

"Sure, just let me know where," Sharice answered.

John kissed her on the cheek and hugged her once more before making his way out of the hotel room. Once he was in the hallway, he pulled out a different cell phone and made a call out.

"Hey, it's me," John said to the line.

"It's me, my friend. How are things?" Rico responded on the other end of the phone.

"Fine. And you?"

"Not so well," Rico replied. "I lost two more assets in Houston. It's a fuckin' disaster out there."

"That bad, huh?" John responded as he started walking down the hall.

"Yes. This thing… it seems like it was too much too soon. At this point, I can't pull it back though. John, I'm looking for your help on this. I spoke to Money, but he's cryin' poor to me. I don't know what else to do," Rico explained.

John was silent for a few moments before a smirk came across his face.

"I know there was some shit between you and my female companion about the job, but I think she's ready now," he replied.

"What changed?" Rico inquired. "I needed her a couple of months ago, and she turned me down."

"All I can say is she did me a solid out here in New York. She's ready, my friend, trust me," John said as he pressed the elevator button.

The two continued their conversation as John tried to negotiate a second chance for one of his most loyal friends.

Chapter 3

Crew Up

At the FBI station in New Orleans, Agents Davis and Daniels are meeting with Deputy Director Evans in the main conference room, giving updates on their Faction case. Evans checked out a few files silently after the presentation as Davis and Daniels looked at each other, wondering what their boss was thinking. While the bureau made several significant busts during the operation so far, no high-level arrests have been made. Their main targets, Faction Bosses Rico and John, have gone untouched thus far in their investigation. After reviewing the files, Evans closed the folder and handed it back to Daniels before scratching his pudgy belly.

"So, I see we're making headway out in Miami limiting distribution on the docks," he said as he leaned back in his chair. "Still, there's no slow down on the streets, which means they're bringing it in elsewhere. Any idea where?"

"Well, according to our informant, it's right here in New Orleans," Daniels answered. "We just haven't been able to locate when and where it's coming in."

"I was under the impression that your informant was one of the top members in this organization," Evans pointed out. "How can he not know where it's going down? Especially in his own city."

Daniels and Davis looked at each other once more before responding.

"Sir... we've come to believe that informant sixty-eight forty is not as important as we thought he was," Daniels responded.

"Yes sir, I mean, he does hold the top rank, but based on the other two, he was nothing more than a place holder," Davis chimed in. "Our guess is the other two bosses distanced themselves from him because he was too loose with things, and right now he's not much of a player on the grand scheme of things. Even his own underboss seems to undermine him."

"That would be Sharice Legget, correct?" Evans asked.

"Yes, sir," Daniels confirmed. "Mike Rashad may be boss by name only, but Sharice is the one who we believe is running things.

"And what does Mike have to say about her?" Evans questioned.

"He believes that she had a local street dealer by the name of Andre White killed in a dispute a little over a month ago," Daniels explained. "He hasn't been seen in that timeframe. It was him that was responsible for that club shooting. It was said the gunman's target was actually Sharice herself, but he missed and shot Sharice's number one, Constance Shaw, instead."

"I see," Evans said, not liking where the investigation is going. "Look, I see a lot of busts limiting drugs, cash, and weapons on the streets. That's good and all, but we have yet to bring in one significant arrest outside of this Mike Rashad, and he seems to be worthless at this point. Either he's lying to us, or he doesn't know anything which in either case, we need to pull any deal we made with him."

"Sir, I agree Mike isn't everything we had hoped, but the last few busts have been on intel that he's provided. I agree, it's not exactly what we want, but it is something," Daniels responded. "A little more snooping on his part could bring us a break in this case. All we need is for Sharice to slip up once, and we can break their whole operation."

"But you said she's cautious. Didn't we bug her recently?" Inquired Evans.

"We bugged her number one, Connie, sir," Davis responded. "We only got the judge to sign off on a warrant for when Connie was in the club. The problem is that Connie was shot and was hospitalized for about a month. The bug ran out of juice, and with the limited manpower we've had, we haven't been able to swap it out."

Evans had heard enough as he waved his agents off.

"Well, the good news is that because of these recent busts, the director has opened the faucet," he said, which excited the two agents. "You guys have been doing great work, but at the end of the day, we're going to need some high profile arrests to justify this increase of funds. Get a list of whatever you need on my desk for approval by day's end."

"Yes, sir," Daniels replied.

Evans made his way out of the conference room as an excited Davis gave several fist pumps.

"Finally! With more surveillance, we actually might be able to bring in this case," he said as Daniels looked on with a smile.

"First thing we need to do is get someone on Connie," Daniels responded. "If she's back on the streets, it's only a matter of time before she does something out of line. I want people on her at all times. We need to also get with a judge to extend the warrant on the bug, and get it swapped out as soon as we can."

Davis nodded his head as he wrote down Daniels's instructions.

"What about John's organization?" Davis inquired. "I mean, Flores is in on Rico's crew, and we're increasing surveillance on Mike's crew. Other than John himself, we don't have much going on his end. What do you want to do about that?"

Daniels was silent as he thought for a few moments.

"Get with the Atlanta office. Have them map out the best solution with John's underlings," he responded. "Right now, I want our attention on Sharice. Flores and the Florida Office can keep tabs on Rico for us. Instead of us working the whole organization as one, we're going to need to have each field office take the lead in their area. With a budget now, I want every office to be knee-deep in Faction business. Also, find out-"

Daniels's words were cut off as his cell phone rings. He took a look at his phone's caller ID and noticed his wife calling.

"Give me a few minutes," he said to Davis, who nodded his head and immediately made his way out of the conference room.

Daniels took a deep breath before answering the line.

"Hey, Christine," he answered the line.

"Hey. Did I catch you at a bad time?" she asked.

"No, I just finished up a meeting," he responded as he leaned back in his chair. "What's up?"

"I was wondering if you had a chance to look at the papers yet," Christine inquired, referring to the separation papers she sent him a couple of weeks back.

Daniels sighed as he shook his head.

"No, I haven't had a chance yet," he answered. "Christine, come on. Why does it have to be this way? We can talk this thing out without all the lawyers and paperwork."

"We've tried that, James. We've tried that for years," Christine responded. "You're married to the bureau, and we both know I will never be able to compete with that. I think it's best that we do this so we can live the life that we want."

"It's not the life I want," Daniels quipped back. "I never asked for any of this."

"Maybe you didn't say it, but your actions sure did," Christine responds. "Look, I'm not here to argue with you right now, just... please look at the papers. I want to get them filed as soon as I can. Can you please do that one thing for me?"

Daniels sighed as he grabbed his head with frustration.

"I'll take a look at them later tonight," he replied.

"Thank you," Christine replied before hanging up the phone.

A defeated Daniels dropped his phone on the table heartbroken. The years he put in have taken its toll on him, and after his actions on his anniversary a month ago, his wife finally decided enough was enough. He had put off looking over the paperwork as long as he could, knowing that once he signed, he and his wife were through. Peering out of the corner of his eyes, he glanced at a photo of Sharice. He frowned because chasing the empress is what cost him his marriage. For his sacrifice to be worth it, he needed to get his target by any means necessary.

Sharice sighed as she sat behind her office desk, grasping her head with frustration as Michelle and Connie were going back and forth with each other standing across from her. The two women traded insults over the death of Sambo as the arguing finally got to Sharice.

"That's enough!" She yelled, calming down her crew members as she tried to make sense of the discussion.

"Fuck, I'm outta the city for three days, and all hell breaks loose!"

Sharice turned her attention to Michelle.

"Now, this guy… this Sambo. Who was he again?" she asked.

"He works uptown, doing this and that. Worked some corners, did minor collections, shit like that," Michelle answered. "He was one of my top earners, Sharice. I go out on collections with this bitch, next thing you know, I'm getting calls on how she killed the nigga for no fuckin' reason!"

"Who the fuck you callin' a bitch?" Connie responded as she squared up with Michelle. "I will beat your thin ass the fuck up all through this office if you keep fuckin' with me!"

"Do it then!" Michelle replied, inviting Connie to make the first move.

Before the argument can escalate, Sharice slammed her fists down on her desk and jumped up from her chair, getting both of her friend's attention.

"I'm not gonna say this shit again! Calm the fuck

down!" She exclaimed, calming the situation once more before turning her attention to Connie.

"Now, what the fuck did you shoot him for?" She asked.

"That nigga disrespected me, Reese, for real," Connie replied. "It's not like the nigga even had the money anyway. We had to fuck him up."

"Yeah, we did! Then I told the nigga to have my money in the next couple of days, and you go back and shoot the nigga? What the fuck for?" Michelle fired back.

Before Connie can respond, Sharice waved her back.

"Wait. Is this that nigga that you always beatin' on and shit?" Sharice asked Michelle. "The one who purposely doesn't have your money so you can fuck him up?"

"Well, yeah, but that's not the point," Michelle responded. "I told him I would-"

"Chelle, I've told you before not to fuck around with him like that," Sharice replied. "How's it gonna look to other folks if you keep going upside the nigga's head to get your money?"

"I mean, it wasn't nothin' I couldn't handle," Michelle

explained. "It was just some shit me and him would do. It was a little kinky, actually."

"Oh, so pretty girl likes it kinky, I see," Connie replied, smirking. "That explains a lot actually."

"Connie, what did I say?!" Sharice said, warning her friend once more.

Sharice sighed as she took a seat back behind her desk. She took both stories into account while trying to decide on how to settle the issue.

"Connie, you pay off from your East corners, fifty percent goes to Chelle for the next three months," Sharice ruled, stunning both Michelle and Connie.

"Fifty percent? Come on, Reese! I'm already struggling!" Connie exclaimed.

"Sambo brought me way more than that!" Michelle quipped as both her and Connie continue to argue their side of the ruling.

"Listen to me. Listen!" Sharice exclaimed, shutting down her friends once more. "Now, I don't need this fuckin' shit! Not today. You've heard my ruling! I don't wanna hear no more about this shit! You got me?"

Both Michelle and Connie nodded their heads.

"You know, we're the highest-ranked fuckin' women in this thing and instead of workin' together to build each other up, y'all heffas sittin' here bumpin' heads all damn day," Sharice preached.

"Reese, it ain't my fault," Michelle quipped back. "She's always-"

"I don't wanna hear it!" Sharice exclaimed, cutting off Michelle's response. "This is what niggas like Money and them want us to do. Keep draggin' each other down. Y'all are playin' right into their hands!"

Sharice was about to continue when there was a sudden knock at her office door. Tracy peeked her head through the doorway and noticed Sharice was holding court in her office.

"My bad, Reese. There's a guy lookin' for you. Said his name is Rico from Miami and that you'd know him," Tracy said, piquing Sharice's interest.

"Send him in," she said before turning her attention to Connie and Michelle. "We're done here."

Michelle turned around and made her way towards the

exit just as Rico was walking in. She accidentally bumped into him but didn't acknowledge it as she walked out of the office, fuming over the decision Sharice made. Rico chuckled as he looked towards Sharice.

"Did I come at a bad time?" He said, referring to Michelle's attitude.

"Not at all, please have a seat," Sharice said as Connie took a seat.

Rico sat next to Connie and had Sharice's undivided attention.

"Can I get you somethin' to drink?" Sharice offered.

"No, thank you," the suave Rico responded. "I won't be here long, just need a moment of your time."

Sharice nodded her head as she leaned back in her chair.

"What's up?"

Rico looked towards Connie before turning his attention to Sharice once more.

"I was hoping we could talk alone," he said.

Sharice nodded to Connie, who rolled her eyes and begrudgingly rose, making her way out of the office. Rico chuckled after he noticed Connie was out of the office.

"That one seems scary," he mentioned, causing Sharice to chuckle herself.

"She's harmless, I promise you. So, what brings you out my way?" A curious Sharice asked.

Rico was silent for a moment, struggling to express his thoughts.

"It's no secret that the Houston operation is falling apart," he explained. "I lost two more of my men out there not too long ago, and I'm afraid I'm running out of options."

"I heard about that. Sorry," Sharice responded.

Rico sighed before continuing.

"About two months ago, I offered you the job of taking control of the operation, and you turned me down," Rico stated.

"Yeah. I had a lot going on then," Sharice quipped. "You said you couldn't wait for me to get my affairs in order with my friend being shot in the hospital and all. You said you didn't have any more patience and needed to move now if I recall."

"And your affairs? Are they in order now?" Rico asked as a sly grin entered Sharice's face.

"They might be," she responded. "But you said you should have never wasted time with me. Do you remember that?"

Rico smiled, knowing what she wanted.

"I apologize if I offended you," Rico responded. "I didn't mean it. I was just so determined to make this work, and I was out of line with my comments."

Sharice smiled as an apology was all she wanted from Rico. She thought about Rico's offer still unsure if she wanted the job.

"Why me? Why now?" She asked. "I mean, I'm sure someone as high up as you gotta have like four or five folks who can handle this shit."

"I did. They're all dead now," Rico explained. "I spoke with John, and he told me how you handled yourself with his New York problem. Said you patched up things that even he couldn't. I need someone like that on this. Someone who can think."

Sharice was quiet as she pondered for several more

moments. She was stronger than she'd ever been as far as her Faction standing. With Rico's vote for boss, she would be able to achieve her ultimate dream.

"Our deal still applies?" She said, wanting verification.

"Yes. You will have my vote for boss," Rico confirmed.

After a few moments, Sharice walked over to Rico and reached out her hand. Rico rose from his chair and shook her hand, sealing their deal.

"Anything I need from you, I get, right?" She asked.

"But of course, Chica," Rico answered.

Sharice nodded her head as she kissed Rico on the cheek before he made his way out of her office. She took a deep breath knowing this move wasn't going to be an easy task.

"I need Bull and Jerome," she said to herself as she walked back behind her desk and took a seat.

In order to win the Houston battle, she would need people that she trusted leading. She wasn't at full force and needed to get her team in order.

Michelle was at her apartment watching TV later that night still bothered by Sharice's earlier ruling. Connie cost her a big chunk of change, and Michelle felt she was offered pennies for her loss. While she fumed at the TV, Theo walked into the apartment and was surprised to see his lover home.

"Hey, babe. You're home early tonight," he said as he closed the front door.

As he walked up to her, he noticed she was in a foul mood. He took a seat next to her with a hint of concern in his eyes.

"Is everything alright?" He asked.

Michelle didn't respond as she stared at the TV with anger in her eyes. Theo was about to try and communicate with her again, but he knew how Michelle can get. She's only going to talk when she's ready, and he didn't want to be at the other end of the attitude she's having. Instead, Theo decided on another approach as he quickly leaned down and grabbed his lover's ankle and began massaging her foot, catching her off guard. Michelle tried to hold onto her anger, but the massage did the trick as she calmed down.

"There we go," Theo said, working her tired foot. "I knew that would loosen you up. You wanna talk about it?"

Michelle sighed as she began to relax a bit.

"It's nothing. My boss just pissed me off," she explained. "It's like there's all this favoritism and shit. I bust my ass working, and she still shows favor to one of the girls she grew up with. It's frustrating as hell."

"Then quit," Theo suggested. "I mean, I never liked you working those late hours anyway.

"It's not that easy," Michelle responded as Theo began working on her other foot. "I like my job. It pays me good money, and I'm really good at it."

"Then transfer to another store," Theo suggested, referring to Michelle's cover story of working at Winn Dixie. "Or see if you can get another supervisor."

"I like my supervisor," Michelle replied. "It's just that bitch that she grew up with that's causing all kinds of issues. She was out on leave recently, and I took up a little more of the store while she was out. As soon as she comes back, my boss tosses her right back into place like everything's good. It's just… It's hard to explain."

Theo could tell that Michelle was frustrated and ended his foot massage. He made his way over towards her and gave her a passionate kiss before looking deep into her eyes.

"I know one way I can get your mind off work for a minute," he said as he worked his hand inside her pants and began rubbing her womanhood.

Michelle was instantly turned on as she bit her lips. Her thighs moistened from his touch.

"If it's only a minute, I'm gonna be pissed," she said, smirking.

Theo chuckled as he continued to stroke Michelle with his fingers. She quickly worked to take off her pants and remove her panties to give her lover full access to her. She then unbuttoned his pants, fighting his every touch along the way. Once he's undressed, she laid back on the couch while Theo mounted her. She gasped as he inserted his oversized manhood in her. He had gotten her warmed up already, so with every stroke, he continued his torment, which excited her, quickly causing moans. Each stroke was perfect in her eyes as it sent shocks throughout her body. He grasped her wrists with one hand and positioned her arms above her head, limiting her movements as he continued to stroke her. He ran his free hand down her arm and into her armpit, driving Michelle wild. She could no longer fight him off as the apartment was filled with her moans once she climaxed. The onslaught continued as Theo continued to punish Michelle's body much to her delight.

The next morning, Sharice made her way toward Bull's home as she pulled up just outside of his driveway. She noticed that the yard hadn't been tended to in quite some time as she walked up and knocked on his front door. After a few moments with no answer, Sharice decided to try the door, and much to her surprise, it was unlocked. She walked into the home and was disgusted with what she saw. There were fast food trash and other items scattered throughout his living room area. The stench also disturbed her when she noticed Bull passed out lying on the couch. She quickly made her way over and tried to lift her friend up.

"Bull! Wake up! Wake up!" She said, trying to get a response from him. "Come on, this is ridiculous!"

After a few taps to his unshaven face, Bull slowly woke up, surprised to see Sharice trying to pull him up.

"Sharice? Is... is that you?" He asked, trying to see what's going on around him.

"Yes, it's me! What the fuck is this?" Sharice responded as she pointed to the trash in the living room. "This place is a pigsty, and oh my god, how in the hell did you mix up shit just right to generate that odor? I mean, seriously Bull, what the fuck?"

Bull finally sat upright on the couch as Sharice took a seat next to him, trying to make sense of everything.

"I'm sorry, I've... I've just been a little busy, that's all," he replied as he rubbed his eyes, still trying to wake up.

"I ain't no doctor, Bull, but this shit can't be healthy. It just can't," Sharice responded, showing concern for her friend. "You've been trippin' since that Ritchie shit. It's almost been two months, Bull. I know the shit was hard, but you gotta let it go and get it together."

Her words fell on deaf ears as Bull tried to raise from the couch. He was off balance, falling back down, frustrating Sharice.

"Bull, look at me," she said, trying to get her friend's attention.

Bull slowly turned to Sharice, who was furious with him. "You got to get over that shit! I know you were close to the guy, but-"

"Close? Close?!" Bull exclaimed like he was offended. "I fuckin' loved him, Sharice! Loved! We grew up together as kids. You don't understand shit!"

Sharice sighed as she backed down. As much as she needed one of her top guys, she couldn't imagine the heartbreak he's going through, especially since she couldn't bring herself to kill her childhood friend.

"Okay, maybe I don't know how you feel," Sharice admitted. "But it's almost been two months. You have to move past it. I'm hearing you're making sporadic collections and shit. You're becoming an easy mark."

Bull lowered his head in shame. While he understood

what Sharice was trying to say to him, he was still full of guilt from killing his longtime friend.

"Look, your name used to ring out on them streets," Sharice told him. "If you keep this up, you're gonna lose everything you worked so hard for. Is that what you want?"

Bull didn't respond. Sharice realized she was wasting her time with her old friend.

She was about to walk off when she turned and looked at her old friend once more.

"At the end of the week, I'm headin' out of town for a job. I'm not gonna lie, I really need you on this. If you're there by Thursday, we can forget all this shit and move on," she said, hoping her friend was hearing her. "If you're not there, I'll assume you're no longer with us, and as far as I'm concerned, our relationship is done."

Those words hurt Sharice, but Bull still didn't give her the response she had hoped. After a few moments, Sharice exited out of Bull's home and headed back to her car. She took one more look at her friend's house. Through all her stern words to him, she still was concerned for his wellbeing. She started her car and quickly pulled off from the road.

Hours later, Sharice pulled up on the side of the road in an old rundown neighborhood in the downtown area. She looked over to a street corner and noticed several drug dealers working in the area. After a few moments, she exited the vehicle and made her way to two men who were standing just outside of the alleyway, overseeing the operations.

"Hey, yo," she said with a smile as she approached the men. "I'm lookin' to get with Jerome. He around?"

"Don't know no Jerome," one of the dealers answered. "If you need somethin', get with one of the young bucks down the way."

Sharice chuckled as she looked at the two dealers. One was muscular with a t-shirt on and jeans with his gold teeth shining. The other was more laid back with a simple button-down shirt, and Dickies. She looked around once more, observing the corner being worked with precision. She was impressed at the operation. It reminded her of her days on the corner.

"This is nice," she said, turning her attention back to the dealers. "Look, get on your phone, and tell Jerome that Sharice is here to see him. He'll take the call, trust me."

"I said I don't know no Jerome," the muscular dealer repeated as he checked out Sharice. "Maybe I can help you with a thing or two, ya heard me."

The other dealer looked on suspiciously.

"Hey, did you say your name was Sharice?" He asked.

"Yeah."

He quickly froze up, pulling the muscular dealer to the side.

"Nigga, do you know who you fuckin' with right now?" He said as he quickly pulled out his phone and dialed Jerome's number.

The muscular dealer looked on with confusion as the other dealer waited patiently.

"Yo, it's me. Sharice is out here sayin' she needs to get with you," he said to the phone, waiting on a response. "Alright, I'll let her know."

He hung up the line and approached Sharice once more, nervously.

"I just hit him up. Said he'll be here in about fifteen. Can I get you somethin' from the corner store or somethin'?" he asked.

"Nah, baby. I'm good. I'm gonna wait over in my car on the corner over there," she said before walking off.

The laid back dealer breathed a sigh of relief as the muscular dealer approached him with confusion.

"Nigga, what the fuck is wrong with you?" He asked. "Why you freezin' up over a bitch?"

"You know who the fuck that is, nigga?" the laid back dealer replied as he explained to the muscular dealer what's going on.

After the explanation, the muscular dealer looked on at Sharice, who entered her car, stunned that he was talking to the most powerful woman in the Faction.

Twenty minutes later, Sharice was sitting in her car surfing the internet on her cell phone, waiting for the arrival of her former lover. Jerome arrived at his corner and approached his dealers that were overlooking the area. They pointed him to her car on the corner. He smiled as he made his way over to her. He noticed that she didn't see him just outside her car door window, and he watched as she continued to surf on her phone. After a few moments, he tapped on her window, startling her as she looked over and finally noticed him. She smiled as she lowered her window.

"Boy, you scared the shit out of me," Sharice responded as she put her phone away.

"Wasn't it you that told me to always pay attention to my surroundings?" He questioned. "What if I was some crazy nigga lookin' to chop your head off?"

"Well, I figured I was on safe grounds with your crew," Sharice responded as she looked over towards his corner. "I mean, they look serviceable."

Jerome looked back at his men as well and chuckled.

"If you say so," he responded before turning his attention back to Sharice. "So, I ain't heard from you in a minute. What you doin' in my neck of the woods?"

"It hasn't been that long."

"Well, last time we spoke, you all but kicked me out your house," Jerome recalls referring to the last time the two were together.

"I don't remember it that way," Sharice replied, smirking. "Get in, I need to holla at you about somethin'."

Jerome nodded before making his way to the passenger's side, entering the vehicle. The first thing that hit him is the scent of her perfume, which grabbed him. It was the scent that always reminded him of her, and with it came the memories of their past relationship. He also noticed that the skirt on her business outfit was riding a little high on her thighs as she sat in the car. He smiled at her as he got comfortable. Sharice raised her car window before turning her attention towards her old lover.

"So, you remember the Houston job that our Miami friend wanted us to handle?" She asked Jerome, who nodded his head. "Well, it's back on. Bull's head isn't right lately, and I need someone who can help lead me through this shit. You wanted to come last time, so I'm wonderin' if you still wanted to do it."

Jerome was silent as he thought for a moment, causing Sharice to hold her breath anxiously awaiting a response from him.

"As I recall, you didn't want me on the job," he responded, smirking. "You said you didn't want me to be a distraction, remember?"

"And as I recall, you forced your way on the trip anyway," Sharice fired back with a smile. "So, I'm a woman of my word, and will allow that deal to hold if you're interested."

"So, I'm not a distraction anymore?" Jerome questioned.

"I mean, we had fun together, Rome. I think we can do this job without all that extra," Sharice answered, causing her former lover to chuckle.

"Girl, please," he quipped, confusing Sharice. "First, you come here seekin' me out with that sexy ass outfit tryin' to get my attention."

"Sexy outfit? This is just my-"

"Then you over here wearin' that perfume that you know I love," Jerome continued, cutting off Sharice. "You doin' all the shit to get my dick hard, and then gonna talk about we can do the job without all the extra."

Sharice shook her head with a smile on her face in

disbelief.

"Oh my god, you are so full of yourself, aren't you?" She asked. "First of all, this isn't my sexy outfit, or whatever you wanna call it. I always wear this. Secondly, I can't help it that my perfume gets your dick hard. That seems like a personal problem right there. I didn't wear it lookin' to drive you wild. Trust me, if I wanted to do that, I would do it."

Jerome didn't believe her since he knew her tricks. Anytime she's needed something from him, she did exactly what she's doing now, making sure to draw him in. The two have been playing this game for years, and both knew how to get what they wanted from each other. Jerome nodded his head as he noticed the slick grin filling Sharice's face.

"Whatever you say," he responded. "So, what's the game?"

Sharice sighed as she calmed down a bit.

"Our Miami friend has been gettin' his ass kicked out there," Sharice replied. "He lost two of his guys recently, and it's starting fall apart. He offered me to pick it up and fix the shit. I got muscle from him, but I need niggas with a brain out there. Bull is still strugglin' with this Ritchie shit. I can't go in there half-cocked or niggas will light me up too. I need someone I can trust out there helpin' me run this shit. Someone who I know has my back. Someone who wouldn't want a hair harmed on this sexy body."

Sharice posed, which caused Jerome to burst into laughter.

"See! Yo' ass ain't no good!" He replied. "I knew you planned this shit out. I fuckin' knew it!"

"What?" Sharice responded with a look of innocence in her eyes. "I promise you, I didn't, for real. Since you had it on your mind though, I figured I'd go ahead use it. I mean, if that's what it takes, you know."

Jerome sighed as he took a look at her once more. While he did notice the flirtation in her eyes, he also noticed something else that he hadn't seen in her in a long time. Desperation. He could tell she really wanted him on this job, and while she was joking her way through it, she was desperate. After a few moments, he slowly nodded his head.

"Alright, I'm in," he said, giving relief to his old lover. "But I'm gonna say this. If you try and hit on me while we on this job, I'm gonna-"

"Give me the dick and shut the fuck up," Sharice responded, smirking.

"Not what I was gonna say," Jerome responded. "But I do like the way you think."

"Well, Rome, you won't have to worry about that. We're gonna have our hands full with these Houston niggas to be thinkin' about all that. I tell you what, once we've done the job, how about we make a promise to celebrate? I'm talkin' a weekend in Vegas or somewhere. Just the two of us, and whatever happens, happens," a flirtatious Sharice responded.

"And what if I can't wait that long?" Jerome fired back as he checked her out once more.

"Once we're in Houston, we're all business," Sharice responded, leaving an opening for Jerome.

"Well, we're not in Houston right now," Jerome replied just as Sharice hoped he would.

"No, we are not," she responded. "How about we hook

up tonight? I wanna meet with the crew tonight and let them know what's goin' on, and after that, we can do whatever."

Jerome nodded his head as he looked at Sharice suspiciously.

"You can't tell me you didn't come out here to tease my ass," he quipped. "It's all good though. I'll make you pay for it tonight."

Sharice giggled as Jerome exited out of the car. Before closing the door, he turned back to her.

"What time we meeting tonight?" He asked.

"I'll text you and let you know," she replied.

Jerome nodded his head and walked off as both he and Sharice had each other on their minds. For Jerome, he was wondering why the sudden change in his old flame. The last time they were together, she let him go, and now all of a sudden, she's being flirtatious towards him. It was confusing, to say the least, and although he's enjoying her sudden advances, he's still concerned wondering why. Sharice, on the other hand, had struggled after their last night together, wondering if she made the right move. She thought back to what Michelle told her one night about having someone in her corner who knows who she really is was a bonus, and that she shouldn't let Jerome get away. She's been lonely ever since, and really missed her old lover's touch. She didn't know how to approach him afterward until this job fell upon her lap. It gave a usually stubborn Sharice a reason to make contact, and she wasn't gonna waste time getting back with the man that she loved. After pondering a few things, she started her car and pulled out of the neighborhood, getting her mind back to business.

Later that night, Sharice was sitting at the bar area of her club, checking out the atmosphere. The place was jumping almost filled to capacity. As she bobbed her head, Tracy walked over and handed her a drink. Sharice took a quick sip of her drink when something caught her eyes from the distance.

"Oh shit," she said, smirking when she noticed Agents Daniels and Davis in the club sitting at one of the tables on the floor.

Unlike their normal suit and tie outfits they normally

wear, the two agents are wearing civilian clothes trying to go unnoticed. Sharice chuckled as she called Tracy back over from behind the bar.

"Check that shit out. Over there at table ten," she said as she pointed out the two agents to her friend.

Tracy looked over and noticed the agents as well.

"They don't seem like the normal club hoppers," she responded. "What are they? Cops?"

"Feds actually," Sharice responded. "Same ones that came and visited me after all that shit went down with the shooting."

"Oh yeah, now I remember," Tracy responded as she peered at them once more. "Damn, they look hella different without them suits on. What you want me to do?"

Sharice thought for a moment before a smile entered her face.

"Send them a bottle of Cristal," Sharice responded with a sinister grin. "Make sure they know it's from me."

Tracy nodded her head and rushed off to execute her friend's requests. Sharice watched as Tracy walked over with a bottle of Cristal and a couple of glasses to the agent's table. They were surprised by the champagne offering as Tracy pointed back towards Sharice, who, in turn, waved at the agents from her bar stool. Daniels took the bottle as he and Davis made their way through the crowd towards Sharice.

"Ms. Legget. Thank you for the champagne, but we can't accept it. We're still on duty," Daniels said as he placed the bottle on the bar.

"You're on duty dressed like that?" Sharice quipped as she checked out both agents. "I mean, you stick out like a bitch in that shit. What, did your bosses cut your undercover clothes budget or what?"

"We all can't show off our bodies like you," Agent Davis chimed in, causing Sharice to smile.

"What's the matter? You want some of this body?" She asked as she posed and crossed her legs.

Davis didn't respond, but Sharice caught him checking out her legs and smirked.

"We're not here to play games with you," Daniels responded. "We're here checking out the establishment for any illegal activity. That's all."

Sharice ignored Daniels as she continued to flirt with Davis.

"So, what's a girl gotta do to get an agent's attention off business, and onto her?" She asked as she pulled down her revealing top just enough to keep Davis' attention. Daniels shook his head as he watched his partner be swayed by Sharice's beauty.

"We heard you were in New York recently," Daniels said, turning his attention back to Sharice. "Care to comment about your trip? It'll make our jobs a lot easier."

"Sure, I was down there to catch a Giant's game," Sharice responded, irking Daniels.

"Come on, Sharice. It's not even football season," he replied.

"I know, right! Imagine my surprise. I went all the way there for nothing," she said before turning her attention back towards Davis. "So, how about next time I'm in New York, you come out, and we can catch the game together? If it happens not to be the season again, we can spend the entire time in the hotel doing, I don't know. I guess I'll let you decide."

Davis was about to comment as he continued to leer at Sharice before Daniels waved him back.

"Of course, the trip would be on me," Sharice added. "I know the bureau isn't payin' y'all much of nothing. It'll be my little treat to my new friends."

"Are you offering us a bribe, Ms. Legget?" Daniels asked.

"Bribe is such a nasty word," Sharice responded, smirking. "I'm just tryin' to have fun, that's all. You guys seem a little uptight, and I think you could use the break."

Daniels smiled and nodded his head.

"Enjoy your night. Catch you later," he said as he and Davis made their way back towards their table.

As Davis looked back, Sharice waved to him and blew a kiss in his direction.

"What the fuck is the matter with you?" An infuriated Daniels said to his partner. "You're over there acting like a mindless idiot!"

"What? I'm just having a little fun," Davis responded, trying to calm his partner down. "I'm just playing with her head to see if I can catch her slipping."

"I hope she didn't catch you slipping," Daniels warned as he continued to monitor the club.

The smile on Sharice's face quickly dropped as she turned to Tracy.

"Look, I gotta get out of here. I don't like those fucks snoopin' around," Sharice said. "If any of the others come looking for me, tell them I'm moving the meet to the shop. They'll know what I'm talking about."

Tracy nodded her head as Sharice quickly finished her drink and got up. As she's about to walk out of the club, she's met by Jerome, who smiles at her.

"Whoa, what's up, Kiss? I thought we was meeting tonight," he said before Sharice grabbed him by his arm and led him out of the exit.

"I'll fill you in along the way," she replied as she pulled her old lover towards his vehicle.

About an hour later, Sharice and Jerome were sitting silently at a beauty shop in the west bank area of the city waiting for the others to arrive. The shop was closed, but it was one of the many businesses Sharice used as a front that was available to her. She was sitting patiently when there was a knock at the front entrance. Sharice nodded to Jerome, who walked over and peeked out of the closed blinds. He unlocked the door for Michelle, Connie, and James, who all walked in the shop, confused. He locked the door after everyone is in as the crew all gather around Sharice, who was sitting in one of the styling chairs.

"Hey, y'all. Sorry to switch venues like this, but we had some Feds in the joint, and I didn't feel comfortable tellin' y'all what I'm about to tell you," Sharice said, causing concern to the others. "Almost two months ago, Rico offered me a job out in Houston to get our thing up and runnin' out there. With that shit with Dre, I wasn't able to take him up on his offer. He hit me up recently and told me things aren't goin' as planned and offered me the gig again. I've decided to take it this go-round."

Michelle and Connie were stunned with the news while James nodded his head with approval.

"Is this gonna get you your stripes?" he asked, referring to Sharice becoming boss.

"Not if I fuck it up," Sharice responded, smirking. "I'm

not sure how long this is gonna take, so I'm gonna be out of the city for a while until it's done. These H–Town niggas seem to be a pain in the ass, so I'll see how it goes. With that being said, I need to make sure shit out here runs smoothly so I can focus on Houston. So, while I'm out of town, Michelle, you're gonna be the top dog runnin' shit."

A big smile grew on Michelle's face. The news upset Connie, who couldn't believe what she just heard.

"What the fuck, Reese? How you gonna pass me up for this bitch," Connie fired back before looking towards her adversary. "Your ass ain't built for this shit!"

"I guess we'll see, now won't we?" a sly Michelle responded, smirking.

Before Connie could respond, Sharice interjected.

"Look, that's enough, you two!" Sharice exclaimed, calming her two female crew members down. "Now, Connie, you're not in charge because you'll be with me out in Houston."

Connie was stunned once more with Sharice's decision.

"You want me in Houston?" She asked for

confirmation. "Why?"

"Because I'm shorthanded right now," Sharice explained. "Besides, there may be a lot of action down there, and we know how much you love puttin' in work."

The rest of the group chuckled to themselves as Connie nodded her head.

"I'm down for whatever. Let them H-Town niggas talk shit. I got you," she replied.

"Good. Now, Chelle, I'm trustin' you to keep shit running out here. You and James partner up and work out collections and whatnot," Sharice said, looking towards the duo. "This is some shit y'all gonna have to be on point with."

Michelle and James nodded their heads with understanding. Sharice turned her attention towards Connie and Jerome.

"You two, get to packin'. I wanna be out of here Thursday night," Sharice instructed. "Once we touch down, Rico has a guy there that will let us know what's what. We'll figure out the rest and start planning after that. Any questions?"

Her crew all shook their heads with their instructions being clear.

"Alright, give me and Chelle some space," she instructed.

Connie gave her boss a look before making her way out of the shop, followed by Jerome and James. After they're gone, Michelle took a seat in the chair next to Sharice.

"Look, I'm not sure how long I'm gonna be out here for this," Sharice said. "I've worked hard to get this city running just the way it keeps me under the radar. Them Feds are stickin' their nose in my business again lately, and it's got me a little nervous. Make sure you're careful. They popped up in the club earlier tonight just loungin' and shit. If they're not afraid to be seen like that, they may be workin' somebody on the inside."

Michelle nodded her head as Sharice continued.

"Also, Money might come by askin' questions and shit about the business," Sharice pointed out. "Look, I know we work for the nigga, but every time he pokes his nose in and sees what we're doing, he tries to put his little spin on it, and it ends up fuckin' up the business. I keep the nigga

139

paid, so he doesn't have to ask questions, but if he does come around tryin' to see what's what, tell that nigga nothing. Be as vague as possible. Last thing I need is him stickin' his nose in my shit and fuckin' it up. The old way of doin' things don't work anymore. He doesn't understand that. He just needs to kick back and enjoy the money. I don't care if he is the boss, tell his ass nothing, ya dig."

Michelle chuckled as she nodded her head.

"I got you, Reese. I won't let you down," Michelle replied.

Sharice nodded as she leaned back in her chair.

"I ain't gonna lie, Chelle. You movin' up in this game rather quickly," Sharice said. "Truth be told, this should be Connie's job as my number one, but you have a way of doing things with a little less flare. That's a good thing this day and age. I don't trust my business to just anyone. Still, this shit ain't easy, and while you're runnin' things, you're gonna have to make some tough decisions. Are you sure you're up for this? It's okay if you're not. I can make other plans if I need to."

"I've been ready for this, on the real," Michelle confidently responded. "I'm not gonna let you down."

Sharice pondered her thoughts for a moment before slowly nodding her head.

"Alright, but as they say, be careful what you wish for," Sharice responded.

Michelle nodded her head as the two continued to discuss different points of the business Michelle needed to look out for.

About an hour later, Connie was sitting with her friend Nicole at an all-night daiquiri shop in New Orleans East. The sidewalks were filled with customers as men flashed their expensive vehicles hoping to get the attention of the scantily dressed females in the area. As the party filled atmosphere raged on with music blasting in the background, Nicole leered at several females trying to get Connie's attention, but she could tell her friend wasn't in the party mood as she watched Connie pick at her daiquiri.

"Why you trippin', girl?" Nicole asked as she adjusted her long blond hair to better see her friend.

"I ain't trippin'. Just got a lot of shit on my mind," Connie responded before taking a quick sip of her drink.

Nicole shook her head with disbelief. She surveyed the area once more, making eye contact with several females. She wanted to make sure her booty shorts and revealing top caught everyone's eyes. She was a little disappointed as only the men were looking her way. One male tried to approach her, but she quickly waved him off.

"Bye, nigga," she said before the male can get a word in.

As he quickly made his way off, Nicole turned to her friend once again, trying to understand her mood.

"Come on, Cee. We used to do our thing at this spot," Nicole pointed out. "I know it's been a minute, but I know you remember who we used to pick up a hoe or two and hook up at the Friendly Inn. Those were the day, boo! Now, all we do is sit here and watch you mope all night. I mean, seriously, what the fuck is goin' on?"

Connie sighed as she finally answered her friend.

"Sharice did this half-ass ruling against me over that new bitch Michelle," Connie replied, causing Nicole to roll her eyes. "Then she got the nerve to let that same bitch be in charge while she babysits my ass in Houston. Can you believe that shit?"

"You know what I can't believe? Every fuckin' time we go out, you gotta bring work with you," a frustrated Nicole fired back. "I mean, can we have one night without you mentioning Sharice? Is that too much to ask?"

"I'm sorry if I'm ruinin' your mood, but the shit is stressin' me out," Connie replied before taking a deep breath.

Nicole could tell her friend was struggling and backed down.

"I'm sorry, boo," she said. "I didn't mean it like that. I know you be on it with her, and that's gotta be some hard shit."

"You don't know the half of it," Connie responded after sipping on her drink. "She's draggin' me to Houston like I'm not worthy of runnin' shit. I been down with her since day one, and her ass still don't trust me. She's known this bitch Michelle for like three months and already givin' her the keys and shit. I took a bullet for her ass, and this is how she fuckin' treats me?"

"It's fucked up, I know," Nicole chimed in, putting her arm around her friend. "But ain't shit gonna get fixed by you stressin' on it. You need to focus that energy into somethin' else. Like tryin' to find the next bitch to hook up with, ya dig."

Connie giggled as she nodded her head. The two friends rose from their seats and joined the crowd in the parking lot, looking for women to get their night started with. At a table overseeing the entire area, an undercover FBI agent wearing civilian clothes was monitoring Connie from a distance. He had an earpiece in and gave an update while keeping his eyes on his target from afar.

Back at Sharice's home, she and Jerome were interlocked in a passionate sex session in her bedroom. As Jerome worked his magic on her, Sharice was almost in tears taking the pleasure that was being dealt out to her. Her emotions were running wild as she tried to make the moment last as long as she could. After several more strokes, Sharice finally gave in to the pleasure as her body tensed up with a powerful orgasm taking over. Jerome was breathing heavily as he finished up himself before rolling over to the side. He looked towards Sharice with a smile on his face as the two were breathing heavily.

"Well, shit, I can tell you've been denied for a while," he said, causing Sharice to giggle.

"Whatever, nigga," she playfully responded. "I ain't a hoe like you. I don't fuck just to be fucking."

"Oh, so I'm a hoe now?" Jerome asked before poking Sharice on the side of her stomach, causing her to laugh.

"Jerome, don't please," she begged him as he started to tickle her. "Please stop! Stop! Stop it!"

"Take it back!" He commanded as he continued to torment her.

"Okay! Okay! I take it back! I take it back!" Sharice screamed out in between laughter, trying to fight her way from her lover.

Jerome laughed as he ceased his assault to a worn-out Sharice. After a few moments, he reached out to her and tried to bring her in close. Sharice was cautious initially but eventually made her way over to her lover as the two looked at each other, trying to figure out what the other is thinking.

"I have a question," Jerome said, disrupting the silence. "Why did you ask me to come on this trip?"

"Ask you?" A confused Sharice responded. "As I remember it, you threatened to tickle me if I didn't let you go, or do you not remember that shit."

"Yeah, I remember that," Jerome responded with a slick grin. "What I'm talkin' about is now. That was for some shit we set up way back that never came. You could have left here, and I wouldn't have been the wiser."

"I keep my word, Rome. I said you could go. When it came back up, my word to you didn't change," Sharice explained.

"Nah, it's somethin' else," Jerome pointed out to a confused Sharice. "I mean, you was talkin' about how I'd be a distraction and shit, and wouldn't even let me be a part of your crew officially. Then all outta the blue and shit, you offer me to roll with you, and even hooking up like this. What's all this about, really?"

Sharice sighed, struggling with expressing her feelings

to her lover.

"Michelle," Sharice replied, confusing Jerome. "I guess I never realized how lonely I am."

"So, you thinkin' about hookin' up with Michelle now?" Jerome joked. "'Cause I'd be down if y'all wanna hook somethin' up, for real."

Sharice looked at her lover as is she's turned off by him.

"You see, that's why I called your ass a hoe," she fired back, causing him to laugh.

"My bad, my bad, I'm sorry," an apologetic and playful Jerome responded as he pulled Sharice in closer.

"Look, it's just... I don't really have anyone close to me, and although I'm out here chasin' this shit, I'm alone with it all. I spoke to Michelle at the club one night about it, and she's out there doin' her thing with a whole man at the house waiting for her every night," Sharice explained. "I almost called you that night after me and her chat. I... I don't know. It just sucks to not have anyone close to you who doesn't know you, you know."

"Get out of here. What about Tracy? You and her are

close," Jerome pointed out. "And as crazy as she is, you have Connie too. It's not like you're lonely in that sense."

"Well, first off, Tracy and I are close, but I keep her as far away from the business as I can," Sharice explained. "I don't want her involved. She just handles the club. She doesn't know what all goes down on the streets. As far as Connie is concerned-"

Sharice stopped midsentence. She knew the real reason she and Connie were distant was because of Lavina's death. She didn't want to share that with Jerome. After a few moments, she smiled before continuing with her thoughts.

"Well, Connie can't provide me some things like you can," Sharice responded as she grabbed Jerome's shaft, successfully deflecting her thoughts.

"Not for lack of trying, I'm sure," Jerome pointed out, referring to Connie's obsession with Sharice.

Sharice giggled as she started to stroke Jerome's manhood, much to his delight.

"I'm not gonna lie, I'm scared," she admitted. "But havin' you here, next to me… I'm willing to give it a go.

That is if you're willing to have me."

Sharice continued to stroke Jerome, getting him erect once again. She smiled, knowing she had him right where she wants him.

"So, what do you think?" She asked as she continued to slowly fondle him. "You think this can work?"

"Yeah, I think I'm down," Jerome responded as bliss filled his body.

"Nigga, I could ask you to eat my ass out right now, and you'd agree," Sharice fired back, smirking. "That's alright. I'll let you sleep on it. But for now, it seems like you ready for round two."

Sharice quickly mounted Jerome and placed his shaft inside of her, surprising him. Sharice started grinding on him as he tried to control her as best he could.

"Wait! Wait!" He pleaded to her.

"Nah, nigga. You tickled me earlier. I then told you about that shit," Sharice replied with a sinister grin on her face, ignoring her lover's pleas. "You bet not cum quick 'cause I ain't gonna stop 'til I'm fuckin' ready!"

Sharice started grinding on Jerome with force as he

struggled to keep up with her. She doubled down as she reached down and ran her nails on his sack, driving him wild. A cryptic smile filled her face because the torment had just begun for her lover.

The next morning, Sharice was sitting in her kitchen on a stool next to her island as she and Jerome ate the breakfast she had prepared. She smiled as she watched her lover enjoy his food, still in his underwear. Sharice couldn't help but notice his bulging muscular build as she took a quick sip of her orange juice.

"Why you gotta sit here lookin' like that?" She said, catching his attention.

"Like what?"

"Sitting in your draws, like you wanna go another round," she answered.

"Girl, you ain't tired?" Jerome responded with a chuckle. "I gotta go get my folks together and shit. Can't be leaving out of town all half-cocked as you would say."

"That's not the cock I'm worrying about," Sharice responded as she opened up her robe. "I know you ain't gonna turn this down, are you?"

Before Jerome could respond, there was a knock at Sharice's front door. Sharice picked up her phone and checked out her security camera app. She sat stunned as Jerome looked for answers.

"Who is it?" he asked.

"It's Bull," Sharice responded, still stunned.

"Alright. Let me get dressed and get outta here," Jerome responded as got up from his stool.

Sharice tied up her robe and fixed her hair quickly before making her way to her front door. She opened the door for Bull, who was stunned to see her still in her robe.

"Shit! Sorry, Reese, I thought you were already up," he said. "I can come back later."

"No, Bull, it's fine. Come on in," Sharice responded, waving him in.

Bull nodded as he walked into the home. Sharice led him over to her living room, and the two took a seat across from each other.

"Look, again, I'm sorry to bother you this early, but I just needed a minute," he explained.

"Yeah. Look, I have something I wanted to say to you as well," Sharice said.

"Please, let me go first," Bull replied. "Look, I know I haven't been around these last couple of months. I've been unreliable, and my behavior has been inexcusable. I won't let that shit happen again; you got my word on that."

Sharice shook her head with a slight grin on her face.

"Bull, what I was gonna say was-"

"No, let me finish," Bull interrupted. "I know it had to be done. Without gettin' to specifics, I knew it had to be done when I brought it to you. I hope that alone proves my loyalty."

Before Sharice could respond, Jerome walked over and motioned to Sharice that he's leaving. Sharice nodded her head as Bull looked at Jerome as well as the two nodded to each other before Jerome made his way out of the house.

"Jesus Christ, I really interrupted your morning," Bull said. "I'm sorry, Reese. I didn't know. You can call him back in, and I'll-"

"For fuck's sake, Bull, can I get a word in please?" Sharice responded, causing Bull to back down. "What I was gonna say is… look, I'm sorry the way I came at you the other day. You are a big reason I am what I am, and I shouldn't have come at you that way."

Bull sighed as he eased up a bit. Sharice could tell he's still a little stressed over the situation.

"Look, I wasn't thinking clearly. I shouldn't have never put you in that position," she responded referring to the hit on his best friend.

"All due respect, I was the only one who could have done it," Bull reminded her. "It had to be done that way."

"No, it could have done a thousand different ways. I just chose the easy route not considering how it would hurt you. If I was in your position… I don't know. I don't think I could have did what needed to be done," Sharice replied. "Look, I shouldn't have gave you an ultimatum. Take all the time you need to get yourself together. When you're ready, get with me, and we'll get you back runnin'."

Bull took a moment to think about Sharice's words. He could see that her intentions were genuine, and he appreciated her looking out for him through the struggle.

"Thanks, boss lady," he said, smirking. "Look, I'm

ready to get back into action. You said you have a job you need me for? When do we start?"

A smile grew on Sharice's face as she nodded her head.

"You ever been to Houston?" She asked her longtime friend.

"Once or twice," he answered.

"Then pack up. We're heading out this evening. I'll get you up to speed later," she said as the two stood up.

They shared a hug with each other before Bull made his way out of the home. Sharice was ecstatic to have one of her key guys back in the game, and for the first time since accepting the Houston job from Rico, she felt she had a great chance to bring it all together.

Chapter 4

Lessons Learned

In the early morning hours, Michelle was lying in her bed, flipping through the channels trying to find something of interest on to watch on her TV to battle her insomnia. Theo was tossing and turning in bed next to her, trying to sleep, but the sound of the TV was disturbing him. Michelle finally saw something on the news that piqued her interest.

"Police are investigating a shooting on the corner of Earhart and Claiborne that left three dead overnight. Witnesses say it's an ongoing dispute between rival drug gangs in the area that has the neighborhood on high alert, keeping the residents stuck in their homes during the later

hours," the news anchor reported as Michelle paid special attention.

After a few moments, Theo had enough, turning to Michelle.

"Babe, please. Can you turn the TV down a little?" He requested. "I gotta be at work in the morning."

Michelle didn't respond since she's focused on the news story. The corner where the shooting took place is run by dealers who worked for the Faction. She knew this type of negative attention could hurt their standing and decided she needed to meet with the culprits to settle this dispute before things got out of hand.

"Michelle? Hello?" Theo said, annoying his partner, who finally snapped out of her gaze.

"What?" She responded.

"The TV. Please? I gotta be up in a few hours," Theo requested once more.

"Oh, my bad. I'm... I'm sorry," Michelle responded as she cuts the TV off.

She lied down on the bed, still wide awake, thinking about her next move.

The next day, Sharice and her crew arrive at the Budget Inn Suites, where Rico's crew set up their main base of operation during the war. She was disgusted looking around. The hotel was run down and falling apart all over. As she exited the vehicle, the smell of the surroundings hit her like a bag of bricks. She couldn't believe this is where they were set up at.

"Rico's gotta be kidding," she said to Connie while surveying the area. "I can't stay in this shithole. Get on the line and see if there's a Sheraton or something close by 'cause this ain't gonna work."

Connie nodded her head as she took out her phone and started searching.

"Anyone else wants me to look for somethin'?" She asked Jerome and Bull.

Neither responded as Connie shook her head in disappointment.

"Y'all some cheap niggas I swear," she said while continuing to search over the phone.

As they continue to walk in the parking lot, Sharice noticed several of Rico's crew standing outside looking at

157

her and her crew. She could tell by the way they were looking at her that they weren't too enthused about a woman leading the charge. Sharice decided to nip it in the bud early as she whistled and waved the men in. After they've all gathered, Sharice stood in the center of the group and addressed them.

"My name is Sharice, and I'm leadin' this job right now," Sharice said as she noticed one of the group members translating her words in Spanish for those who didn't speak English. "I know a lot of you don't approve of a female leadin' this shit, but if you could get the job done, then I wouldn't be here. What I want, I get, and if you have a problem takin' orders from a woman, then you can get the fuck outta here and head back to Miami or wherever the fuck you're from."

Sharice looked around as the interpreter continued to translate her words.

"This is Connie, Bull, and Jerome. If any of them give you an order, you do it," Sharice continued while pointing out her crew. "From now on, nobody does shit unless one of us instructs you. Got it?"

Rico's crew all remained silent as several of them nodded their heads with understanding. Sharice dismissed them as she led her crew to her room. As she walked into the room, she shook her head at the basic setup. From the orange carpet to the stained walls, this hotel room was as low budget as it gets. Sharice sighed, wondering why she offered to take the job in the first place.

"What the fuck, Rico," she said to herself while Bull and Jerome checked out the rest of the room.

"Well, I can tell you by the look of things, Rico chose this spot because it's low key," Bull said as he looked out of the window. "There's no security cams, no families here, and judging by the way our friends are hangin' out with their guns, not much of a police presence. Honestly, not a bad spot."

"It smells like piss in here," Sharice pointed out as she walked towards the bathroom.

She cringed because the funky smell is strongest in the bathroom as she looked around. It looked as if it hasn't been cleaned in months with toilet paper scattered on the floor and leaky faucets on both the sink and the shower.

She slowly backed away from the bathroom, sighing as she turned to Connie.

"Please tell me you found somethin'?" She asked her friend, looking to find somewhere to stay at.

"Yeah, there's a Hilton about fifteen minutes away," Connie answered as she looked on her phone. "Using your Latoya I.D., right?"

"Yeah. Make sure you get three rooms," Sharice instructed.

"Aw, you're spottin' us a room?" Connie asked before Sharice rejects her notion.

"Hell no! Get your own rooms," Sharice responded. "See if all three of the rooms are shared. Set them up for at least the next week. We'll figure some things out after that."

Connie shook her head but placed the order as Sharice handed her a credit card. She then turned her attention to Jerome.

"Go out there and bring in Eddie," she instructed. "Rico said he'd be our contact in this dump. Let's see what he has for us."

Jerome nodded his head as he exited the room. Sharice sighed as she took a seat on the corner of the bed. She pulled out her phone and searched for several places in the area, hoping to continue her daily life without much change. As she searched, Jerome returned with Eddie, Rico's main contact. He was a small skinny guy with long hair. He didn't look fierce at all in Sharice's eyes. *It's probably the reason they're struggling,* Sharice thought before she rose from the bed to greet him.

"Eddie, I assume," she asked as she shook his hand.

"Yes, ma'am," he responded with a strong Hispanic accent.

"Please, just Sharice," she responded, offering him a seat at the desk before retaking her seat on the corner of the bed. "So, Rico told me you're the last man standing out here. What happened?"

Eddie sighed before going into his story.

"We've been battling back and forth with the Rock over corners for the past month," he explained. "We were making ground when his men took out two of our guys last week in Sunnyside."

"The Rock?" Connie asked as she took a seat next to Sharice.

"Yeah, he's the big man out here," Eddie responded. "He controls about eighty percent of the dope in the area. He has soldiers ready to go to war at the drop of a dime. The few corners we do run down here are constantly being harassed by his people."

Sharice thought for a moment before continuing the conversation.

"Tell me about the other twenty percent," she responded. "If he controls eighty, what's up with the others?"

"Simple pushers and cornermen," Eddie answered. "Nothing big."

"Maybe, but together they could hold some weight," Sharice pointed out. "Tell me how the Rock operates. How does he get his product?"

"From what I could find out, he's importing his supply from Mexico," Eddie responded.

"Could be cartel," Bull responded.

"Yeah, most likely, but I don't know exactly which

cartel," Eddie replied. "By cutting out the middleman, and with the territory he's running, he's at least pulling one and a half to two million a week. Easily."

Sharice tapped her leg as she thought for a moment.

"Does he have any issues with law enforcement?" She asked.

"No. From what I can tell, he has the law and several politicians in his pocket," Eddie answered. "It's pretty laid back here. All you need to know is who to grease to get things done."

"Interesting," Sharice responded as she thought for a moment. "What about his crew? Tell me about them."

"He has a lot of heavy hitters on his crew, but his two most important men are Troy and Double R," Eddie answered. "They are the ones who make shit happen in the streets. Nobody talks to Rock without talking to them first. I'm more than certain they were responsible for the Sunnyside hit."

"So, they're at his side for the most part?" Sharice confirmed to a nodding Eddie.

Sharice looked towards Connie and Bull as she thought

about her next move.

"Okay, Eddie, I need you to get word to this Rock," Sharice said, turning her attention back to him. "I want a sit down with him here in the next day or so. I just wanna talk. No tricks or shit. I'm flexible with time, so whatever works for him, works for me."

Eddie was stunned by Sharice's instructions.

"You wanna set up a meeting?" He asked.

"Yeah, what's the problem?" Sharice asked.

"I don't know. I mean, I thought we were here to muscle this guy out," Eddie responded. "No disrespect, but he's killed a lot of our crew."

"Did you or any of your crew try and sit down with the man?" A confused Sharice asked.

Eddie shook his head, stunning Sharice who is in disbelief with his answer.

"Well, that's probably why your crew keeps getting' shot up," Sharice pointed out, upsetting Eddie. "You don't just show up to somebody's city and try to muscle them out. It makes them desperate. Plus, they have the home-field advantage. No disrespect to you and yours, but this is the exact way you lose a battle. I'm not sayin' we aren't gonna have to cap some folks, but you meet with your enemy to see them face to face. See if there's a weakness. Once you learn about them, you'll be better equipped to fight them. This shit you're givin' me doesn't help with the battle."

Eddie was still upset with the sit down but nodded his head with understanding.

"Now, I want to do a little more research on his corners and the area," Sharice said as she turns to Connie. "Get together two groups. The first group, send them out to the various corners, projects, and neighborhoods that the Rock runs. They are there to collect names only. No shootin'," Sharice instructed. "The other group send to check out five-o. We need to figure out how we can get the law on our side."

Connie nodded her head as Sharice turns her attention back to Eddie.

"Thanks for the intel, Eddie," she said. "We will keep in touch."

Eddie nodded his head before he got up and made his

way out of the room, followed by Connie.

"So how 'bout I take the law crew, and you take the corner crew?" Bull asked Jerome, who chuckled.

"Oh, so I gotta sit up in the car lookin' at project niggas all day while you get to watch the cops in the safe area?" He pointed out jokingly. "That's like borderline racist, for real."

"Well, I think it'd be a little strange to see a white guy in the middle of the projects, don't you?" Bull responded.

"White privilege at its finest," Jerome responded, causing Bull to laugh.

Sharice chuckled herself, rising.

"Look, be careful, guys," Sharice warned. "We ain't shit out here. We might get caught up real quick. These stupid sons of a bitches then already fucked us up here. If the Rock was smart, he'd hit us quick and hard."

"Yeah. You gotta wonder what Rico was thinkin' with this," Bull responded.

"Well, I'm outta here. I'm gonna head over to my hotel. Hit me on the burna if you need me. Please enjoy the toilet bowl," Sharice said as she grabbed her purse and walked out of the room.

Jerome and Bull chuckled to themselves as they both made their way out of the room as well to join the rest of the crew.

At a local New Orleans FBI safe house, Agents Daniels and Davis were sitting in their conference room with Faction boss 'Money' Mike going over several different photos and other items.

"Yeah, that's that nigga right there," Money said, confirming what Davis and Daniels suspected on one of the photos he's looking act.

"Good," Davis responded before looking towards Daniels. "Should we get the Miami office to bring him in?"

"No. Let's see what else we can find out before moving in," Daniels answered, knowing that Flores is still undercover within the Miami organization. "I mean, we got what we need to take him anytime we want. Let's see where he leads us."

Davis nodded his head as he took the picture back from Money and added it into his file. Daniels turned his attention to Money, who was looking as though he's bored.

"You've done good today, Mike," he said to his informant. "It would be better for us and you, however, if you could get us more information on John and his organization."

"I then told y'all I don't have that type of relationship with him, or the rest of the wops," Money responded. "The shit y'all askin' about is hard to come by."

"Sharice has a relationship with him," Daniels responded. "Speaking of which, our sources say she was with him in New York a few days ago. Any idea why they were there?"

Money shrugged, frustrating Daniels.

"Hey, I gave y'all that when it happened," Money pointed out. "So don't give me the stink eye and shit."

"What about now? I hear Sharice is out in Texas. What's going on there?" Daniels fired back.

"I told y'all about that shit too!" Money exclaimed. "I told you Rico came to me on that shit. He's tryin' to get our business out there in Houston and wanted to use her to set that shit up. Y'all the ones slippin', for real."

Daniels chuckled, shaking his head in disbelief.

"Let me ask you this, who is running her crew right now?" Daniels inquires, confusing his informant.

"I... well, I'm not one hundred percent, but-"

"You don't have a fucking clue, do you?" Daniels asked the stuttering Money. "How you became the boss of anything boggles my mind. Sharice leads you around by the nose, and you let her. My guess is the only reason she keeps you around is so you will take the hit when the hammer drops."

Money frowned, offended by Daniels's words.

"Naw, you got the shit twisted," he fired back. "I run shit. If I tell that bitch jump, she asks how high. I set this shit up, so she is the face everyone knows while I'm lying back in the cut safe from all this shit."

"And yet here you are," Davis responded, smirking. "A lot of good that did."

"In case you were wondering, Michelle was left in charge from what we can tell," Daniels pointed out to a confused Money.

"Who?"

Daniels grabbed his head in frustration before responding.

"Michelle. Sharice's right hand while Connie was in the hospital," he explained.

"Oh! You mean redbone with the long hair?" Money responded, finally understanding. "She's a piece of ass, for real."

"Yeah, well why don't you go down to the club and talk to that *piece of ass*," Daniels responded as his frustration grows. "Maybe she can give us something that can help bring down Sharice."

Money nodded his head with understanding.

"Hang tight, we'll get you a ride back," Daniels said as he nodded to Davis to meet him outside the conference room.

Both agents made their way out and closed the door behind them.

"Any word from Flores?" Daniels asked.

"Not much. Pretty much corroborating what Mike has told us. She's still trying to earn Rico's trust, so I'm sure you know what that means," Davis answered, referring to

Flores' history of sleeping with her marks.

Daniels sighed before walking off, frustrated with how the operation is going thus far.

Later that evening, Michelle's sitting on a bench at the lakefront staring out into the abyss. The setting sun reflected from her sunglasses as she sat in silence awaiting the arrival of two of the crew leaders that were part of the altercation she observed on the news the night before. After several moments, two cars pull up and park across the street from her. Big Rob exited the first vehicle with a frown on his face as he noticed K Dub exiting the other vehicle. K Dub chuckled to himself as he watched Big Rob jogging across the street, seemingly out of breath because of his weight. Michelle noticed both dealers making their way towards her and rose to greet them.

"You're late," she snapped at them as they both approached her.

"My bad, we thought you was on the other side," K Dub responded as Big Rob tried to catch his breath.

"Why the fuck would I be on the white side?" Michelle

questioned. "You know what? Never mind. I asked you fools here to find out what happened the other night. I gotta see this shit on the news? What the fuck is goin' on?"

"What's goin' on is this nigga took two of my people out," an enraged Big Rob responded. "He's breakin' the property lines."

"Nigga, please!" K Dub snapped back. "This nigga talkin' about property lines and shit, and he don't even have anyone on the block usin' the muthafucka. Prime real estate, and ain't nobody been on the block in weeks!"

"Nigga, what I do with my property ain't got shit to do with you!" Big Bob said as the two are getting heated.

Michelle stepped between them to calm the situation down.

"Fuck all that shit!" She yelled, grabbing their attention. "What matters is this shit needs to be settled. A fuckin' bystander was hit as well, and that's the type of shit we don't need!"

"A what?" Big Rob asked.

"She means somebody who don't have nothin' to do with nothin'. Damn, you a stupid nigga," K Dub responded.

"Alright, enough of that name callin' shit!" Michelle warned. "Like y'all niggas five years old and shit. The point is your shit is causin' us shit, so now we gotta step in."

"Step in? Where the fuck is Sharice on this?" K Dub asked. "She told me she'd be here to settle all disputes. Why are we talkin' to you?"

"For real," Big Rob responded. "Where she at?"

"She's outta town dealin' with some other shit. I'm here, so you're gonna have to deal with me," Michelle explained. "Do we have a problem?"

Both K Dub and Big Rob were silent as Michelle continued.

"So, you said he was on your territory?" Michelle said, looking at Big Rob.

"Fuck yeah!" Big Rob exclaimed. "Check it out, my nigga Andre was pinched 'cause of some nigga he dropped a few months back. He ran that corner and shit, and the next thing I know, this high yella bitch here has his crew sellin' on my block!"

"First of all, you betta watch that shit before I beat your fat, Jell-O puddin' eatin' fuckin' ass," K Dub threatened, causing Michelle to slightly smirk. "Second, this nigga ain't tellin' the whole truth. That nigga Andre was picked up damn near a month ago, and ain't nobody been on the block since then! Territory belongs to whoever claims it! Since he wasn't usin' it, I set up my own people on it. I made sure we was respectin' the lines. He didn't have a corner nowhere close to there. My people was mindin' they business when his folks rolled through startin' shit. All my folks did was defend themselves."

"How are we startin' shit when it's our corner to begin with?" Big Rob fired back. "It ain't your territory to just be startin' shit!"

"Why not, nigga? You wasn't usin' it!" K Dub retorted.

"Yo, Michelle! You got a rulin' on this shit, or what?" Big Rob asked as both he and K Dub looked towards her.

Michelle didn't say anything for a moment as she tried to figure out what to do next. After a few moments of silence, she finally addressed the two dealers.

"Alright, so the block was Big Rob's shit initially, right?" She asked.

"Hell yeah," Big Rob responded.

"Why weren't you doing anything with it then?" She fired back, catching him off guard.

"I was busy with other shit! I didn't have time to set back up after Andre left," Big Rob explained.

"Yeah, your ass was busy, alright. Busy watchin' money walk away," K Dub responded. "He didn't want the shit or the money that came with it!"

Michelle was silent once again because she's not sure how to handle the situation. Both dealers could see in her eyes that she wasn't confident.

"Alright… look, I'm gonna hit Sharice up and run this by her to see what she wants to do," she said, upsetting the dealers.

"What the fuck? You said you was the woman with this shit," K Dub reminded her.

"Yeah, I mean, what are we payin' y'all niggas for?" Big Rob chimed in. "Y'all promised y'all would handle shit like this!"

"Hey, take it easy!" Michelle fired back. "Now look, I'm gonna reach out and see what she wants to do about all this. I need you two to play nice until I can hit her up. No fuckin' shooting! You understand?"

K Dub and Big Rob begrudgingly nodded their heads before walking off back to their cars. Michelle breathed a sigh of relief before pulling out her cell phone and dialing Sharice.

Sharice was talking on the phone while getting settled in at her hotel room, which is a far cry from the run-down motel she left from earlier. She rolled her eyes as she plopped down on the bed, trying to get comfortable.

"Michelle, I understand... look, you need to make a decision," she said, grabbing her head, frustrated. "That's why I left you in charge... look, Michelle, handle it. I'm not there, you are. I can't... look, I gotta go. Just take care of it... later."

She breathed a sigh of relief before tossing her phone next to her. Just as she closed her eyes and was about to relax, there is a sudden knock at her door. A confused

Sharice slowly walked over to her bag and pulled out a gun before approaching her door. She looked into the peephole, lowering her weapon to the side when she noticed Jerome standing outside of her door. She opened the door to a smiling Jerome.

"How in the fuck did you know what room I was in?" She asked him.

"Girl, please. You know you can't hide from me," he responded, smirking. "So, you gonna let me in or what?"

Sharice opened the door for her lover as he walked in and looked around the room.

"Damn, this is nice," he said. "I can see why you not messin' with us poor folks."

"Anyway, is there a reason you're here? I was just about to call it a night," Sharice responded as she watched her lover get a feel for the place. "We got a lot of shit to do tomorrow, so you should be turning in yourself."

"Don't mind if I do," Jerome replied before plopping down on the bed.

Sharice approached him with a smile, looking down at him with her hands on her hips.

"Excuse me?" She said, looking for an explanation. "What do you think you're doing?"

"Calling it the night," Jerome responded. "Gone head and get into those pajamas. I'll just order up some room service since I haven't eaten."

Jerome reached for the phone when Sharice quickly walked over and grabbed the phone from him, putting it back on the receiver. Jerome responded by grabbing his lover by the waist and rolling her onto the bed, much to her surprise. He quickly mounted her and secured her wrists over her head, causing her to giggle.

"Really, Rome?" She said while looking into his eyes. "You see, this is why I didn't want you here when you first asked me. You play too much, and you're very distractive right about now."

"Girl, please. You like the attention, you always have," Jerome replied. "You need a nigga to take your ass over every now and then. You're so used to runnin' shit all the time that you don't know what it feels like to not have control."

"Oh, and you're the one who is gonna teach me to let

loose?" She asked with a sinister grin.

"Well, it's a challenge. Maybe my most difficult one yet, but I'm down," Jerome responded before moving in close and kissing his lover.

Sharice tried to wrestle her arms from Jerome's clutches, but his grip was too strong. She had no choice but to accept the passionate kiss she was receiving, being helpless in his hands. The two were just about to get going when Sharice's phone began to ring.

"Wait, that's the burna phone," she said, trying to get Jerome's attention. "I gotta answer it."

"Only if you promise to go to dinner with me tonight," Jerome responded with a slick grin.

"Fine, fine! Now let me get it before it stops ringing," Sharice responded.

Jerome released Sharice from his hold as she quickly reached over and picks up her phone.

"Hello… yeah… now? Okay… okay, I'm on my way," Sharice said, hanging up the phone.

"Rock wants to meet in the next half hour," Sharice responded, looking at her disappointed lover. "We need to hurry."

"I have a rock too, you know," Jerome responded, causing Sharice to burst into laughter.

"Yeah, well, your rock can wait," she responded as she jumped out of bed and headed to the bathroom to straighten herself out.

Almost an hour later, Sharice was sitting back at the motel looking at the time on her phone, becoming agitated because Rock hadn't arrived at their meet yet. She was sitting on the corner of the bed with Connie and Bull waiting patiently with her.

"This nigga ain't comin'," Connie said, breaking the silence. "I think he played us, or he's about to start some shit. We really need to bunker down before we get caught slippin'."

"Relax, we have a crew out there looking over the spot," Bull reminded Connie. "If this was a setup, we'd hear somethin' and be able to react."

Connie sighed as she began pacing the room. Sharice herself was becoming frustrated as she folded her arms.

"I'm givin' his ass ten more minutes, and I'm out," she said. "Maybe Connie is right. Maybe this is their plan to get us all together and monitor us. We could be settin' ourselves up here."

"Or maybe he's makin' sure that this isn't a set up himself," Bull pointed out. "Don't forget, he doesn't know you. He might think you're tryin' to set him up and is being overly cautious. I know I would."

Before Sharice can respond, the hotel door opened and Jerome walked in.

"He's here," Jerome announced.

Sharice quickly rose from the bed while Jerome let in Rock and two of his crew members Double R and Troy. She quickly took note of all their faces, finally meeting the men behind the street fame. She can tell where Rock got his nickname from as he's built solid with his muscles bulging through his tight shirt. He reminded her of Kimbo Slice with his dark complexion and bushy beard. Sharice smiled as she greeted her guests.

"Hello, gentlemen," she said, approaching them. "I'd offer you a seat, but due to the accommodations here, you can see we're-"

"Cut the bullshit," Rock said, cutting off Sharice. "You requested my presence. What is it that you want?"

Sharice shot a look at Rock for a moment before backing down.

"Business it is," she said before taking a seat on the corner of the bed once again.

Rock took a seat across from her at the desk area with Double R and Troy standing by his side. Sharice quickly took them in as she had Bull, Jerome, and Connie standing by her side.

"Here's the thing, Rock, or The Rock. Not sure what to call you actually," Sharice said, smirking. "Either way, you know who I'm representing here. You know who we are, and me and my organization are here to set up shop in your city."

"You Faction niggas are some bold muthafuckas," Rock responded, smirking. "You think you can just run in another nigga hood and take over, and expect us to lay down like some bitches?"

"For real. Where they do that shit at?" Troy chimed in.

Troy was the skinniest of the trio, and also light-skin. *He still carried himself well for a lightweight,* Sharice thought, but he wasn't overly intimidating to her. The one who gave her the most concern was Double R, who seemed to look at her obsessively during the discussion. He kept a dead stare at her as she noticed the scar running down his dark-skinned face. Sharice noticed him clutching his fists as if he's trying to contain himself.

"Look, you did a nice job lasting as long as you did," Sharice responded, trying to move the conversation along. "I know there's been a lot of shit goin' down with the fools who was runnin' this thing before me, but we don't have to go there, for real. Let's settle this shit now, and we can all go home happy."

"Settle this?" Rock responded with a chuckle. "Alright, I'm gonna make this shit easy for you. You don't want me to stop droppin' your people, tell your bosses to get the fuck outta Houston. Ain't nothin' here for y'all. Better pull that shit in Dallas or somewhere."

"Come on, Rock. You know that ain't happening," Sharice replied. "We can work out a deal where you'd be makin' out like a bandit."

"I'm doin' that now," he quipped.

"Yeah, but at what cost? You're droppin' my people, we're droppin' yours. It's a simple numbers game, boo," Sharice pointed out, getting comfortable. "I have major money and three cities full of niggas ready to go to war. As big as you are in Houston, we both know you don't have the resources to keep up."

"Yeah! So why don't you drop this fuckin' act before we wipe you and your fuckin' punk ass crew out!" Connie exclaimed.

Sharice turned to her with rage in her eyes.

"Connie! Enough!" She fired back before turning her attention back towards Rock.

"Excuse my friend here, she can get a little excited," she said to her rival. "So, how about it, Rock? Why don't we sit down and settle all this without the bloodshed? You know you can't win this thing."

Rock chuckled to himself, getting up from his chair.

"I guess we gonna see, ain't we?" He responded as he motioned for his men to leave.

Double R was the last to leave. His eyes were fixated on Sharice, making Bull and Jerome nervous. He slowly made his way out of the room as Bull closed the door behind them. Sharice immediately jumped up from the bed and got into Connie's face.

"What the fuck was that, Connie?!" She exclaimed, looking for answers.

"What? I'm sayin', there's too much talkin' goin' on," Connie responded. "We need to let these niggas know we ain't out here for all that talkin' shit!"

"This is the exact reason the bosses don't respect you," Sharice fired back. "You can't go runnin' into a fight all the damn time! There's a way to do things!"

"Oh, come on, Reese," an unconvinced Connie responded with a chuckle. "This nigga ain't gonna give shit up, and you know it! This sit down was a bad idea. We should have took them niggas down when we had the chance! We had them niggas here!"

"That's why I'm the fuckin' one who calls the fuckin' shots, and not you!" Sharice fired back, getting into her friend's space. "I know what the fuck I'm doin' here, and if you can't handle that, you can take your ass back to New Orleans!"

Bull walked over, trying to calm the friends down.

"Okay, calm down," he said, getting between the two. "The fuckin' enemy is out there."

"Fuck this! I'm outta here," Connie fired back as she grabbed her jacket and walked out of the room.

Jerome walked over to Sharice and tried to calm her down as well.

"Look, you know how she is," he said. "Just… just let it go."

His words fall on deaf ears as a rage-filled Sharice grabbed her purse and made her way out of the motel as well.

Back in New Orleans, Michelle was cuddled up with Theo on their living room couch watching TV. Their couple's time was short-lived as Michelle's cell phone suddenly rang.

"Hello?" She said, answering the phone.

"Hey, what's up?" James responded, shocking

Michelle.

"Hold up a second," Michelle replied as she got up from the couch, confusing Theo.

She made her way into the kitchen before going back to the phone.

"What the fuck is the matter with you?" Michelle whispered. "I told you I was spending the night with Theo."

"Fuck that nigga. I wanna see you," James replied, confusing Michelle.

"Nigga, are you hearin' anything I'm sayin'?" She whispered back. "I thought you had the kids tonight anyway?"

"Nah, baby mama actin' a fool once again," he responded. "But fuck all that. Would you rather have the big dick or a short memory?"

Michelle smiled as she looked back behind her before responding.

"You know what I want," she whispered back, falling for James' flirtatious ways.

"Yeah, I know. You want the big dick, don't you?"

"Yes," Michelle responded with a giggle.

"I wanna hear you say it," James quipped.

"Boy, I'm not sayin' that shit," Michelle replied, being careful not to speak too loudly.

"Say it, and tonight I'll make sure to do that thing you like," Jerome replied, causing Michelle to bite her lip.

"You better not be playin' with me," she responded. "You better do it, or I'm gonna be pissed."

"Say it and your wish is my command," James responded.

"I want the big dick," Michelle quietly replied with a giggle.

"I can't hear that shit! Say it louder," James commanded.

Michelle rolled her eyes as she looked behind her once more.

"I want the big dick," she responded a little louder than previously.

"Louder damn it!"

"Look, nigga, he's in the other room, that's the best you gonna get," Michelle fired back.

"Yeah, alright. Meet me at my spot," James responded.

"I'm not playin' with you! You better do that thing," Michelle replied, smirking.

"I got you, shorty. Oh, do me a favor, pick up some Black and Mild's on your way over," James responded, causing Michelle to roll her eyes.

"Oh, so I'm stoppin' for shit now?" She asked.

"Just do it!" He exclaimed.

"Nigga, I don't know who you think you hollerin' at," Michelle replied with an attitude.

"Don't sweat that, baby. Only one hollerin' tonight is you. I'm out. See you when you get here," James responded before hanging up the line.

Michelle smiled with a sinister look on her face. As she turns around, she's startled by Theo, who's standing behind her. He looked at her suspiciously as Michelle gathered herself.

"Hey, what's up?" She asked.

"I was gonna ask you the same thing," Theo quipped back. "What's going on?"

"Oh, it's nothing. Just some problems at work I need

to take care of," Michelle answered.

"It's funny how your job only calls you at night," Theo implied as Michelle backed away, becoming defensive.

"What are you tryin' to say?" She asked with an attitude.

"I'm not saying shit! I'm just curious, that's all," Theo fired back.

Michelle ignored Theo as she walked past him into her room. She located some clothes and started getting dressed. Theo followed her as the argument continued.

"Look, I told you about this when we started dating! You said it wasn't a problem!" She pointed out.

"It's not a problem! I'm just sick and tired of every time I get some alone time with you, you have to run out and do this and that!" Theo responded.

"What the fuck you want me to do?" Michelle questioned. "It's my fuckin' job, okay!"

"It's the middle of the night! Let them find someone else to do this shit!" Theo pleaded with his love.

Michelle put on her shoes and shook her head as if she's offended.

"Look, I don't have time for this shit right now. I'm out," she said as she quickly walked past Theo out of the bedroom and out of the apartment.

Theo had a look of frustration in his eyes as the lack of attention he had been getting lately was becoming a problem.

The next day, Rock and a few of his crew members, including Troy and Double R, were at a local restaurant dining outside for lunch a little after noon with each other. Another crew member entered the area and took a seat as he handed Rock an envelope. Rock took the envelope and motioned the crew member to leave as Troy and Double R turned their attention towards their leader. He looked at it for a moment before tossing it on the table.

"A little light," he said before digging into his food once more.

"Them Faction nigga still makin' shit rough in Sunnyside," Troy responded. "They got some crews runnin' scared and shit."

"Is that a fact?" Rock responded, leaning back in his

chair. "Any nigga who ain't down for the cause needs to be dealt with asap. We not gonna let these out of town niggas dictate our corners. You put the word out, any nigga roll through here light again ain't rollin' out here on they feet."

Troy nodded his head with understanding.

"So, what do you want us to do about the bitch?" Troy asked, piquing Double R's interest.

Rock thought for a moment, scratching his head trying to figure out his next move.

"I don't know just yet," he replied. "She didn't seem like the rest of these spics we then dropped. She seems to know her shit."

"Come on, dude. She's just a broad. What can she fuckin' do to hurt us?" Troy responded with a chuckle.

"The rest of them niggas came out guns a-blazin' and shit," Rock pointed out. "They didn't give a fuck. This bitch, she came at us tryin' to feel us out and shit. Being respectful. She's smart. Never underestimate your opponent, Tee. Believe that."

Troy shrugged as Rock thought for a few moments.

Troy became impatient as he gave his thoughts on how to handle things.

"Tell you what, let's just off this bitch and go on with the rest of our day," he suggested. "If she's as smart as you say she is, let's not waste time gettin' her out of the picture."

"Patience, my nigga. Patience," Rock responded, disappointing Double R, who sat back in the chair frowned up.

Rock noticed his attitude and chuckled.

"What's up, Double R? You seem mighty quiet over there," he responded. "What, you think I'm trippin' not takin' out the bitch too?"

"I wouldn't mind a lil' action with her, you feel me," Double R responded, causing Rock to laugh.

"Oh, you diggin' shorty?" Rock asked, causing Double R to nod his head. "Well, don't blame you. She's a piece of ass alright. Look, I hear y'all niggas. Let me learn about shorty a little more, and then we'll see where we go from there."

Both Troy and Double R were disappointed with their

boss' ruling.

"I will throw y'all a bone, though," Rock responded, catching his friend's attention. "That dike bitch, the one with the smart ass mouth. How about we teach her a lesson that she'll never forget?"

Double R's eyes lit up with the news as Rock waved him off.

"I don't want her dead, you feel me. Just roughed up a little," he instructed. "I want Ms. Boss lady's full attention on this one. Make sure you send a message that she'll never forget."

A smile grew on Double R's face and Troy nodded his head as well. Before Rock could continue the conversation, Aisha, his girlfriend, made her way over to the table. Double R stood to offer his seat, which the sexy Aisha acknowledged before sitting down.

"Hey, boo. What y'all doin' over here?" She said with her Texas drawl.

"Ain't nothin'. Just going over a few things, that's all," Rock responded. "You wanna taste or somethin'?"

"Let me get a long island," she replied before grabbing

a menu. "What's good here?"

Rock shrugged as Aisha looked over the menu. Double R stole a few glances at his boss' lady. She was stunningly beautiful, albeit ratchet with her tight top, capri pants, and tennis shoes. Her essence blew in his face at the slightest breeze with her perfume intoxicating him. Her shoulder-length hair slightly flowed during the breeze as well, as Rock caught a glimpse of his crew member peeking at his girl.

"Hey, why don't y'all give me and my girl some space right now?" he said. "We'll pick this up later."

Troy nodded his head as he and Double R made their way out of the dining area. Rock shook his head as he turned his attention back to Aisha.

"I swear that nigga Double R scares me sometimes," he said. "Nigga loses his mind over pussy."

"Well, that's fine, bae," Aisha replied, smirking. "He can lose his mind with this pussy. Means I have his attention, and as long as I have that, we ain't gotta worry about him."

"As long as that pussy don't touch that nigga, we ain't

got no problems," Rock responded, admiring his woman's caramel skin. "Now hurry up and order, shit. It's gettin' a little hot out here."

Aisha giggled as she took a look at the menu once more, trying to find something to satisfy her appetite.

Later that night back in New Orleans on the block that K Dub and Big Rob were fighting over, there was high activity. The once vacant block is now busy with drug activity and fiends. A few blocks away, a local dealer frowned looking at the busy area when Big Rob's SUV pulled up beside him and lowered his window.

"What the fuck? We're not workin' that block, are we?" He asked when he noticed the traffic in the area.

"Nah, that's what I was tryin' to tell you," the dealer responded. "I came rollin' through here and saw that shit. I know you told us to chill, but how we gonna let some niggas take our shit like it ain't nothin', ya heard?"

Big Rob got out of his vehicle to get a better view of the block. He was confused until someone caught his eyes.

"What the fuck, that's one of K Dub's people!" He

angrily explained as he continued to watch from a distance. "This nigga here can't seem to follow directions."

"I didn't know who it was. That's why I called you here to see what's up," the dealer replied as he looked on at the block as well. "So what we gonna do about this shit?"

"I promised ol' girl I wouldn't do shit 'til she got back with me," Big Rob replied, fidgeting with his beard. "That nigga did too, but as you can see, some of us ain't following the rules."

Big Rob took out his cell phone and was about to dial Michelle when he paused. He put his phone back in his pocket with a vengeful look in his eyes.

"You packin'?" He asked his dealer.

"Nah, but the B.G.S is," the dealer responded, pointing towards a car in the distance with several of their crew members sitting and awaiting their orders. "Just say the word, and clear that bitch out, for real."

Big Rob thought for a few moments trying to make a decision. He looked at the block once again when his rage suddenly took over.

"Tell them niggas to strap up. I don't want none of

them niggas walkin' away from that corner unscathed," he responded, much to the delight of the dealer.

"I got you, nigga," the dealer responded before running over to the other crew members and jumping in the car with them.

Big Rob got back into his SUV and settled in to watch the action from a distance. On the corner, one of K Dub's dealers was getting irritated with a fiend, who was on the corner with her six-year-old daughter.

"Come on! I'm tellin' you I'll come back around tomorrow with the five dollars," the fiend argued.

K Dub's dealer was disgusted with her appearance because of her missing teeth and sores over her body.

"Get the fuck outta here, you disgustin' bitch!" he responded, pushing her away. "What you need to be worried about is takin' care of that baby!"

The fiend continued to plead with the dealer, trying to get her next fix at a discount. The conversation was short-lived as Big Rob's crew drove to the curb and opened fire on everyone in the area. The gunfire sent everyone on the corner scattering as best they could, but Big Rob's crew made sure that nobody walked away from the corner unscathed as ordered. After several moments, Big Rob's crew quickly pulled off much to their boss' delight, who watched the hit from his SUV. He chuckled to himself as he started his vehicle and quickly pulled off as well, leaving the once active block in silence. In the aftermath of the hit, seven people were killed lying on the ground, including the six-year-old daughter of the fiend.

In Houston, Sharice and Jerome were eating at an elegant restaurant in the city. The nice romantic atmosphere filled the area as the two lovers sat in their private booth. Jerome noticed Sharice picking at her food as if she was distracted.

"What's the matter?" He inquired. "You don't like the pasta?"

"Huh? No, it's fine. I... I just have a lot of shit on my mind," Sharice responded.

"Well, I'm here if you wanna talk about it," Jerome replied. "I mean, I didn't bring you out here to mope."

An offended Sharice shot Jerome a look.

"I'm sorry if I'm ruining your fuckin' meal," she snapped back with an attitude. "I'm over here stressin' out and shit, and you're all in your feelings about fuckin' dinner?"

"Whoa, whoa, just... I'm sorry, okay?" Jerome responded as he looked around to make sure nobody heard them. "I didn't mean it like that, it's just... you looked upset, and I was trying to get you to let me in. I didn't mean to set you off. My bad."

Sharice sighed as she dropped her fork.

"Hey, I'm sorry," she responded. "I'm just... I can't explain right now. I didn't mean to trip."

"It's cool. I know you're stressed and shit with all this. I'm here if you wanna talk about it. I'm not just here for muscle and dick, I can do other things, ya dig," Jerome replied with a smile.

Sharice loosened up a bit as well, smirking.

"It's this thing with Connie," she responded, opening up with her feelings. "I can't believe she did that shit yesterday. She was just out of line. I don't know why I brought her down here for this. She just goes off over the slightest thing."

"Well, it's not like I didn't tell you that shit a million times," Jerome pointed out. "She's been holdin' you back for years. She's unstable."

"She's my friend, Jerome. I love that girl," Sharice snapped back.

"Alright, fine. I get it," Jerome responded, waving her off. "Sounds to me like you're trying to convince yourself that you love her. Just an observation."

"Look, if you don't wanna talk about it, why the fuck did you ask?" Sharice fired back.

She was about to get up from the table when Jerome tried to convince her to stay.

"Sharice, please. Stay. I'm sorry," Jerome pleaded.

Sharice sighed, trying to calm herself down. There was an uneasy silence between the two as Sharice took a quick sip of her wine.

"Reese, you need to relax. You're workin' too hard. These niggas are gonna go down, so you don't need to keep stressin' over it. You need to work out that frustration," Jerome said before taking a sip of his drink.

Sharice rolled her eyes, knowing at what Jerome was hinting at.

"Is that all you can think of? Gettin' a piece of ass?" Sharice snapped back.

"That's not what I'm sayin'," Jerome argued.

"You know what? I don't need this shit," Sharice replied before finishing her drink. "I don't even know why I let you talk me into this shit."

"Reese, will you let me talk?" Jerome responded, being a little more assertive. "Look, I ain't talkin' about sex and shit. Another thing, don't be trippin' on me 'cause you're beefin' with Connie. Whatever fuckin' attitude you have with her, give it to her, not me!"

Sharice was surprised by her lover's response. She had never seen him so direct with her before. She knew how difficult she could be when she's angry, especially with Connie. She never intended to take it out on the man that she loved.

"You're right. I'm sorry," she said while grasping Jerome's hand. "Look at me, Rome. I really am sorry. Fuckin' Connie just brings it out of me sometimes, especially after she-"

Sharice caught herself and sighed, letting go of her lover's hand and eating her food once again. Jerome was confused as he tried to press his lover.

"After she what?" He asked.

"Huh?"

"You were sayin' somethin' about Connie. Especially after she did what?" Jerome asked.

"It's... it's nothing. I was just talkin' out loud," she replied, trying to deflect the questioning.

Jerome could sense something more was up when Sharice looked away from him.

"Is there somethin' you're not tellin' me about Connie?" He asked.

Sharice's emotions were running wild as thoughts of Connie and Lavina filled her head. Jerome refused to let up and continued with his questioning.

"You know, now that I think about it, you and her had a fallin' out before the shootin'," he pointed out. "What was that shit about?"

"You don't know when to stop, do you?" A frowned

up Sharice quipped.

"That's it. I hit a nerve, didn't I?" He questioned.

"You don't know what the fuck you're talkin' about," Sharice fired back.

"What did she do? What the fuck is the big secret?" He inquired.

Sharice shot him a stare that frightened Jerome. All the pent up rage and anger filled her face as she clutched her fists, which concerned him. She started breathing heavily as a few tears slowly fell from her eyes. Knowing that the conversation had taken a turn for the worse, Jerome quickly tried to comfort her.

"Reese, calm down. Just talk to me. Tell me what's goin' on," he said, grasping her hands trying to settle things.

After a few moments, more tears started flowing down Sharice's face as she calmed down. Jerome released his grasp on her hands as she took a napkin, wiping her face.

"Connie killed Lavina," she softly said, letting out months of frustration, shocking her lover.

"She killed Lavina?" a stunned Jerome asked. "Why

didn't you tell us?"

"It wasn't worth mentioning, okay?" Sharice replied as she got herself together. "Matter of fact, don't tell anyone else about this shit."

"For sure, I won't, but what the fuck happened?" a curious Jerome asked.

Sharice sighed as she struggled with her words. Revisiting that painful memory always hurt her, but she did feel a slight relief letting someone know about what's been tormenting her for months.

"Look… it's a long story," she softly responded. "Let's just say she really fuckin' hurt me with that shit. I was ready to move on without her. I was done with the bitch until-"

"She took that bullet for you," Jerome responded, finishing his lover's thoughts. "Now, you feel guilty and shit about being mad at her."

Sharice nodded her head as went into her purse and pulled out her makeup mirror to check her face, making sure her earlier tears didn't smear her eye liner.

"Yeah, I guess," she replied after fixing a few spots

around her eyes. "I looked Lavina's sister dead in her eyes and told her that I would find the person who killed Lavina and deal with them personally."

Jerome sighed, finally understanding the full weight Sharice had been carrying all this time.

"I'm gonna be real with you, Reese. I know she saved your life and all, but that's some deep shit. I mean, if she's crazy enough to cap Lavina, what else could she do?" He pointed out.

"Rome, the girl took a bullet for me," Sharice quipped. "Through all the shit, she fuckin' put her life on the line for me. That should count for somethin', ya know."

"True that but she's caused nothing but stress for you," Jerome fired back. "I mean, when does it end? It's not like this shit is a new thing. She's been stressin' you out for years. Way before this Lavina thing happened."

Sharice sighed because she knew Jerome's words were true. Most of the issues she had running her crew have all been because of Connie. While Connie has been loyal for the most part, she caused more headaches than she resolved. Sharice finally admitted to herself that her longtime friend was a liability.

"What should I do with her?" Sharice asked, seeking answers.

"I mean, if you're not willin' to deal with her the one way we deal with things, I don't know," he responded, referring to killing Connie. "I mean, maybe move her to another crew, and let her be someone else's problem.?

"I can't," Sharice responded, shaking her head. "Money's wanted her dead for years now. If she's not under my wing, he will cap her for real. I... I'm just stuck with her."

"Damn. I don't know what else to tell you then," Jerome responded. "I know if you don't deal with this shit now, you're gonna pay later. I mean, look at what just happened here? What happens if you get all emotional and shit dealin' with Rock? It's gonna cost you in the long run."

Sharice took a deep breath, thinking to herself for a few moments. She looked through her cell phone for a few moments trying to get her attention off Connie when something on one of the news sites caught her eyes.

"Son of a bitch," she responded, upset at what she saw. "Pay for the check, we need to go. Now!"

Jerome was confused but followed orders as he waved to the waitress, asking for the check.

In New Orleans, Michelle was sound asleep at James' apartment in the bed with him after the two have had a night of passionate sex with each other. Her slumber was disturbed when her cell phone suddenly rang. She rolled over to the edge of the bed and picked through a few items before finally locating her cell phone in her pants pocket and quickly answered.

"Hello?" She said in mid-yawn.

"Yeah, it's me," Sharice said on the other line. "I thought I told you to take care of that dispute between those two guys."

"I haven't had a chance to meet up yet," Michelle responded, lying back down on the bed.

"Well, maybe you need to check the news out and see what's been goin' on while you've been sleeping," Sharice responded before abruptly hangin' up the phone.

Michelle was confused as she searched the news on her phone and noticed what her boss was talking about. She frowned as she jumped out of bed and started getting dressed. The commotion woke James up as Michelle turned on the light, looking for her things.

"Yo, what the fuck' goin' on?" He groggily asked.

"I gotta go," Michelle responded, putting on her clothes as she found them.

"Well, can you at least turn off the damn light?" James asked.

"Fuck, nigga! Wait," a frustrated Michelle fired back as she quickly looked for her shoes.

Later that night, Sharice walked into the motel room that Bull was staying at as Jerome stayed outside and checked in with the members of Rico's crew. Bull could tell that she's been stressing out.

"Rough night?" He asked as Sharice sighed.

"Rough as hell," she responded. "How's things been goin' here?"

"Quiet for the most part. I did hear back about who

Rock's supplier is. The good news is it's one of the cartels that Rico is connected with," Bull pointed out. "I figure you make a call to the big guy, and let him know about it. Let him reach out and force them to choose."

Sharice nodded her head with understanding, finally having some leverage over her foes.

"That'll be a short conversation, I'm sure," Sharice responded. "You heard from Connie today?"

"Not since earlier," Bull answered. "Why? You want me to call her?"

"No. Let's just enjoy the silence for a little bit," Sharice responded. "I'll get with her tomorrow. Well, it looks like everything is cool here. I'm gonna head in for the night. You need anything?"

"A fifth of vodka would be nice," Bull joked as Sharice playfully punched him in the shoulder before making her way out of the motel room.

She checked in with Jerome before jumping into her rental car and heading back to her hotel.

At the Davenport Club located in Houston, the music

was blasting, getting the customers' crunk on the dance floor. It was not a big club, but was jam-packed way beyond the maximum occupancy for the building. As the clubbers enjoyed their drinks and socialized with each other, Connie sat at the corner of the bar area, looking miserable as she downed several shots. A male noticed her and walked up to her, trying to get her attention.

"Cheer up. Turn that frown upside down," he said with a flirtatious smile. "Let me buy you a drink."

Connie had a dead look in her eyes, staring at the male. She didn't say anything, but the male quickly got the picture that she's not in the mood for his presence. He quickly backed away from her and headed to the dance floor as Connie turned her attention back towards her drink. Unbeknownst to her, Troy and Double R were watching her from a distance blending in with the crowd. Troy nodded his head to Double R, who took a sip of his drink, keeping an eye on his target.

Early the next morning, a car pulled up to an abandoned warehouse in Houston's warehouse district.

The construction was falling apart, as were the surrounding buildings. The little green it did have in the area was overgrown, signifying the area had not been maintained for quite some time. Troy and Double R jumped out of the car and looked around the area before heading towards the trunk of the vehicle.

"Man, let's hurry this shit up. Sun will be up soon," Troy said as he popped open the trunk revealing a struggling Connie inside. Her ankles and wrists were both tied together with zip cords, and her mouth silenced with duct tape. She tried her best to free herself to no avail. Double R smiled, watching her squirm as Troy looked around once more.

"Come on, nigga! Get her legs and help me!" He exclaimed, trying to get Double R's attention.

As they lifted her from the car, Connie continued to buck as much as she could. They quickly toss her to the ground as Troy ripped the duct tape from Connie's mouth.

"I'm gonna kill you hoe ass niggas!" She exclaimed. "Both of you are dead! You hearin' me?! You're fuckin' dead!"

Double R walked over and grabbed Connie by her chin.

"You know, this bitch don't look half bad," he said, smirking.

Connie spit in his face, causing him to slap her several times before he was stopped by Troy.

"Look, nigga, we ain't got time for all that," Troy pointed out. "What you wanna do here since we can't kill the bitch?"

Double R smiled as Troy caught on.

"You a sick nigga, you know that?" Troy responded, smirking.

"Aye, boss said we can't kill her, but we need to send a message. What better way to send a message to a bitch," Double R responded, looking down on Connie before closing the trunk. "Help me lift her up."

Both he and Troy lifted Connie from the ground and bent her over on the car trunk. Double R quickly snatched down her pants as a terrified Connie fought as best she could. With both Troy and Double R holding her down, she was at their mercy. Double R dropped his pants as well.

"Fuck you! Fuck you!" Connie yelled as Double R

inserted himself inside of her.

Connie's eyes were full of tears as Double R laughed while assaulting his captive.

"Don't stress, shorty," he said after several strokes. "My man here got next. Why don't you tell us who has the biggest dick."

Connie was distraught as Double R continued to rape her while laughing. She tried to remove her mind from the pain by looking at a nearby streetlight shining in the area. Her tears continued to fall as the little fight she had in her slowly faded with every stroke from her captor.

Chapter 5

Truth Hurts

In the early morning hours back in New Orleans, Theo walked into a local Winn Dixie seeking out Michelle. The two hadn't spoken much since they had their falling out a couple of days earlier, and he wanted to have a conversation with her, hoping for common ground. He looked around the front end of the store before heading to the customer service desk and approaching the customer service clerk.

"Hello, excuse me, I'm looking for Michelle Johnson. She's a supervisor here," Theo said, confusing the service clerk.

"Michelle Johnson? Sorry, sir, I don't know a Michelle

that works here," the clerk responded, causing Theo's face to drop.

"Are you sure, cause she was on call tonight and said she was called in?" he replied.

"I'm sorry. The only supervisor here is Gerald," the clerk answered.

"Where is he? I'd like to speak with him," Theo said.

The service clerk pointed out Gerald, who was standing by one of the front end registers. Theo made his way over and greeted the supervisor.

"Gerald, is it?" He said while extending his hand.

"Yes, sir. How can I help you?" Gerald responded as he shook Theo's hand.

"Hey. I'm looking for Michelle Johnson. She's a supervisor here," Theo said, causing Gerald's face to drop.

"Do you have a warrant?" He asked, stunning Theo.

"A warrant? Why would I need a warrant?" Theo asked.

"You're here to request her records, right?" Gerald asked.

"No. I'm her boyfriend. We had a little falling out, and

I came by to apologize," Theo explained. "Why would someone want to request her records?"

Gerald nervously laughed as he tried to backtrack his statement. He could tell Theo had no clue who Michelle really was.

"Oh, I thought you might have been with our main office," he responded. "It's a check they do to see if we would break protocol, that's all."

"Um, okay," a suspicious Theo responded. "Well, do you know where she is? I'd like to have a quick conversation with her, if possible."

"Well, she hasn't been in today, but I can call out and see where she is if you need me to," Gerald answered.

"No, that's okay. I thought this was the store she was on call at," Theo responded.

"Well, she could be on call at several locations we have," Gerald answered.

"So, she doesn't just work at this location?" Theo questioned.

"She works as an area floater," Gerald explained. "She could be at any of our ten locations. I mean, if I hear from

217

her, I can let her know you were looking for her."

Theo nodded his head and walked off. As he exits the store, a million thoughts were going through his mind as he became more suspicious than ever of his mysterious girlfriend.

The sun was beginning to rise at the New Orleans Lakefront as Michelle patiently waited for the arrival of K Dub and Big Rob. She checked her phone once more when she noticed Big Rob and K Dub pulling up together at the same time. She waited in silence as both men approached her, mean mugging each other with every step. After a few moments, Michelle looked both men up and down before starting the discussion.

"What the fuck did I say?!" Michelle exclaimed, getting into both of the dealer's faces. "What did I tell you assholes the last time we sat right here on this fuckin' lake?!"

"Aye, it wasn't my fault," K Dub chimed in.

"You a fuckin' lie, nigga!" Big Rob responded. "This muthafucka went against the ruling! Had his people posted up on the spot after he was told to chill!"

The two dealers traded verbal jabs with each other until Michelle got between both of them.

"You idiots realize there was a fuckin' six-year-old shot dead?!" Michelle pointed out, quieting the two. "Niggas killin' each other ain't nothin' new in the city, but when a fuckin' child ends up dead, that makes nationwide fuckin' news! I can't believe you assholes right now!"

"Look, we didn't know there was a young buck out there," Big Rob responded. "I mean, who the fuck has a child on the corner that late?"

"What are you, fuckin' stupid?" Michelle fired back. "Dope heads are known for bringing their kids out and shit. Them suits already givin' us hell over this shit!"

"Wouldn't have even been a thing if this nigga would have followed orders," Big Rob explained. "That was my block to begin with! This nigga was fuckin' me out of five g's!"

"Nigga, you got one more time to disrespect me before I fuck you up!" K Dub responded as the two dealers squared up with each other.

"I'm right here, nigga! You ain't sayin' nothing but a word!" Big Rob responded as Michelle got between the two once again.

She was pushed to the side, surprising her as she stumbled to the ground. K Dub and Big Rob continued going back and forth with each other. Michelle jumped up from the ground and dusted herself off. With a scowl on her face from the disrespect the dealers dealt her, she took out her gun and fired one shot in the air, silencing both men.

"Enough of this shit!" She yelled. "All I wanna know is who fired the first shot last night!"

"That nigga right there," K Dub responded as he pointed to Big Rob.

"Only because this nigga had his-"

"Thank you," Michelle said before firing a shot into Big Rob's head, killing him and stunning K Dub.

K Dub was silent as Michelle looked over towards Big Rob's bleeding body, making sure he was dead. She then turned her attention to K Dub with her gun still drawn, aiming her weapon at him.

"That corner now belongs to me," she said to a nervous K Dub. "That's the tax you get for disrepectin' my fuckin' ruling! Do you have a problem with that?"

K Dud slowly shook his head as Michelle lowered her weapon.

"There's some bricks and chain next to the bench over there," Michelle responded, pointing towards a nearby bench. "Dump this nigga in the lake and get the fuck outta here!"

Michelle was about to walk off when she quickly turned back around.

"Oh, and K, get someone to eat the charge," she said as a nervous K Dub nodded his head.

"I'll take care of it," he said.

Michelle smiled as she put on her shades and walked off to her car. A relieved K Dub breathed a sigh of relief as he looked at Big Rob's fallen body, trying to figure out how he's going to move the big man in a timely manner.

Back in Houston, Sharice, Bull, Jerome, and a few others from Rico's crew were all in the emergency room after hearing about Connie. Sharice was so distraught by the news that her face was drenched with tears and anger. Jerome had his arm around her trying to comfort his lover, but he could tell that nothing he could say or do would settle her down. As she tried to maintain her anger for the moment, a doctor working the emergency room approached her and the others. Sharice rose quickly to meet him.

"Your friend is going to be alright," the doctor said, reassuring Sharice. "She has a couple of broken ribs and a few other injuries, but nothing serious."

Sharice breathed a sigh of relief, happy to hear that her friend wasn't hurt too seriously.

"Thank you, doc. Can I see her?" Sharice asked.

"Yes, that won't be a problem, but I was hoping I could speak with you privately for a moment," the doctor responded.

Sharice nodded as she took a walk to the other side of the waiting room to speak with the doctor one on one.

"I didn't want to say this around the others, but she was raped pretty badly," the doctor said, stunning Sharice.

"She… she was raped?" Sharice struggled to ask.

"Yes. I don't want to go into the details. I tried to get her to discuss the assault with me, but she won't talk to me about it. By law, with this type of abuse, I'm supposed to notify the authorities," the doctor responded as he noticed Sharice's mood turning for the worse. "I understand you're upset, but getting upset isn't going to change what happened to your friend. The reason I'm telling you is to see if you can convince your friend to discuss this with me or the authorities."

"Have you called the police yet?" Sharice asked.

"Not yet, but I was-"

"Don't," Sharice said, cutting the doctor off. "Let me talk to her before you do. I'll see if I can get her to talk. I know you have to do what you have to do by law, but give me ten minutes with her. Please."

The doctor nodded his head before leading Sharice to the room Connie was in. As Sharice walked in, she noticed Connie lying on the bed with anger in her eyes. The two friends made eye contact as Sharice walked over towards her. Both were trying to control their emotions as Sharice grasped her friend's hand.

"God, Connie. I'm so sorry," Sharice said, breaking the awkward silence. "I wish I could have been there. I could have prevented this shit."

Connie's eyes started to water up, but she remained silent.

"When they said you were in the hospital, I could have died," Sharice continued, tears rolling down her cheeks. "I know we were havin' our issues, but I would never wish anything like this on you. I... shit. Girl, I'm fuckin' sorry."

Connie still didn't respond as Sharice took a seat next to her friend.

"I was happy when they said you were gonna be okay. I thought they roughed you up, and that was the worst of it, but the doctor told me about what they did to you and..." Sharice said, struggling to discuss the sexual assault with her friend. "I... I just don't know. You didn't deserve this shit. I know the game is the game, but this shit here... it's too much."

Sharice looked over to her friend, waiting for a response but didn't get one. She could tell the anger

Connie was feeling as tears streamed down both of their faces. This was part of the game that was difficult for them, and both friend's emotions were running wild. After a few moments, Sharice nodded her head and rose from her seat, preparing to leave.

"I'll let you get some rest," she said before heading towards the door.

"You ain't said one thing I wanna hear," Connie responded, breaking her silence and catching Sharice's attention. "All this 'I'm sorry' shit doesn't mean anything to me."

Sharice turned around and slowly approached the bed once again.

"I'm gonna take care of it, okay?" Sharice responded. "I'm gonna handle it."

"Bullshit!" Connie exclaimed. "If you meant all that shit you was feedin' me, you know what I want to hear!"

"It's been a long night, Connie. Just get some rest, and we'll talk later," Sharice responded to an unsatisfied Connie.

"Fuck that shit! These niggas put their dick up in me!

225

You know what I want!" Connie fired back, trying to draw the emotion out of Sharice. "Don't give me that get some rest shit! Tell me what I wanna hear!"

An enraged Sharice could no longer hold in her anger.

"I'm gonna kill those muthafuckas!" She screamed. "Is that what you wanna hear?! I'm gonna make sure them niggas die slow for this shit!"

Connie backed down, satisfied with what her friend was saying. It was the emotion she was trying to draw out of her. She knew that an enraged Sharice was a dangerous person, and she wanted to make sure Sharice felt every bit of her pain in order to respond.

"That's what I'm talkin' about," Connie responded. "Look, they gonna let me out of this joint in a day or so. Hold off until I get back on my feet. I wanna knock these niggas down myself."

Sharice looked back at her friend and thought for a few moments.

"I'll see what I can do. No promises," she responded. "The doctor has to call the cops on this by law, so be ready for that. Get some rest. I'll visit you later today."

Connie nodded her head as Sharice made her way out of the room back towards her crew. Bull was the first to approach her.

"How is she?" He asked.

"She'll be fine," Sharice reassured him as she led Bull and Jerome outside of the emergency room.

"That's good to hear," Jerome said as they make it to the parking lot. "I got a crew together ready to make a move whenever you're ready. Just say the word."

Sharice was silent as she pondered her next move. She knew Rock would expect her to strike. The move against Connie was done to provoke her into a war on the streets, where in Houston, he had the advantage. After thinking for a few moments, she slowly shook her head.

"Nah, I'm not gonna go that route," she responded, shocking both Bull and Jerome.

"Are you sure? You gonna let this shit slide?" Jerome questioned, irritating Sharice.

"I'm the fuckin' one in charge!" She reminded him. "I'm sick and tired of y'all niggas questioning everything I say! I said leave the shit alone right now! End of story!"

Both Bull and Jerome backed down, nodding their heads. Jerome wasn't happy about the way his lover just snapped at him but remained silent for the moment. Sharice was frustrated and had a headache with everything going on.

"Make no mistake, them niggas ain't gettin' away with this shit. They did this shit expecting me to hit back. Right now, we're gonna hang back until I get shit figured out," Sharice responded, letting her crew in on her thoughts. "Bull, did John ever get back with you?"

"Yeah, he said the police commissioner is friendly," Bull answered. "A couple of years ago, two of John's crew was pinched out here for a money laundering charge. John reached out to a couple of officers he knows out here, and they hooked him up with the commish. Money changed hands, and his boys were out in less than a week."

"Can we get a meet?" Sharice asked.

"We can try, but for what I hear, he's in Rock's pocket," Bull pointed out. "He's not gonna go double dippin', so to speak."

"Well, we'll see how long their money goes when their

supply dries up," Sharice responded. "Spoke to Rico, and he got word to his folks down in Mexico. Told them they're either with us or Rock. Just as I thought, that conversation didn't last long."

Bull nodded his head as Sharice snapped her fingers.

"You know what? Set up a meeting with Rock," she said, stunning her crew members once again. "I'm sure he's heard back from Mexico by now, or will soon. See if we can get a sit-down. Let's make it a few days out. That'll give us a little time to put some things in motion."

"Are you sure you wanna do that?" Jerome questioned. "I mean, what do you expect to accomplish with that?"

Sharice shot Jerome a look, upset that he was once again questioning her orders.

"Bull, give us a moment," she said, turning her attention towards her lover.

Bull nodded his head and walked off as an angered Sharice addressed Jerome.

"What the fuck is wrong with you?" She quipped. "If you fuckin' question me in front of folks again, on everything, I'm gonna send your ass back to New Orleans so quick that it will be like you never left! Who the fuck are you to question me?!"

"I'm just tryin' to understand what's the plan?" Jerome responded. "I'm not tryin' to disrespect you. You're right, I shouldn't have done that in front of Bull, but you don't' seem yourself right now, and it's in this moment that will decide if we win this thing or lose. I don't wanna see what happened to Connie happen to you!"

"Don't worry about me," Sharice stated. "Just do what I tell you to do without all that extra! You got me?!"

Jerome was about to respond but realized he's not going to win this war of words. He slowly nodded his head. Sharice checked her phone notifications and noticed a text message.

"I'm gonna need you to make a pickup tomorrow morning from the airport," she instructed. "It's something I need for the meeting with the commissioner. If Bull is able to pull it off anyway."

"No problem, boss," Jerome responded in a mocking tone.

Sharice shot him a look of anger before walking off

towards her car.

Jerome looked on with concern in his eyes, watching Sharice pull out of the parking lot. What happened to Connie was in the back of his mind, and he wouldn't be able to handle himself if Sharice was put in a similar position. After a few moments with his thoughts, he rejoined Bull, and the two went back into the hospital to join the other crew members in the waiting room.

Back in New Orleans, a little after noon, private detective Batiste was sitting at his desk in his downtown office, going over some paperwork when there is a knock at his door.

"It's open!" he yelled with his strong New Orleans dialect.

Theo walked into the office and was a little put off with the messy surroundings as he approached Batiste's desk. Theo understood the mess once he noticed the detective himself was pretty much a slob with a wrinkled button-down shirt that seemed to be missing a button with a bulging belly and hair that looked like it hadn't been cut in weeks.

"You must be Theo, right?" Batiste said as he stood up and wiped his hands on his pants before offering to shake Theo's hand.

Theo was reluctant at first but shook the private eye's hand eventually.

"Yeah, um, that's me," he said, still uncomfortable with his surroundings.

"Please, have a seat," Batiste replied as both he and Theo take a seat. "So you're friends with my cousin with cousin, right?"

"Yes. Kia referred me to you. Said you're just the person who can help me out," Theo answered. "Said you'd be fair with me when it comes to the rates."

"Well, Kia still owes me money for a job I did for her a couple of months ago, but that's neither here nor there. So as I recall, you want me to check up on your girl who you think might be cheatin' on you, am I right?"

"That's correct," Theo said, handing Batiste a few photos of Michelle from a folder he brought with him.

Batiste looked over the photos and nodded his head

like he was impressed. He looked at Theo, wondering what a girl like that would see in a person like him.

"Cute girl," he said, smirking. "You sure she's with you? I'm just askin' because I'm not trying to be part of a stalker case here."

"I'm in one of the pictures with her," Theo pointed out, growing tired of his interaction with the private eye already.

"Doesn't mean anything," Batiste replied. "After you've been in this game as long as I have, you learn a thing or two about the way people think. I normally don't like to get involved in stalker cases, or worse, domestic disputes. If anything happens to her, I will turn you in myself, are we clear?"

"I would never hurt her," an offended Theo responded. "I love her. It's just... I don't know. Lately, she's been a little distant. Late calls at night, always at work. I went to her job earlier this morning, and it seems like they were covering for her. I don't know. I might just be overthinking things."

Batiste pondered for a moment before putting the

photos on a pile of files on his desk.

"You got all the information I told you to get?" He asked.

Theo nodded his head as he handed the private eye a paper from the folder of handwritten information detailing Michelle's job, license plate number, social security number, and other various details. Batiste reviewed the info and nodded his head with approval.

"My rate is one-fifty an hour, plus expenses," he said as he tossed the paper on the pile on his desk. "If you're good with that, I can get this going today."

"Kia said you charge one-ten an hour," Theo replied.

"That was a family discount rate," Batiste pointed out. "Take it or leave it."

Theo rose from his seat, grabbing the sheet and photos he gave the private eye, preparing to leave when Batiste stopped him.

"Okay, okay. One-fifteen an hour. Best I can do," he offered.

Theo thought for a moment and nodded his head as the two men shook on it. He handed the information back to

Batiste.

"So, how long is this going to take?" Theo asked.

"I dunno. Let me make a few calls and see what I can dig up. I'll let you know if I get a bite or not," Batiste answered.

Theo nodded and quickly made his way out of the cluttered office. Batiste smiled and leaned back in his chair as he took a look at one of the pictures Theo had given him earlier.

"Michelle. What's a cutie like you capable of?" He said to himself before putting the picture down to make a few calls.

At Club Exotica later that evening, Michelle was sitting at the bar having a drink, chatting back and forth with Tracy, who was there prepping for opening later that night. As the two were in mid-conversation, Money walked in and greeted them both with a smile.

"Ladies, lookin' good, I see. Lookin' good," he said as he walked over and took a seat on the stool next to Michelle.

"Hey, Mike," Tracy responded as Michelle rolled her eyes. "You drinkin'?"

"Nah, baby girl. I'm just here to see my friend real quick," he responded, referring to Michelle. "You mind givin' us a minute?"

Tracy nodded her head and walked off as Money turned his attention to a disinterested Michelle.

"So what's good, boo?" He asked, smirking on his face. "How's business goin'?"

Michelle shrugged before taking a sip of her drink. She remembered that Sharice told her not to give Money much info so he couldn't interfere with things and decided to limit much of what she said to him.

"You got the money, right?" She asked.

"Yeah, I got it," he answered as Michelle nodded her head.

"Cool," she replied as she took another sip of her drink.

Money thought for a moment, trying to find a way to continue their conversation since he was wired by the FBI.

"So, Sharice has you runnin' things now I see," he said, making small talk. "How's that going? Being in charge for the first time?"

"I wouldn't know. I'm not in charge," Michelle smartly responded, hoping to end the conversation. "Sharice told me to make sure you got your money, and look after the bar. That's it."

Money looked on to her, confused as he scratched his head.

"Wait, so you're not runnin' shit right now?" He asked, causing Michelle to shake her head. "Then who's runnin' things?"

"I don't know. You may need to get with her on that," Michelle responded, smirking. "I was just told to get you your money, and look after the club."

"Yeah, you said that already," a frustrated Money responded. "I'll get with her on that, cause I need some shit taken care of. She's been slippin' since she made that trip to New York with John, for real. You wouldn't happen to know what went down out there to have her actin' a fool and shit, would you?"

Michelle shrugged once again before taking another sip of her drink. Money realized he's wasting his time with her and got up from the bar. Before he walked off, he walked up to Michelle and smiled, running his hand through her curly hair, making her uncomfortable.

"You know, the way things are going with Sharice, she may not be in the top spot much longer," he said as he looked her over. "I hear your name in the streets more and more as of late. If Sharice *is* on the outside lookin' in, I may need a successor. I know you know more shit than you're givin' me right now, and that's cool, but best believe things are gonna change around here sooner rather than later. It would be in your best interest to make sure I'm satisfied, ya dig."

Michelle shook her head slightly as she gently grabbed Money's wrist and removed his hand from touching her.

"Well, let's hope Sharice keeps us both paid so we can do what we do," she calmly responded before turning away from the Faction boss.

Money chuckled and nodded his head before making his way out of the club. As he exited, he passed up James, who made his way into the club and noticed Michelle sitting at the bar with her back towards him. He smiled as he tiptoed over behind her, making sure he didn't make a sound. He quickly moved in and kissed her on the neck, startling her as she jumped up and faced him.

"Nigga, what the fuck?!" She responded relieved that it wasn't Money who had kissed her.

"Saw you over here looking all vulnerable and shit, and figured I'd take advantage of that," James responded as he took a seat next to her. "Why you all jumpy and shit?"

"I don't know. It was... never mind. You just caught me off guard," Michelle responded as she took a seat back at the bar. "So, what's up? Why you over here?"

James looked around the bar area to make sure they were alone before commenting.

"K Dub got someone to take the charge on the hit," he quietly responded. "They gonna be charged with killin' that lil' girl. Ain't no comin' back from that, for real."

"I know it's fucked up, but them niggas shouldn't have been beefin' like that. I specifically told them to hold off until I heard back from Reese. It's his own fault for that shit," Michelle responded before finishing her drink. "You could have called me to tell me that. You didn't need to come all the way here."

"Well, I didn't come here just to tell you that," James responded with a sinister grin. "I bought you a gift, but first, what's up with you and Money? Nigga passed me up on the way out. Anything I need to know?"

Michelle smiled, turning towards her secret lover.

"That's boss business, ya heard me," she responded. "I'm talkin' high-level shit that don't have nothin' to do with you. Now, what gift did you bring me?"

Michelle curiously looked as she watched James go into his back pocket and pull out a set of handcuffs, surprising her. He looked towards Sharice's office when he suddenly had an idea.

"Ain't no better place to try these out," he said, motioning towards Sharice's office.

"You've gotta be kidding," a stunned Michelle responded. "I'm not tryin' to fuck in an office Sharice then probably fucked in. The thought of it grosses me out."

"Come on, stop actin' like a bitch," James responded as he twirled the cuffs on his finger. "You always said you wanted to get it on a desk and shit. Wasn't that like a fantasy of yours?"

"True, but Sharice's desk? Really?" Michelle responded. "I mean, if she finds out about that shit, that's our ass."

James continued to dangle the cuffs trying to sway Michelle. The tactic worked because she weakened at the very thought of being cuffed and taken advantage of on a desk. After several moments, she sighed, rising from the barstool.

"Fine, but I'm not cleanin' up after this shit," she warned James. "You better make sure everything is as it was when we're done."

"Shut your ass up and get up them stairs," James responded while rising as well.

Michelle giggled as the two began making their way upstairs to Sharice's office.

"By the way, you're wearin' the cuffs first," she quipped.

"Yeah, we'll see about that," James replied before tapping Michelle on her ass.

She was turned on by the rush and hurried up the stairs

with James in hot pursuit.

The next morning Sharice was sitting at a small café located in downtown Houston eating breakfast alone with a briefcase next to her when Police Commissioner Rollins made his way in the area looking around. She noticed him and tried to take him in for the moment. He's an older man with graying hair almost as if he's distinguished, she thought to herself. She was turned off because it was another corrupt black official she had to bribe, which never sat well with her. She had no issues with bribing law enforcement in the past, but it always made her feel a certain way when it came to politics and high-end officials, particularly black officials. It was part of the game, but there was a little piece of her that hated this part. She waved at Rollins, catching his attention as he smiled before walking over.

"You're early," he responded as Sharice got up to greet him. "I heard that about you. Guess I had to see it for myself."

"Well, don't think this is the norm," Sharice responded

as the two shook hands. "I don't know my way around this city, so I wanted to make sure I was where I needed to be. I ordered something to eat, I hope you don't mind."

"Not at all," Rollins responded, motioning Sharice to take her seat.

They both sat down as Sharice took a quick sip of her drink.

"Thank you for takin' the time to meet," she responded as Rollins stopped her in her tracks.

"The only reason I'm here is cause John reached out," he explained. "My time is valuable, so if we can dispense with the pleasantries."

"Fair enough," Sharice responded. "Look, you know about us. You know where we come from, and who we have backin' us. I'm here to talk about those you're currently in bed with and was looking to see if you may be in the market lookin' for someone else to sleep with."

Rollins chuckled as took Sharice in. He was impressed with her well-spoken vibe since he was used to dealing with street dealers like Rock most of the time.

"In my line of work, change is bad," he replied. "Going

from bed to bed can cause problems. I like my sex protected."

Sharice grinned as she got a little more comfortable in her seat.

"I can understand that," she responded, changing to her flirtatious mode. "Protected sex is the responsible way to do things, but every now and then something better comes along that will give you a sensation that sex with a rubber just can't do."

She gave him a look and knew she had his full attention. Rollins was taken aback by her but wasn't willing to buy what she's selling.

"That all sounds nice, but me and my friend have a good relationship. I don't see a reason to change up," he responded to a disappointed Sharice. "I'm sorry if you were promised different."

Sharice slowly kicked her leg out under the table, moving the briefcase towards Rollins.

"Why don't you take a look under the table and see what being in bed with us is all about?" she said. "I know it's more than your friend has to offer; I can promise you that."

Rollins slowly reached under the table and opened the case. He was impressed with the amount of money she's offering him to switch allegiances.

"A half a million reasons to enter the sheets with me," a seductive Sharice continued as Rollins lowered the case and turned his attention back towards her.

"A half mullion, huh?" He responded, tugging at his chin as if he's considering the proposal. "I heard getting in bed with your kind is like selling your soul. Sounds like thirty pieces of silver if you ask me."

"Getting into bed with us is nothing like you heard," Sharice answered. "Especially with me. I don't bite, and I'm very gentle. Your friend isn't gonna be able to afford you anyway in about a week or so. You might as well get in on the ground floor with someone better, don't you think?"

Rollins was silent as he considered Sharice's proposal. He had heard about the allure Sharice brought to the table and knew she used it to her advantage to sway men to her favor. He thought he was beyond reproach, but found her essence and beauty swaying him all the same. After a few moments, he slowly nodded his head, much to her delight.

"So, what is it that I have to do for a half-million reasons?" he asked.

Sharice smiled as she went into her purse, pulled out a sheet of paper, and handed it to Rollins. He pulled his glasses out to read the list.

"All I want you to do is your job," Sharice responded, smirking. "Nothing more. I'll have another list for you tomorrow."

After checking out the list, Rollins looked at Sharice suspiciously. She responded with a look of reassurance as he took off his glasses and placed them back into his case.

"So, are we in bed together?" Sharice asked, looking for confirmation.

Rollins slowly nodded his head as the two shook hands, solidifying their deal.

"Good choice," Sharice responded. "So, you're gonna make me eat here alone?"

"Are you covering?" Rollins asked, causing Sharice to giggle.

"I think I can dig a little deeper for breakfast," she replied.

Rollins got comfortable, grabbing a menu, and looking it over. This part of Sharice's plan went as well as she had hoped. With the law now being on her side, she had Rock right where she wanted him for the moment.

Later that night, Detective Batiste was parked across the street from Club Exotica, sipping coffee and listening to the radio as he monitored the club. He was mid-sip when he noticed Michelle and James casually walk out of the club, sharing a few kisses with each other. Batiste grabbed his camera and snapped a few shots of the two, making sure he got pictures of James having his arm around her, and a few shots with the two kissing.

"Well, Theo, it seems your lovely lady is a cheat," he said to himself as he snapped several more shots. "Too bad too. She's a lovely piece of ass."

He continued to shoot photos watching the as the two entered a car and pulled off when his cell phone suddenly rang. He checked the caller id, recognizing his law enforcement connection and smiled as he quickly answered the line.

"Russ. Hey, thanks for getting back to me so quick. So how's life going? Feds still giving you shit?" He asked before laughing. "Yeah, I bet. Well, you're a bit late. I was lookin' for something on that girl I sent you earlier, but I saw with my own eyes what I needed to see, so there's-"

Batiste's words are silenced as his police contact filled him in on Michelle's background and history. He was stunned hearing about her criminal history and her association with the Faction crew.

"You're shittin' me. You have got to me shittin' me," he responded as he took a look at some of the photos he just shot on his camera.

"Son of a bitch," he said as a million thoughts ran through his head.

His police contact continued to fill the private eye's head with tales of investigations, stunning him with each word.

Later that night, Theo was outside of Batiste's office

impatiently waiting for the detective to arrive from his earlier stakeout. After a few moments, Batiste hurried over with his keys out and several folders in his hand.

"Sorry I'm late. I had to make a stop over by the seventh district precinct to pick up a few things," he explained as he opened the door.

Theo didn't respond as the two made it into the private eye's office and took a seat over by his desk. Batiste was trying to get himself together as Theo eagerly awaited the information he was looking for.

"Well?" Theo asked. "Did you find out anything? You said it was important."

Batiste sighed, hating to break the news to Michelle's boyfriend.

"Look, normally I'd drag this thing out since I'm paid by the hour, but I came across some information that you need to hear," he explained. "This can cost you your life, and in turn, my life."

Theo was confused as Batiste continued.

"Let me ask you this. Do you know what your girlfriend does for a living? Really?" He asked. "I mean, did you know about her background before asking me all this? 'Cause if you did, you owe me a lot more than what we agreed."

"What are you talking about?" Theo questioned. "Are you telling me she's not an area manager for Winn Dixie?"

Batiste was stunned with the naivety of Theo. He was certain that Theo knew about her double life, but looking in his eyes, he realized he was in the dark about her background as well. He took a deep breath before breaking the news to Theo.

"Your girlfriend doesn't work at any grocery store," he said, stunning Theo. "Well, on the books, she technically does. She gets checks sent to her bank account, but she doesn't step foot in the store. It's what we in the world call a front."

"A front? I'm not understanding," a naïve Theo responds. "That's something that a criminal would use, and I know Chelle isn't a criminal."

Batiste shook his head as he handed Theo the files he came into the office with. Theo read over several reports, stunned about the double life Michelle was leading. He learned about several murders she's suspected of, and other notable crimes, wondering who this woman he'd been dating for the last couple of years was.

"I…I'm not understanding," he stuttered, reviewing the paperwork. "How did you come into this? Where did you get this paperwork from?"

"I reached out to a contact on the force," Batiste answered. "I was just looking for some background on your girl, but I didn't expect to find any of this shit."

Batiste can tell Theo was at a loss for words looking over the files.

"Your girlfriend is a top-level member of an organized crime outfit," he said, trying to rip the band-aid off. "They're into drugs, prostitution, and murder. They run the crime in this city and several others. We're not talking about the Jets and the Sharks here. These guys are the real deal."

Theo had enough and he slammed the files on Batiste's desk.

"This is bullshit! It has to be!" He exclaimed. "She's like fifteen pounds with clothes on! She couldn't hurt anybody!"

"Well, according to the files there, she's a suspect in over a dozen murders, and that's just the bodies they know of," Batiste pointed out to a panicked Theo. "Look, when you've been in the private eye game as long as I have, you see things. She may not have killed all those folks that she's accused of, but where there's smoke, there's fire. I'm just sayin'."

Theo, on the verge of a breakdown, took a moment to process everything he just learned. Nothing about her personality spoke towards any of what's showing in the file. He wondered how he could have missed it. Batiste could tell Theo was still trying to wrap his mind around what he's just learned.

"Look, I know this is some terrible shit to find out, but better, you hear it now from me than in a courtroom," Batiste explained, putting the files away. "Trust me, you're better off."

Theo, struggling to maintain his emotions, finally asked the one question Batiste had failed to answer.

"Is she cheating on me?" He asked, stunning the

private eye.

"Are you insane?" Batiste quipped. "After everything I just showed you, you're still interested in all of that?"

"Please. I… I know she's whatever she is, but I still need to know if she was cheating on me or not."

Batiste sighed as he took out his camera and motioned Theo to join him behind the desk. Once Theo walked over, he showed him several of the photos he snapped earlier of James and Michelle walking out of the club.

"I'm sorry, okay. She runs with a circle where this thing is normal," Batiste pointed out. "You need to walk away from this thing if you can. I know it sucks cause she's a looker, but you don't wanna be around when the hammer falls, trust me. And that's if you're lucky. If a rival gang finds out your boo has a weakness for you, you could be in danger. Just let it go, man."

Theo continued to look at the photo of James kissing his girl as rage filled his eyes. He was heartbroken, and even with her background, nothing hurt him more than Michelle cheating on him.

Back in Houston, a couple of days later, Rock and Aisha are walking hand in hand through a car dealership, checking out several vehicles together, laughing and joking. As they made their way through the lot, they noticed both Double R and Troy waiting for them at the far end. As Rock approached, he could tell that they were bothered by something.

"What's up?" Rock asked as he dapped both his crew members.

"You ain't hear? Ronnie, Darrius, and Fat Boy all got locked up on charges," Troy said as Rock began walking back to the main lot.

"What they get them for?" He asked, checking out a few vehicles during his stroll.

"Possession with intent and weapons charges," Troy answered. "Now you know them niggas don't carry no weight. It's bullshit. Either the cops set them up or-"

"Or it's her," Rock said, finishing his friend's sentence.

"I was thinkin' the same thing," Troy admitted as Rock stopped and checked out another vehicle that caught his attention.

"Here's somethin' else you don't know. I called Ruiz tryin' to set up another shipment, and he told me that we've received our last shipment from them," Rock said, stunning both Troy and Double R. "From what I heard, them Faction niggas use him as a supplier too. Just a matter of numbers. He don't wanna lose them, so he cuts us loose."

"Nigga, we gonna run dry in about a week," Troy responded as Rock calmly faced him.

"Less than that," Rock replied. "He did say if we took care of the problem, he would hook us back up, but until then, we're outta the loop."

"So what we gonna do, nigga?" Troy asked. "Look, I know you like shorty and all, but this chick bringing us down like a bitch right now. It's time to take care of her."

Aisha, Double R, and Troy all looked towards Rock, who was thinking silently for several moments.

"Shorty wants to meet with me tonight," Rock said as he scratched his head. "My guess is that she wants me to know it's her that did this shit. Fatboy, Ronnie, and Darius are all muscle. She knows that; she did her homework. Try and soften us up before she strikes. If she got them pinched, that means our guy is no longer runnin' with us."

"You mean the commissioner?" A panicked Troy responded. "Bruh, if they got him on the payroll, we're fucked!"

"Shorty wasn't the only one doin' homework though," Rock responded smirking. "Found out who she really is, and if I'm right about this, we can end this thing real quick."

Rock had everyone's attention as he continued.

"She's really a big thing in the Faction. I'm talkin' bout she runs New Orleans, for real," Rock explained. "That nigga who is over her is a joke. She's the real boss out there, and if that's the case, them sending her here to deal with this shit meant it was a last-ditch effort to get this shit together."

Rock looked at Troy and smiled.

"You right, nigga. It's time we take shorty out," he said, which put a smile on Double R's face. "But I want a last fuck you to all them Faction niggas to let them know we ain't to be played with. She left her homegirl in charge while she was out here dealin' with us. I wanna send a couple of guys out there to cancel that bitch. Shorty has this club in N.O. where her crew all hang out at. Get some guys down there to watch that spot. As soon as ol' girl shows head, do what needs to be done."

Troy smiled as he nodded his head. Rock turned his attention to Double R.

"I know you been waitin' for this, nigga," Rock said, smirking. "The bitch is all yours. She's at the Hilton. One of our people works there and already has a key for you to get into the bitch's room. I'll meet with her tonight while you set up. No mistakes."

Double R's eyes lit up knowing he's been given the task of killing Sharice.

"What about that suave nigga she be with that you told me about?" Aisha asked, smirking. "What's his deal?"

"That's ol' girl's boo thang," Rock responded with a slight chuckle. "He might be a problem if we hit his girl, for real. Troy, you're up on him."

Troy nodded his head as Aisha interjected.

"Nah, boo. I got this one," she said. "I'll take care of it.

Fast, quick, and in a hurry."

Rock thought for a moment before slowly nodding his head with approval.

"Troy, you back her up," Rock instructed. "That leaves that Italian nigga, and the bitch in the hospital."

"That's gonna be tough to get in that hospital," Troy pointed out. "Even if she didn't have a crew in there protecting her, there's still all types of cameras and shit in there. No way to take her out without being seen."

"Yeah, I know. Same with the Italian nigga. He ain't left their stronghold since he got here. Probably coordinating everything from there. Send some people to keep an eye on them as best they can. If we get a chance, then we do them too, but our top priority is the bitch, her boo, and her homegirl back home. Let's try and get it done all at once," Rock instructed.

Aisha smiled while hugging her man tight as both Double R and Troy continued to listen to their leader's plan on how to end the war with the Faction once and for all.

Chapter 6

Blood on the Streets

It's early evening and Sharice was helping Connie get her things together in the hospital. Connie was upset and she let Sharice know it with a scowl every time the two made eye contact. Sharice took one more look around the room to make sure everything was taken care of.

"Looks like we're good to go here," she said, much to Connie's disgust. "Do you need anything else or-"

"How can you call yourself my friend after the shit you pulled!" Connie exclaimed, cutting off her friend.

Sharice sighed because she knew this conversation was inevitable.

"Look, I'm still workin' on it, okay?" Sharice

responded. "I promise you we are gonna get those assholes who did this to you. We just… we need to take it slow right now."

"Two of that nigga's soldiers fuck me and you're saying we need to take it slow?!" An unconvinced Connie exclaimed. "Fuck that! I'll go after these niggas myself once I'm outta here!"

"No, you're not!" Sharice fired back. "You're leavin' from here straight to the airport and heading back to New Orleans!"

Connie stopped gathering her items and quickly approached Sharice.

"So that's it? You're gonna side with the asshole who did this to me?" Connie asked. "Shit, Sharice, I thought we were better than that. You're gonna actually sit down with this nigga and make a deal. I can't believe you right now."

Sharice sighed as she put her arm on Connie's shoulder, trying to reassure her of her intentions.

"Connie, I've never lied to you. Not once," she replied to her friend. "I will take care of it. Right now, my plan is working. We need to lay back and let things chill for a moment. I just need a little more time."

"I heard about the arrests and cuttin' that nigga supply off," Connie said. "If you gonna go at the nigga, now's the time to do it. What are you sittin' down with him for? I mean, say he does agree to settle now that you then worked him over. What happens next?"

Sharice was silent as Connie turned away from her friend.

"That's what I thought," Connie responded, grabbing one of her bags.

"He can settle all he wants to," Sharice responded as she walked over and jumped in Connie's face to show her how serious she was.

"Look at me! They will pay for everything they did. I put that on everything," she stated.

Connie was hesitant at first to believe her because Sharice was always about money first. This time, however, as she looked at her friend, she could see a sense of hurt in them. This wasn't the typical money-driven Sharice. This was vengeful, looking for payback Sharice. Connie eventually nodded her head.

"Alright, I'm gonna believe you on this one," Connie responded. "It's all on you then to make this shit right."

The two friends shared a hug with each other for a moment before Connie picked up her cell phone from the table next to her bed.

"Why do I gotta go back though?" She asked her friend. "Let me stay here with you. I'm feelin' better and shit. You could use me."

"No, you're goin' back home," Sharice reiterated. "I need you to keep an eye on Michelle. Her crazy ass then killed Big Rob for no apparent reason."

"Are you serious?" A shocked Connie responded with a slight smirk.

"Yeah. I need you to get a message to her directly. Maybe you were right. She wasn't ready to run things out there," Sharice said when she noticed the sinister grin filling her friend's face. "What's so funny?"

"I thought I'd never live to see this day," Connie answered with a snicker. "The day where Sharice said the words 'Connie, you were right'."

Sharice rolled her eyes and folded her arms as Connie

continued.

"Nah, don't roll your eyes on this," Connie joked. "I mean, it's a trip! Normally it's 'Connie, you've fucked up' or 'Connie, that's not right.' To hear you say that shit is fuckin' amazin', for real."

"Yeah, well, maybe I just found someone who fucks up more than you," Sharice pointed out, causing her friend to laugh.

"Oh, so you have jokes, I see," Connie responded as Sharice finally managed a smile as well.

She embraced her friend once again before the two made their way out of the room. Jerome walked over and grabbed Connie's bag from her before Sharice pulled him to the side.

"Make sure she gets on that plane," she said.

"I got you," Jerome responded. "I'll be back in time to join you at the sit down tonight."

"You're not coming," Sharice replied, stunning her lover. "Rock wants to meet at this park somewhere, not the hotel. Just me and one person he said. I'm gonna let Bull ride with me on this one."

"You and one other person? Are you really goin' for that shit?" Jerome argued. "He might be settin' you up!"

"Maybe. I'll have some back up out of sight," Sharice assured him. "With a few more of his muscle soon to be locked up, this nigga doesn't have a prayer, and he knows it. I doubt anything jumps off, but I'm rollin' with Bull, and that's the end of it."

Jerome looked at Sharice suspiciously.

"You're still pissed I spoke out in front of the group, aren't you?" He responded.

"No, it's not that. Me and Bull have been doin' this thing for years. I just feel a little more comfortable with him sittin' in on this. Don't take it personal," Sharice said, trying to explain herself.

Jerome didn't want to hear anything she had to say, so he quickly walked past Connie and the others to head out of the hospital. Connie looked on confused as she walked over to Sharice, seeking answers.

"What's he trippin' on?" She asked her friend.

Sharice didn't give her any answers as she headed out to leave the hospital as well. Connie shrugged it off and followed shortly after.

Back in Michelle's apartment in New Orleans, she and Theo were sitting down for dinner, but there was tension in the air between the two. Michelle sipped her drink and looked at her boyfriend, who struggled to make eye contact with her. It was the first interaction between the two since Theo had learned the truth. Even with all his knowledge, he wanted to hear the truth from her mouth. Michelle, noticing there was an uneasy feeling between the two, questioned her lover.

"Is everything okay?" She asked.

"Everything is fine," a monotone Theo responded.

"I mean, you really haven't touched your meal. Did I overcook it?" Michelle asked, trying to see what's really on Theo's mind.

"No, I just had a late lunch. Not really hungry," Theo replied, trying to keep his emotions in check.

Michelle nodded as she took a sip of her drink once again. Theo decided to interrogate her to see if he could get her to confess her atrocities.

"So, how was work last night?" He asked, trying to make conversation.

"You know. Same old, same," Michelle responded before taking a bite of her meal.

"Really? You know, I passed by, and they said you weren't in," Theo responded.

Michelle took a sip of her drink quickly as she tried to come up with an excuse.

"Which store did you go to?" She asked.

"The one on Carrollton," Theo answered.

"Well, that's why then. I was at the East location for most of the day," Michelle responded, thinking the questioning was done.

"Well, that was my second choice," Theo responded, catching Michelle off guard. "I went over there as well, and they said you weren't in."

Michelle nervously took a sip of her drink, trying to hide her feelings from her lover.

"Well, I was there. Somebody new probably didn't know who I was, or I was at lunch. I'll have a talk with them tonight," she said, causing Theo to nod his head.

"Tonight? You're going back in?" He asked.

"Yeah. Boss is out of town, so I have to make sure this truck coming in is signed for and stocked," Michelle responded, dropping her knife and fork.

"I see," a suspicious Theo responded. "Well, I need to head home anyway. How 'bout I drop you off?"

"No, that's fine," Michelle quickly dismissed. "I'm not sure how long I'm gonna be tonight, and I'd rather have my car with me. Tell you what, how about we hook up tomorrow night? Have us one of those romantic nights like we used to?"

Theo was silent for a moment as the photo of Michelle cheating jumped in his head. He wanted to jump across the table and rip her heart out after what she did to him. After calming his emotions a bit, he slowly nodded his head.

"Tomorrow it is," he said with a forced smile on his face. "I'm going to go ahead and head out. Need to get an early start on a few things for work."

"Huh? What about dinner?" Michelle asked, referring to his full plate.

"I'll take it to go," Theo responded as he grabbed his

plate and headed to the kitchen.

Michelle followed, watching Theo looking for Tupperware in her cabinet.

"Is there something wrong?" she asked, trying to understand her lover's actions.

"No, everything is fine with me," Theo responded as he scraped his plate into a bowl he found. "What about you? Is there something you want to say?"

"Like what?" A confused Michelle asked.

Theo smiled as he sealed up the bowl, kissed Michelle on the cheek before grabbing his keys, and heading out of the apartment. Michelle was still confused with what just happened as she walked back over to her dining room table to finish her meal.

In Houston, Sharice and Bull pulled up to a local park and observed the area for several moments. Bull was reluctant to take the meeting with Rock in an unknown area, but Sharice felt pretty comfortable with everything going on. She was about to exit the car when Bull pulled her back in.

"Just a sec," he said as Sharice closed her door. "I'm still not feelin' this meet. Why set it up with just two people? I mean if he wanted just one on one time, he could have just said that."

"It's because he thought I'll feel safe with one of mine around," Sharice pointed out. "Thinking I'm just some weak bitch who can't handle herself. He's not the first to think like that."

"I don't trust him," Bull quipped. "I think this is a setup. You really think he's gonna keep his word and show up with one other person? I'm tellin' you, it's a setup."

Sharice considered Bull's words when she noticed Rock and one other member of his crew pull up in the parking lot as well. Sharice checked around to see if anyone else was with them. The coast seemed clear for a moment as both she and Bull watched their rival exit his car and take a seat at a park bench. Sharice sighed as she opened her car door once again.

"Just keep a look out, okay?" She told her trusted associate. "If you are right, and this is a hit, be ready to move."

Bull nodded his head as the two exited the vehicle and make their way over towards the bench Rock was waiting for them at. As soon as Sharice arrived, Rock's associates moved in to pat her down. Before he can lay a finger on her, Bull stepped up and stood between the two.

"I'm packin' just like you're packin'," Sharice said to Rock. "No need to do all this shit."

Rock thought for a moment before nodding his head to his crew member. Sharice took a seat on the bench next to Rock as the two gazed upon a long-abandoned area.

"I grew up not too far from here," Rock said. "I remember when this place was the shit as a kid. Ice cream trucks, little gatherings, and shit. This used to be the spot comin' up. Got my first piece of ass over there behind those bleachers. Yeah, this used to be the spot for real."

Sharice looked around the old rusted out playground area and bleachers that are falling apart. The area was a far cry from what Rock described.

"Change. It comes so fast that you don't realize it until it's over," Sharice responded, remembering her grandmother's home and how it changed for the worst due to her drug dealings. "The thing is change is inevitable. If you don't embrace it, it can swallow you whole. Mind if we have this conversation without the help?"

Rock chuckled as he nodded his crew member off. Sharice did the same. Bull hesitated for a moment, before him and the Rock's crewmember left the area. Sharice took a deep breath before continuing.

"I see you didn't bring one of your normal guys with you," Sharice pointed out. "I figured you'd bring at least one of them to the meet."

"After what happened, I think it would have been in bad taste to do that," Rock responded, referring to the attack on Connie. "No need to bring all the emotions and shit out."

"True. Business is business, and I get that, but your guys crossed the line," Sharice fired back. "There's a way to do things. You certainly have my attention now though."

Rock looked at Sharice and smiled.

"Is that a fact?" He replied. "Look, I'm not gonna get into who started what with this shit. What's done is done. I see you've been a little busy yourself. Gotta admit, cuttin' me off from my supplier was a genius move, but we all know suppliers are a dime a dozen. I'll be back in business before your next hair appointment."

"That's tomorrow, actually. You gonna be back in business tomorrow?" Sharice mocked, causing Rock to chuckle.

"I guess not," he replied. "I see you took out a few of my heavy hitters too. You know those charges won't stick, right?"

"They will stick long enough for me to do what I need to do."

"And what is it that you're needin' to do?" Rock asked.

"If necessary, take you and your whole organization out," Sharice responded.

Rock thought for a moment. He knew he already had his plan in place to take out Sharice, but didn't want to tip his hand.

"You said if necessary," he responded. "Does that mean there's still a deal to be made?"

"There's always a deal to be made," Sharice responded as she glanced over towards her rival. "But you knew that when I first sat down with you. You chose this path, not me. How we proceed from here is up to you."

Rock chuckled once more, impressed by Sharice's demeanor as he leaned back on the bench.

"So, Ms. Sharice, what are our options now?" He mockingly asked. "What deal can we come to terms with?"

"Simple," Sharice responded with a sinister grin. "Same deal I offered when I sat down with you. You become one of us. You run the territory like you've been doin' only we get our share using our supply. You're basically one of us."

"Yeah, but with a lot less money," Rock pointed out.

"True, but I'm sure an ambitious man such as yourself would find other ways to close that gap," Sharice quipped. "Those were the terms I was set to offer you before we started the whole thing, but now there is somethin' else I'm gonna require."

"Oh yeah? What?"

"Two of your crew violated my girl," Sharice pointed out as her tone changed. "Now whether you ordered them to do it or not is irrelevant. What is relevant is in order to accept this deal, those two niggas must be turned over to me."

Rock chuckled at the notion of selling his friends out.

"And there it is," he replied. "You see, that's why you can't have women runnin' shit. Y'all get in y'all's feelings real quick. If I was prepared to settle right here, and now, you would let a little thing as what happened to your friend let the deal fall apart. Somethin' tells me if Money was here, or even Rico, that they wouldn't let things like that fuck up the deal."

"Well, they're not here. I am. I speak on their behalf," Sharice responded, becoming a little more aggressive with her tone. "Something tells me if my girl was a nigga, she wouldn't have been raped either. We can go round and round with this shit, but honestly, it's a waste of time for both of us. Those are my terms. Your other option is we take it to the streets. Let's see how you do when that money dries up. I'm in it for the long run. The question is, are you?"

Rock nodded his head smirking. He can tell he struck a nerve with Sharice talking down to her because she was a woman.

"Can I think it over?" Rock humbly asked.

"You got 'til tomorrow night," Sharice answered as she rises from the bench. "After that, the deal is off the table."

Rock nodded his head as he rose from the bench as well. He checked out Sharice with a glance and smiled.

"It's too bad you didn't come up out here," he said. "Me and you could have run this fuckin' city. Probably get twice as much money partnering up out here."

"Is that a proposal?" Sharice asked, grinning.

"It can be," Rock responded as he approached her. "Just say the word, and I'll buy the ring right now."

Sharice giggled as she checked out Rock's solid frame. She gently rubbed her hand down his chiseled chest and impressed with what she saw.

"Nigga, you can't even afford to take me out to dinner," she fired back before walking off back towards Bull.

Both her and Bull got back into their car and pulled off as Rock's crew member rejoined him back by the park bench. Rock nodded his head as he took out his cell phone, dialing Double R, who answered quickly.

"Yeah, it's me. She's headin' your way now. Probably get there in about a half-hour," he informs.

Double R was sitting in the Hilton lobby when the call came through. He smiled as he hung up the line and approached the check-in attendant at the front desk. The attendant recognized him and looked around before handing him a key with the room number written on it. Double R nodded his head as he took out an envelope filled with cash and handed it to her. The attendant quickly counted the money and nodded her head with approval. Double R quickly made his way towards the elevator to head up to Sharice's room.

Once in the room, Double R looked around and checked for the best position he could conceal himself to get the drop on his target. He wasn't looking for a quick kill, rather to incapacitate her so he could take his time with her. What happened to Connie would be a far cry from what he had planned for her. As he checked out the room, he noticed Sharice's suitcase lying on top of the bed. He walked over, unzipped it, and poked around until he saw a pair of Sharice's panties in the bag. He took the panties from the bag and sniffed them like he was infatuated with her. After several deep, obsessive breaths, he placed the panties back in her bag and zipped it up as it was prior. He took a seat on the corner of the bed, waiting for his prey to arrive.

Back in New Orleans, just outside of Michelle's apartment building, Theo was watching his lover's apartment from his car, hoping to get answers. He took a sip of his bottled water when he noticed Michelle making her way out of her apartment. He watched as she jumped into her car and pulled off. Theo quickly started his vehicle and followed Michelle out of the complex and onto the main road.

As Theo continued his pursuit about twenty minutes later, he was confused as he noticed Michelle driving into the airport terminal.

"What the hell is she going to the airport for?" He

mumbled to himself as he watched her pull off to the curb at the arrival terminal.

He quickly pulled off to the side as well, watching his lover closely.

A few minutes later, Connie walked out of the terminal with her bag in hand when she noticed Michelle's car. She tossed her bag into the back seat of the car before joining Michelle in the front. Michelle could tell Connie had a rough time in Texas, noticing several bruises filling her face.

"Damn, you alright?" Michelle asked before Connie shot her a look.

"Just drive," she responded, not wanting to discuss what happened to her.

Michelle shook her head but pulled off to head out of the terminal. There was an uneasy silence between the two rivals before Connie addressed Sharice's concerns.

"So, I heard you took out Big Rob," she said, which caused Michelle to shoot her a dirty look.

"So?" She responded. "It's not like he was connected and shit. He started that whole thing with that six-year-old gettin' killed."

"Don't tell me about it. Sharice is the one tryin' to figure out what the fuck is goin' on out here," Connie pointed out. "She's concerned that all this unnecessary shit will cause heat."

"So what if it does!" Michelle fired back, getting aggravated. "The city is like in the top five of murders all the time! What's one more dumb ass nigga gonna do?!"

"It's not the point. She wants that shit limited!" Connie responded. "If other outside niggas kill each other, then it is what it is. The shit we could have prevented though is what she's talkin' about. And then you took the corner after all that? What the fuck is wrong with you?"

"I did what needed to be done!" Michelle exclaimed, tired of the criticism thrown her way. "One nigga got dropped, one nigga lost his corner. That's how I settled it!"

"By makin' yourself more exposed running another corner that you're unfamiliar with?" Connie responded, catching Michelle off guard. "Sharice don't want us too exposed out there, which is why we only have limited corner responsibilities. You don't know that block, or the niggas runnin' it. They could sell you out with a quickness. The niggas working our shit have been vetted, so to speak so we know what we're dealin' with. That was a rookie mistake, for real."

Michelle was silent because Connie spoke the truth, which infuriated her to no end. She hated that Connie made sense, and her pride won't give Connie the satisfaction knowing she was right. After a few moments, Michelle let go of that pride to respond to her bitter rival.

"Alright, so I'll give the corner to K Dub," she responded. "Let it be his headache, and charge him twice the rate to run it."

"You don't want that nigga havin' no more power," Connie replied, frustrating Michelle even more.

"Okay, then what do y'all want me to do then?!" Michelle fired back. "You say I shouldn't run it, then you say I shouldn't give it away! What then?!"

"Never said you shouldn't give it away," a calm Connie responded. "I'm sure you got some crew folks under you that's been doin' their thing, right? Someone you trust? Offer it as a gift to them. Let them run it, and you get your money off the top. You let them take all the risks, and make sure they keep your name out of it. Them niggas don't need to know who's runnin' shit. It keeps your member's morale up, and lets you see if they got what it takes to run they own shit."

Michelle sighed and nodded her head cause once again, Connie was making sense.

"Look at you talkin' about moral and shit," Michelle responded, smirking. "Who knew you could be so thoughtful."

"Happy niggas make the most money," Connie pointed out. "Besides, they the ones on the corner, not me. A boss bitch lets the rats take the risk while she chills sippin' on champagne. Speakin' of which, drop me off at the club. I'm meetin' my homegirl there."

"Sharice said to bring your ass home," Michelle responded before Connie turned and looked at her.

"Save that shit for them corner niggas. Like I said, I need a drink," Connie repeated.

Michelle sighed as she nodded her head with approval.

"Normally, I'd argue with you, but I think I need a

drink too," she said before pulling out her cell phone and dialing James. "Yo, it's me... yeah, I have Connie in the car. Look, I'm in a pissy mood right now... yeah, it's like that. Meet me at the club. We can get a few drinks and make a night of it... alright. See you in a bit."

Michelle hung up the phone as Connie looked at her suspiciously.

"Y'all two fuckin', ain't y'all?" Connie inquired, smirking.

Michelle chuckled, refusing to respond as she continued down the freeway heading to the club. Theo continued to follow her from a distance, unbeknownst to her.

Sharice and Bull pulled up outside of the hotel and made their way into the lobby. As Sharice passed the front desk, she noticed the attendant looking at her strangely. The two made eye contact momentarily before the attendant looked away, drawing the suspension of Sharice.

"You see that shit?" Sharice said to Bull as she pushed the elevator button.

"What?"

"The way that front desk lady looked at me. Like she knows who I am."

"What? Get outta here," Bull responded before peeking around the corner and checking out the attendant. "I think you're being paranoid. If anythin' she's probably checkin' you out for all the wrong reasons. You do seem to attract those kinds."

Sharice smirked as the elevator arrived. As both she and Bull entered into the elevator, the desk attendant took out her cell phone and dialed Double R.

"Yeah, she's on her way up, but she's not alone. Another guy is with her," she said once he answered the line.

"Alright, I'm headin' out. I'll be in the bar. As soon as the nigga she came with bounce, let me know," Double R responded before hanging up the line.

Moments later, Sharice and Bull exited the elevator, just missing Double R leaving out of the room and around the corner. Sharice walked into the room and looked around, still feeling something was off. Bull walked in and took a seat on the bed as he checked his cell phone. He looked up and noticed that Sharice was still a little uneasy with everything going on.

"A lot of guys would kill to be in this position," Bull said, referring to him sitting on her bed.

"Yeah, I bet they would," Sharice responded as she placed her purse on the computer desk.

"There's one particular guy I know that would love to be here right now," Bull said with a sneer filling his face.

Sharice sighed as she took a seat on the bed next to Bull and took off her shoes.

"You think he's pissed at me?" She asked.

"He just wants you to be safe, Reese. He's just lookin' out for you the best way he can," Bull answered.

"I'll be fine," Sharice quipped as she rubbed her sore feet.

"I know you will, but to be fair, if you was my girl, I'd wanna make sure you're safe too," Bull pointed out. "It's different in this thing of ours, and these mopes could make a move at any time."

"I know, I know," Sharice responded, tired of the preaching she was receiving.

Bull chuckled. He could tell he was getting on Sharice's nerves.

"So, how's everythin' workin' out with that?" Bull questioned. "I mean, are y'all gonna jump that broom as y'all say?"

Sharice chuckled and shook her head.

"Come on, Bull, you know me," she responded. "What makes you think I'm even capable somethin' like that?"

"I get that, but you can't let this thing run you twenty-four-seven," Bull responded. "You're gonna miss out on some of those nice things."

"Didn't bother you." Sharice pointed out.

"Yeah, it did," Bull responded. "That's why I'm warning you. If I could take it all back, there'd be a lot of shit I'd change. Havin' a wife and kids, it would have been nice. Now I'm an old man for the most part with nothin' but my work to keep me busy. Learn from me. You don't want this life, Reese."

Sharice let Bull's words repeat in her head for a couple

of moments as she smiled at her friend.

"I know, I know. That's just my two cents," Bull continued.

"Yeah, but you gave me a dollar's worth there, didn't you?" Sharice quipped with a smile.

Bull nodded his head, getting up from the bed.

"Guess I'll head out," he said.

"Alright. Hey, do me a favor and check out that attendant on your way out," Sharice replied. "I know, I might be paranoid, but just give her a quick glance."

Bull nodded his head as he walked out of the hotel room. Sharice took a deep breath before opening up her suitcase. She's caught off guard because things seem out of place in her case. She pulled out the panties that Double R had sniffed earlier suspiciously and felt something was off. She checked through several other items before receiving a text from Bull saying 'All good' referring to the attendant. She texted Bull back, saying 'hang around outside. I'll let you know when you can go. Keep out of sight'. She then made her way into the bathroom and started up a shower.

In a local Houston strip club, Jerome was sitting at the bar area watching the strippers on stage from a distance. It was a hole in the wall establishment with lower end strippers, but it was just the place for someone trying to stay out of sight and to themselves. He was sipping on his drink, being entertained by the show when Aisha, wearing booty shorts and heels, walked into the club and smiled when she noticed her target. Her face was made up and she was scantily dressed to make sure she caught the attention of every man or woman in sight. She walked over and noticed that Jerome seemed a little down as she took a seat next to him.

"Hey, baby. Buy me a drink?" She flirtatiously said.

"Maybe another time," Jerome responded, ignoring her.

"Come on, boo. You seem like you need a friend to talk to. I wouldn't mind being that friend," she replied as she crossed her legs, purposely intertwining with his leg.

Jerome turned, looked at her for the first time and was impressed. He gave her a good look before pulling his leg back, breaking their connection.

"You seem like a nice chick and all, but I'm not about that," Jerome responded. "I'm sure there are plenty of niggas up in here willin' to keep you company."

"There are, I'm sure. But I'm not here for that," Aisha responded. "I saw you over here lookin' like you were down and out, and figured it must be a girl got you this way. When my ex left me, I know it was hard as hell for me to move past that shit. I was just like you, at the bars with my girls mopin' around. I just couldn't get back out there, and it took the kindness of a stranger walkin' over to me buyin' me a drink and talkin' to get me outta that funk. I'm just returning the favor."

"So, based on that example, shouldn't it be you buyin' me the drink?" Jerome quipped, causing Aisha to giggle.

"Well, I ain't that friendly," she responded. "Some things are what they are, but I am here if you wanna just chat."

Jerome chuckled as he raised his hand to call the bartender over.

"Hey, let me get another one of these, and whatever my friend here wants," he said. "I didn't catch the name."

"Sade. And I'll have a vodka, straight," she said as the bartender walked off to fill her order.

The two started conversing with each other, which lead to laughing and joking. Their interaction distracted Jerome from noticing Troy walking into the club and observing the two from the dark end of the building.

Back in New Orleans, Michelle and Connie pulled up outside of Club Exotica and made their way towards the entrance. Across the street, checking out the club was Freeway, one of Rock's crew, and three other crew members sitting in a car, waiting to make their move on Michelle. Freeway noticed Michelle and Connie exiting the vehicle and was confused as he pulled out his cell phone.

"Son of a bitch," he said as he dialed Rock's number and waited for an answer. "Yo, we over here at the spot, and ol' girl just ran through, but I think that other bitch that was roughed up back there is here too. What you want us to do?" He asked as he listened to his leader's instructions. "Yeah, alright, we'll take care of it."

He hung up the phone before turning his attention towards the crew members sitting in the back seat.

"Y'all go get another car and meet us back here," he instructed. "The chick that just walked in with our girl is y'all's responsibility. Take that shit away from the club though. Rock said the Feds be on this bitch hot. We'll keep a lookout 'til y'all get back."

The two crewmembers Freeway addressed both nodded their heads and exited the vehicle. Freeway got comfortable as he looked at the driver with a smile on his face.

"We lucked up with that shit," he said before looking out towards the club once more.

Just down the block, Theo, who pulled up moments ago, also parked on the curb watching the club on the lookout for Michelle.

Inside, the club was packed as always as Michelle and Connie made their way through the crowd towards the bar area. They took a seat as Tracy greeted them from behind the bar.

"What's up, ladies? Y'all look like y'all then had a

rough night," Tracy said before noticing the bruising on Connie's face. "Connie? What happened to your face? I thought you were in Houston?"

"I just got back," Connie responded. "Could you bring me a scotch? The good shit."

Tracy had a look of concern on her face but nodded her head and walked off to fill Connie's order. Michelle looked at Connie and could tell she was still a little down about being back. Sharice always told her to try with Connie, so she decided to attempt to spark a conversation with her adversary.

"Look, back in the car, that was some real shit you told me," Michelle admitted. "I know I can be difficult, but I wanted to tell you I appreciate the advice."

Connie didn't respond as Tracy returned with her drink. After she downed it, she handed the glass back to Tracy.

"Another one," she said before looking towards Michelle. "Look, it ain't nothin'. Sharice can be really strict over this shit. Been with her for years. I know how she thinks. You got skills, I ain't gonna lie. I've been waitin' for this shit all my life, and I'm not about to let a bullet or you take my place, ya dig?"

Michelle frowned as Tracy returned with Connie's drink. Once again, she downed it in one shot and rose from the bar. She walked up to the VIP area as Tracy and Michelle observed a shell of the woman they know.

"No disrespect cause I know y'all go a ways back, but your friend there can be a real asshole when she wants to be," Michelle said, turning her attention towards Tracy. "I guess after what happened to her though, she has the right to be moody."

"What happened?" Tracy inquired.

"Shit that will keep you up at night," Michelle responded before looking back towards the crowd.

Tracy, knowing she wasn't going to get an explanation beyond that, sighed before walking off to attend to customers. Michelle's face lit up when she noticed James walking in the front door. She made her way over and greeted him with a kiss before leading him back to the bar area to share a drink with him.

Back in Houston, a car with Troy and Aisha pulled up to an abandoned, rundown neighborhood. They both exited the vehicle and looked around the area before heading over towards the trunk. Troy unlocked the truck to reveal a passed out Jerome tied up in it. Troy looked at Aisha and shook his head.

"Shit, girl. How much shit did you put in his drink?" He asked.

"Enough that he didn't make a peep," Aisha fired back. "What does it matter anyway? We got him, right?"

Troy shook his head as he worked to lift Jerome's body from the trunk. He tossed him on the ground before closing the trunk and looked around the area once more. Jerome grunted but didn't respond much beyond that. Troy crouched down, slapping Jerome on the face several times trying to wake him.

"Hey! Wake the fuck up!" He said while repeatedly slapping him.

Jerome finally came to as he looked around groggily.

"What... what's goin' on," Jerome struggled to say as Troy stood above his captive.

"What's goin' on is your exit party," Troy responded as he took out his gun from his belt strap. "You New Orleans niggas should have stayed in that dump city of yours."

Jerome didn't respond as he struggled to remain coherent. Troy chuckled as he looked at the sad state his rival was in.

"You know, I could have just busted a cap in your ass the second we pulled up, but I wanted to put your mind at ease and let you know my man Double R is takin' care of your girl," Troy gloated. "Thing is though, he's very particular when it comes to the women, ain't that right Aisha?"

"Yeah, he's a freak for real," Aisha chimed in.

"What happened to that dike bitch ain't nothin' compared what he's gonna do your girl," Troy said, angering Jerome. "Yeah, my guess is he's gonna split that ass in two. Good thing is she'll join you eventually. When she does, ask her about how Double R wore that ass out!"

"Fuck you, muthafucka!" A rage-filled Jerome responded as he tried to rise from the ground, only to fall back over. "I'll kill you! Don't you touch her, nigga! I'm warning you!"

Troy laughed, aiming his gun towards Jerome, only to be stopped by Aisha.

"Hold up! I told Rock I would do it," she said, confusing Troy.

"What the fuck does it matter?" He asked.

"Because I said I was gonna do it, nigga! Now give me the strap and step aside," Aisha commands.

Troy shook his head in disbelief but did as he was ordered. When Aisha raised the gun, he could tell she had no experience cause she was holding the gun sideways with one hand.

"Aye, this ain't the movies, for real," Troy said as he walked up to her and corrected her grip.

He aimed the gun right towards Jerome's head, who was still fighting the effects of the drug.

"Alright, just pull the trigger, and look out for the kickback," Troy said as he backed away from Aisha.

After a few moments, a jittery Aisha took a deep breath and looked into the eyes of her target. She eventually built up the courage to pull the trigger, firing a shot to Jerome's head. The blast surprised her, forcing her to take a step back and break her heel on one of her shoes, sending her tumbling to the ground. Troy was in tears laughing at an embarrassed Aisha, who jumped up and dusted herself off.

"That shit ain't funny, Troy!" She exclaimed while gathering herself.

Troy wiped his face as he walked over to Jerome's body to check to see if he's still alive. The bullet went through the front of his head, blasting out the other side of his skull, which was shattered. After a few moments, Troy nodded his head as he walked over and took the gun away from Aisha.

"Well, that nigga dead," he said, getting back into the car.

Aisha looked over her handy work and was a little startled with what she's done, but eventually made her way back into the car. Troy quickly sped away down the block leaving Jerome's corpse there to bleed alone.

Around forty minutes after their arrival to Club

Exotica, Michelle and James exited the club laughing and joking with each other, catching the attention of both Freeway and his driver, and also Theo, who was heartbroken seeing the warmth between the two. Rage filled his face as he looked to approach them, but realized he didn't have a weapon to protect himself in case things get physical. He grunted as he started his car, quickly pulling off and passing up Freeway and his crew member.

"There's ol' girl now, yo," Freeway said as the driver started the car. "Let's wait a little and follow them. See if we can catch them slippin' along the way."

Michelle and James got into her car and pulled off down the road. Freeway's car made a U-turn and quickly followed. James was smiling as he looked at Michelle, which confused her.

"Why is you lookin' at me like that?" She inquired.

"I don't know. Just happy to see you, that's all," James admitted, smirking. "I thought you was gonna be with that square nigga tonight."

"Had every intention to, but then Sharice called me to pick Connie's crazy ass up. He was actin' funny today anyway, so I was like fuck it," Michelle responded.

"You's a lyin' muthafucka," James responded, smirking. "You just wanted the big dick, that's all."

"Nigga, everythin' ain't about sex. You know that, right?" Michelle replied as she stopped at a red light.

"Let me see. Lame nigga? Or big dick? Gee, I wonder what I would choose?" James fired back, acting like he's thinking.

Michelle chuckled as well when she looked over to her left to see Freeway lowering his window with his gun drawn.

"Get down!" She yelled to James as Freeway opened fire, destroying the window.

He fired several more shots littering the car door, making sure there would be no survivors. After a few moments, he slowly hopped out of the car and motioned the other crew member to join him. The crew member pulled out his gun and joined Freeway as they cautiously approached the car to confirm that the hit was complete. As Freeway peeked into the window, Michelle fired a shot into his head, killing him. James jumped out of the other side of the car and opened fire on the driver, who tried to escape. The driver fell lifelessly to the ground as Michelle kicked open her car door. She checked her head, which was bloodied from the glass that cut her. James noticed the blood on her brow.

"Shit, you okay?!" He asked before quickly checking her out.

"I'm fine, just a scratch," she said as she walked over to Freeway and crouched over him to check his pockets.

James looked over at the car and the bullets holes on the car door, confused.

"How in the fuck did we survive this?" He asked as he continued to assess the damage.

"I had metal plates inserted into my doors for just this occasion," Michelle explained as she pulled out a cell phone from Freeway. "You didn't notice how she always rides low?"

James shook his head with amazement as he put away his gun.

"Well, excuse me, Ms. James Bond," he jabbed as he joined her next to Freeway. "Maybe next time, add some bulletproof glass."

Michelle used Freeway's thumb to unlock his phone and checked out the number listed on it.

"Eight three two area code. What the fuck?" She questioned before wiping the phone and tossing it to the ground.

"Where's that at?" James asked.

"Houston," Michelle responded before panicking. "Oh shit! Connie! Get her on the phone! Let's go!"

Michelle hurried back into her car as James pulled out his cell phone to call Connie before getting in as well. The bullet filled car screeched as it headed down the road.

Connie was at the daiquiri shop with her friend Nicole when her cell phone suddenly rang. She checked the caller ID and sent the call to voicemail. She was still down and out with everything going on. Several tables down in the packed shop were two of Rock's crew members watching her closely, looking to make their move. Nicole was having the time of her life, laughing and joking with folks passing by when she noticed Connie's down mood.

"Girl, what's up with you?" She said, trying to cheer her friend up. "Look, I know you're pissed with Sharice and all, but every time we go out, you're like this. You need to loosen up a bit. Enjoy the moment! You can mope around when you're at the house."

"I'm just sick of this shit!" Connie exclaimed. "I've given my life to this shit, and I'm still treated like a fuckin' child! People hurt me, Nicole. I mean they really fucked me up. All I get from Sharice is '*I'll take care of it*'. If she were in the same situation you know god damn well she would handle it. Or send me to do it. I swear, I'm gettin' tired of not being able to do what I wanna do, for real."

Connie's phone rang once more and she saw that it was James calling again. She sent the call to voicemail once more before taking a sip of her drink. Nicole could tell she was frustrated more than ever, so she hugged on her friend.

"Cee, forget about that shit," she said. "Look, you and I both know that this shit between you and Sharice has been boilin' over. I know you don't wanna hear it, but maybe it's time you move on from that shit and do your own thing."

Connie looked at Nicole as if she's offended.

"Do my own thing? Like what?" She questioned. "There is no own thing. I don't know how to do shit else but what I'm doin', and Sharice and the Faction are the only folks out here doin' just that. I wouldn't last five minutes out there on my own. They got this city on lock, ya heard me."

"Maybe another city then?" Nicole suggested. "I mean they don't run every city. I'm sure you can find a spot to call your own somewhere else and build that empire I know you got floating in your head."

Connie giggled at the suggestion as Nicole's attempt to change her friend's mood was working. It was always a dream of Connie's to get her own thing working, without the help of anyone. She loved Sharice but always being in her shadow, frustrated her to no end at times. While starting her own hustle in another town was tempting, deep down in her heart, she knew she wouldn't be capable without the backing of a major figure. At the end of the day, she was a woman, and she knew that she would never garner the respect she needed to become the top dog by herself. Sharice fought hard to get where she was, and it wasn't something Connie wanted to waste time or effort into doing on her own. As she sipped her drink and fantasized about a life where she's the boss, her cell phone rang again, disturbing her thoughts. She checked once more and noticed it's James calling.

"What the fuck?!" Connie uttered to herself as she finally answered the phone. "What, nigga! I'm tryin' to chill and shit! What do you-"

Connie's face dropped as James explained to her what went down earlier. She cautiously looked around the area trying to see if anyone is scoping her out. Out of the corner of her eyes, she noticed the two members across the way who were eyeing her hard. She didn't make it obvious that she noticed them as she smiled, making the call look casual.

"Yeah, I think I see two," she said with a slight grin. "I'll meet you back at the club... no, don't sweat it. By the time you get here, either I'll be dead, or they will. I'll get back to you."

She slowly lowered her phone and casually watched

the men looking in her direction. She turned to Nicole, who was bobbing her head with the music.

"Hey, I need you to do somethin', and you're not gonna like it," Connie said before going into details on what she needed to be done.

Nicole became nervous after hearing what was required of her but nodded her head.

"I'm really not dressed for this shit," she responded.

"Don't worry, you'll be fine. You ready?" Connie asked.

Nicole quickly finished her drink and sighed before nodding her head. The two friends get up and headed over to the women's bathroom. Rock's crew noticed the movement and decided this was the perfect time to take out Connie. They made their way through the crowd and headed over towards the bathroom area. They stood just outside the bathroom with a full view of the entrance. Their hands were clutching their guns inside of their jackets, waiting for any movement. After several moments, Nicole walked out of the bathroom, laughing on her cell phone, nonchalantly walking past Rock's crew. They ignored her because she was not their target, and continued to remain ready for Connie to exit. Nicole turned around, slowly pulled a gun from her purse and opened fire, hitting one of the crew members from behind. Everyone in the shop began to panic and scatter in the area once the shot was fired. The other crew member turned and was about to pull out his gun when Connie burst out of the bathroom and fired several shots of her own, killing the member. Nicole was a nervous wreck as she dropped the gun on the ground, shaking. Connie walked over to the crew member Nicole had injured, and noticed he was still breathing. She quickly ended his life by firing a couple of more shots before checking out both men.

"You alright?" She asked her nervous friend before picking up her discarded gun.

"I... I... I shot him," Nicole stuttered.

"Yeah, but I killed him. You don't have to sweat it," Connie responded. "Come on, we need to get out of here before someone comes lookin'."

Nicole was frozen, looking over the crew member she shot. It was her first time using a gun, and she thought she had killed him initially. Connie noticed her friend still stunned. She walked over and grasped her hands, taking the attention off of the fallen men.

"Look at me. We need to go, okay?" Connie calmly stated. "You didn't do anything. I killed that man. All you did was wing him. Now let's go."

Nicole slowly nodded her head as Connie led her out of the area and into her car. Connie drove the car with Nicole, still shook over the events, and unable to focus. A smirk came across Connie's face because she felt alive for the first time in a while.

Back at the club, Connie settled Nicole in the VIP area before making her way into Sharice's office. Michelle and James jumped up when they noticed her walking in.

"Fuck, Connie! You can't call and let us know you're alright?!" Michelle said, causing Connie to smile.

"Gee, I didn't know you cared," Connie mocked before taking a seat in the office. "It was two hitters. Not the two I wanted, but it's a start. You sure them niggas were from Texas, and no other shit we might be in?"

"Nah, I checked one of my guy's cell phone. It's definitely a Houston area code," Michelle confirmed, leaning on the nearby desk. "So, how'd you get out alive?"

Connie sighed before shaking her head with regret.

"My girl, Nicole," Connie admits. "I had her run interference while I took care of it. She shot one of the guys, but I took them both out for good."

"I'm confused, she shot one of them niggas?" James inquired. "Cause I met her before, and she don't seem like the type that's strapped."

"I gave her my back up piece to use," Connie answered, grabbing her head in frustration.

"Back up piece? Christ, how many guns you packin'?" An amazed James questioned.

"Two on me, and another two in my ride," Connie replied. "Keep them out of view in case the cops wanna jack me up."

James chuckled as he shook his head.

"Christ, I'm runnin' with Double O Seven and John Wick. I feel so weak right now," he joked as both Michelle and Connie managed a smile.

Connie looked around the office when something hit her.

"Shit! Did anyone try and call Sharice? They could be movin' on her too!" She responded.

"Yeah, we did. Several times. She's not answering her phone," Michelle answered. "I tried Jerome too, but didn't get an answer."

"What about Bull?" Connie questioned.

"You know how Bull is. He's on a burna phone. He doesn't carry his real phone on him," Michelle pointed out. "But, yeah, I did try him too just to see. No answer. You were just out there; do you have his number?"

Connie got up and checked her pockets when she realized she didn't have her phone with her.

"Shit! Where's my phone?" She said as she looked around the area. "Fuck! Please tell me I didn't leave it at the daiquiri shop!"

"Just… just calm down, okay," Michelle responded, trying to settle Connie down. "Why don't you go check the car. If you did leave it at the shop, we'll deal with it. I'll try and call Sharice again."

Connie nodded her head as she rushed out of the office. Michelle dialed Sharice once again, trying to get in touch with her leader before something tragic happened to her.

Back in Houston, in Sharice's hotel room, her cell phone was vibrating on the nightstand next to the bed. Double R quietly crept into the room, making sure that didn't make a sound. He gently closed the door and turned his attention towards the bathroom, where he heard the shower running. He tiptoed around the room and noticed her cell phone ringing as well. He ignored it as he placed his hand on the bathroom doorknob. A slick grin filled his face as he readied himself for the confrontation. He drew his gun, ready to enter when suddenly the closet opened, revealing Sharice with a gun of her own drawn with Double R's back towards her. She fired two shots, one in Double R's back, and another in his leg that sent him crashing into the wall in front of him yelling out in pain. Sharice quickly leaped out of the closet and over towards her fallen foe, grabbing his gun away from him before he can make a recovery. The grimacing Double R grunted, and turned over on his back to face the woman he was obsessed over. Sharice feeling no threat from him any longer, smiled as she quickly grabbed her cell phone and dialed Bull.

"Yeah, it's me. I had a visitor... No, I'm good. Do me a favor, circle around the parking lot real quick to see if he's alone. If there is nobody else, there's a Walmart just down the road. Get disposal kit number eight... Yeah, I know, I know. I'll take care of it. If you see anyone else, let me know. And come through the other door... yeah, that one."

Sharice hung up the line and sat on the edge of the bed, towering over Double R, who was still struggling to breathe. She grabbed a pillow and quickly placed it on his stomach to muffle the sound of a gunshot she executed, causing him to scream out once again.

"I remember you," she said with a sinister grin on her face. "You were at the meet when we first sat down with your boss. You were lookin' at me all strange and shit. I've seen those looks before. Mainly perverts or rapists. My girl told me you were the one that raped her. She didn't need to tell me though. I knew."

Sharice crouched down and used the pillow to muffle Double R's screams as she pushed her gun into his exposed belly wound. After several moments of him squirming, she pulled back and removed the pillow from his face. She had a sadistic smile on her face as she checked out the damage she'd caused.

"You know, it was a good plan, I gotta admit," Sharice said as she took her seat on the bed once again. "Set me up while I was out meetin' with your boss. It was almost perfect. Somethin' tells me y'all weren't expectin' Bull to come back with me. Had he not, I'd be dead, or at the very least part of whatever sick shit you had planned."

Sharice noticed something in Double R's pocket and crouched down once more to see what it was. She chuckled as she pulled out a set of handcuffs.

"I see what you had planned," Sharice responded before standing above her enemy. "It was perfect. I wouldn't have been the wiser, even after Bull left. If you hadn't gone into my bag and took out my panties, I wouldn't have known shit."

Double R was grimacing in pain as Sharice slowly lifted her skirt to reveal her panties.

"Were these the ones you just had to get a whiff of?" She teased as she spread her legs to make sure Double R had a good view. "Is that what you wanted to see?"

Double R tried to ignore her taunts, but couldn't help himself as he looked up and was blessed to see what he longed for. Sharice smiled as slowly lowered herself on top of him and started to unbuckle his belt.

"I know you're bleeding here, and it's pretty painful, but I always wondered if a nigga can still get hard under this much stress," she said as she opened his pants. "I saw it on a movie once, and I swore it was all bullshit. I mean, who could get hard and shit after they've been shot? Just didn't make sense to me."

After Sharice opened his pants, she jerked them down as far as she could before exposing his fully erect manhood. She looked at him as if she's impressed.

"Well, I guess the movies were right in this case," Sharice said as she slowly began rubbing Double R's manhood. "You know, what you did to my girl, it was pretty fucked up, and it's sad to say, but you're not gonna live past tonight. I'm feeling good though, so here's what I'm gonna do. I'm gonna let you bust that last nut before I send you on your way. How's that sound?"

Double R didn't respond as Sharice teased his manhood once again. He fought her as best he could, not wanting to give her the satisfaction.

"Come on. If you don't tell me you want it, I'm gonna stop," Sharice teased as she took his manhood and began rubbing it on her sweet spot, just outside the panties he was obsessed with earlier. "Come on, I need to hear you ask for it. It'll be the last one you ever feel, so say it."

Sharice slowed down because she could feel he was on the brink of releasing himself. During the act, she's smeared herself with blood from the wounds of Double R. None of it mattered because Sharice wanted her prey to give into her. Double R grit his teeth from being filled with both pain and pleasure simultaneously. Sharice released her grip on his shaft and looked as though she was disappointed.

"Oh well, I guess no last release for you," she

responded before reaching for her gun that's laying on the bed.

"P...please. I... I want it," Double R murmured, much to Sharice's delight.

"I'm sorry, I can't hear you," she responded, smirking. "Can you repeat that for me?"

"Please, I want it," Double R answered slightly louder.

"Come on, my nigga. This is the last time you're gonna bust a nut here! Say that shit like you mean it!" Sharice commanded.

"I want it! Please! I... I want it!" A loud Double R spat out, causing Sharice to giggle.

"That's what I'm talkin' about," she replied as she began to slowly stroke his shaft again.

With one hand on his shaft, and the other hand teasing his sack, Double R was in a state of bliss. The life-threatening wounds didn't seem to bother him anymore since the hand job he was receiving had taken over his body. Sharice's touch was executed to perfection as Double R struggled to last as long as he could, knowing it will be the last time he felt anything. Just as his body tensed up and he's about to release for the final time, Sharice quickly grabbed her gun and shot him right in his groin, causing him excruciating pain. The pain was so dreadful that sounds weren't even coming out of Double R's mouth as the shock took over his body. A sadistic Sharice smiled as blood from the blast splattered on her face.

"It seems I blew my load before you did," Sharice mocked before rising from the ground.

She took her heel and stomped into Double R's groin, looking to inflict as much pain possible.

"Now, we have a little time before clean up. I have a couple of questions about my friend Rock, and you seem to be the perfect person to ask," she said. "So, let's begin. Shall we?"

Sharice continued to torture her victim just as she promised Connie she would. The muffled screams filled the hotel room as Sharice made sure to cover his face whenever inflicting any pain on her prey.

Thirty minutes later, Bull returned with several bags and enters the hotel room. As he walked into the adjacent hotel room Sharice was in, he was stunned when he sees the damage Sharice has caused to Double R. As she turned around, he's left speechless with all the blood she was covered with. What surprised him, even more, is that Double R was still alive through everything.

"Bout time," Sharice said as she carefully walked over to him. "I thought this nigga was gonna die before you got back."

"Sharice… I… I…" Bull replied, trying to put together a full sentence.

After a few moments, Sharice gave up trying to wait for Bull to pull himself together.

"Look, I need to get out of this shit. You got the cleaning supplies?" Sharice asked.

Bull handed her the bags he brought in with him still trying to get his mind off what he's seen. Sharice quickly sifted through the items.

"Alright, cool. I'm gonna get cleaned up and-" Sharice stopped mid-sentence when she noticed Bull wasn't paying any attention to her. "Bull! For fuck's sake, please!"

Bull snapped out of his gaze of his boss's handy work

and gave Sharice his attention.

"Rig the sprinklers, wipe off all handles, and anything else I could have touched. I'm gonna take a quick shower and clean out the bathroom. Let's move!"

Bull nodded his head as he quickly got one of the chairs and stood on top of it to rig the sprinkler system. Sharice quickly stripped out of her blood-soaked clothes and got into the shower. As the water ran down her body, the blood cleansed itself from her and dripped into the below drain. She used shampoo to make sure the grime was out of her hair and rinsed off rather quickly. As she dried herself off, she glanced at herself in the mirror. She was horrified by what she saw. The blood may be gone from her body, but the image of it still weighed heavily on her. After a brief look, she turned away and began cleaning the bathroom.

Several minutes had gone by as Sharice opened the door and carefully made sure she didn't touch any blood-stained carpet or wall. In her hand was a garbage back containing her bloodied clothes. Sharice took a deep breath as she went over ever last detail to make sure she was covered when she stopped in her tracks.

"Were there cameras in the hallway?" She asked.

"I don't know, I didn't pay attention to that," Bull answered.

"Fuck! If there is, they got me walkin' in this room. Let me take a peek real quick," Sharice replied before making her way out of the room and into the hallway. She cautiously checked out the entire hallway but didn't see anything visible. She made her way back to the other room she rented just to make sure if there was a hidden camera anywhere, there was footage of her walking into that room to cover herself. She quickly made her way over to Bull, who was waiting to make his next move.

"Was there one?" He asked.

"Not that I can tell, but let's leave out next door just to make sure," Sharice responded as she looked over towards Double R's fading body.

"I wondered why you took out three rooms," Bull responded as he picked up several bags.

"You always taught me to keep them guessin'. Remember?" Sharice responded, smirking as she quickly looked around the room once again. "We ready?"

Bull nodded his head as Sharice looked at Double R one last time.

"Well, we gotta go, boo," she mocked as Bull lit some paper.

The room had been soaked with lighter fluid, with globs of it on Double R's body. Bull handed Sharice the paper as she took a long look at her enemy.

"Bye, bitch," she said before tossing the paper onto Double R's body.

The fire spread quickly as Bull and Sharice rushed to the next room and closed the door. Sharice grabbed her suitcase, and a few other items before both she and Bull exited the adjacent hotel room. Both were calm as they hit the elevator button. As soon as it opened, they entered, noticing that the smoke from the room was starting to fill the air. Once in the lobby, the fire alarm went off, alerting the rest of the hotel of the fire. Sharice noticed the front desk clerk and growled. She was about to approach her, but Bull pulled her back.

"We gotta go, Reese. We don't have time for that," he said.

Sharice calmed down and nodded her head before both her and Bull made it out of the hotel into their car. Bull pulled off quickly out of the parking lot as Sharice finally breathed a sigh of relief. As she was getting herself back together, she checked her phone and noticed Michelle had called her seventeen times.

"Damn, Chelle, seventeen times? Really?" She said to herself as she dialed her number. "Hey, It's me... yeah, yeah, I'm good... Wait, what?"

Terror entered Sharice's face after she heard about the attempt on her crew's life and realized she had not heard from Jerome.

"Bull, where the fuck is Jerome?!" She exclaimed.

"He took off before the sit-down," Bull recalled. "Probably just to clear his mind. Why? What's wrong?"

Sharice tried to speak, but nothing came out of her mouth. She hung up the phone with Michelle and quickly dialed Jerome's number, praying he would answer. After multiple rings, the call went to voicemail. She hung up the line and called over and over again, hoping the worst had not happened.

Chapter 7

Game Over

A few days after the attempt on Sharice's life, back at the New Orleans FBI Headquarters, Daniels was on the phone at his desk, stunned with the news he was receiving.

"Son of a bitch!" He exclaimed, slamming his phone down before making his way towards Davis' desk.

Davis was on his computer stunned by the same information he received via email as well when Daniels approached him.

"Are you seeing this?" Daniels asked.

"Yeah, checking it out now. How in the hell did we miss this?" Davis responded while reading the memo. "Says here we got a body in the Hilton in Houston where

Sharice was staying at, another one of her people found dead in an abandoned neighborhood, and another four dead down here thought to be connected to the Faction as well."

"Whatever is happening in Texas is spilling over here," Daniels deduced. "Get Flores on the phone, and get somebody to pick up Mike. This 'I don't know what's going on' shit has gone on for too long."

Davis picked up his desk phone and began making calls as a frustrated Daniels made his way back towards his desk.

About an hour had gone by, and Daniels and Davis were in the conference room looking over several files when the conference phone began to ring. Davis answered the line.

"Flores, is that you?" Daniels asked.

"Yeah, it's me," she responded as Davis walked over and closed the conference door.

"Is it safe to talk?" Daniels asked.

"Yes, it is. Probably more safe than it's ever gonna be," Flores gloats. "I got him. I got him on tape!"

Daniels and Davis were stunned as they surround the

speakerphone.

"You got Rico on tape?" Daniels asked to verify.

"Yep! Me and the boss were having a date night in his humble establishment while his wife was out of the country. While we were eating diner, a few of his lieutenants came in and disturbed us, needing to talk about something. He asked me to give them a moment, which I did. I tried to get in their business as much as I can, but they kept their conversation close. None of them, however, realized I left my phone nestled in my purse on the dining room table!" Flores explained. "He gave several orders that your informant confirmed, and not through anyone, but the man himself. We got him, guys! We got him!"

Daniels breathed a sigh of relief as he sat back in his chair.

"Is there any way we can tie any of this back to what's going on in Houston?" He asked.

"Houston? What happened there?" Flores questioned.

"Two dead, one on Sharice's side and one on their competition. In New Orleans, four dead, all looking like they're Texas natives," Daniels explained. "I know Rico was in charge of that move. Anything heard on your end about it?"

"No, not really," Flores responded. "I did overhear that he sent someone out there a few days ago to deliver something, but by the time I was able to get free, the guy was already on the plane. I filed it under my report."

Daniels pondered for a moment, trying to add things up.

"If he was on a plane, it had to be money," he responded. "Rico's sending money to Houston. Maybe it's a payoff or something."

"Maybe. Anyway, I'm late for my club job. Gonna put in my two weeks to make it look official. Hopefully, we'll be snapping the cuffs on Mr. Rico soon," Flores said with glee. "If I hear anything else, I'll keep you updated."

Daniels hung up the line and nodded his head with approval. Davis could tell he was still a little disappointed with the news.

"What's the matter?" Davis asked his partner. "We just landed Rico. Between him and Mike, we have two-thirds of the Faction bosses in custody. I know it's not John, but it's something."

"No, we'll have one boss in custody," Daniels corrected. "Mike is a patsy. Always has been. The real boss is out there in Houston right now cleaning up shit."

Before Davis can respond, there was a knock at the conference door as an agent peeked his head in.

"Hey, informant sixty-eight forty is in. You want him in interrogation?"

"No, bring him here," Daniels responded.

The agent nodded his head and walked out to retrieve Money Mike. He returned several moments later with Money, who was cuffed and confused about what's going on.

"Bruh, what the fuck is this shit?" He asked as Daniels waved off the agent and turned his attention to Money.

"Sit the fuck down," Daniels commanded, tired of playing games with the Faction boss.

"Yo, what about these cuffs? This shit is uncalled for, for real," Money responded until he saw the seriousness in Daniels's eyes.

He slowly took a seat as Daniels leaned towards him.

"Mike, this is bullshit," he said to a confused Money. "I have dead bodies popping up all over the city, people dead in Houston, and money being transported across state lines! There's no fucking way you can't know what is going on, being that you're a fucking boss!"

"Hey, chill out. I just heard about that shit not too long ago myself," Money responded. "I mean, they didn't send Sharice there for the coffee, or whatever the fuck Houston is known for. She had a job to do, and she did it! We've been doin' this shit for months now, and y'all still ain't grabbed Rico with all the shit I then gave y'all! Don't be gettin' on my ass cause y'all got niggas gettin' on your ass!"

Daniels growled. He was getting more and more frustrated with the Faction boss.

"You know, maybe this isn't going to work," he said. "You're right, we've been going back and forth with this for months. Maybe it's time to pull you and let a judge see if you've lived up to your end of the deal. Of course, they're going to ask our opinion on the matter. What do you think, Davis? You think the man has lived up to his end?"

Davis chuckled as he shook his head.

"The deal was for full cooperation. I just don't feel we're getting that," he responded.

"What the fuck y'all niggas want?!" A frustrated Money fired back. "I gave y'all what I know! I did exactly what I was told to do!"

"We want Sharice!" Daniels exclaimed. "We want her on tape talking about the murder of the witness to John Bianchi, or any of the other hundred murders she's involved in! I want her on tape, and I want the shit by the end of the week, or you can kiss that deal goodbye. Are we clear?"

Money frowned as he's being backed into a corner. He didn't have the relationship with Sharice that he needed to seek out the information the Feds were asking for. He nodded his head, even though he had no idea how he was going to pull it off.

"Fine. I'll get that murder, or some shit on the girl. Y'all some cold muthafuckas I swear," Money responded as Daniels backed down.

"Before we cut you loose, answer me this," Daniels responded. "What would Rico send money to Sharice for? According to our sources, he sent a large sum of cash to Texas. I thought John handles the money."

"If he sent her some shit, that came out his end," Money explained. "Any big shit goes through John, especially if it's money for a shipment. It could be some shit to pay folks off. We normally take care of that shit on our own."

Daniels and Davis looked at each other, wondering if Money was right.

"Sit tight, we'll be right back," Daniels responded as he and Davis walked out of the conference room.

"Payoff does sound plausible," Davis said as Daniels continued to think silently.

"Yeah, but to who? If money did exchange hands, then we have an even bigger grab than we thought," Daniels replied just before his cell phone rang.

He checked the caller Id and sighed.

"My wife," he said. "Get somebody to bring Mike back, and get on the phone with the Houston office. Find out what they know. Maybe they can tell us what the fuck is going on out there."

Davis nodded his head and made his way back into the conference room. Daniels answered his phone and starts conversing with his wife as he made his way back towards his desk, grabbing his head with frustration with each word.

Back in Houston, Rock was sitting on a stoop in one of his most secure and busiest dope corners overseeing things from his crew members. With the hit missed on Sharice, he was on high alert and took refuge in the safest neighborhood he could think of, one that he knew he couldn't be touched at. He was smoking a cigarette when out of nowhere, several cop cars pulled up in the area, disrupting business and sending Rock's crew scattering. Rock didn't budge as one of the police officers walked over to him, smirking.

"Jalen Johnson," the officer said, calling Rock by his real name. "We have a warrant for your arrest."

Rock chuckled as he stood up from the stoop and

walked over to a nearby wall. He placed his hands on the wall as another officer walked over and searched him.

"What? Did I forget to pay a parkin' ticket or some shit?" Rock nonchalantly asked. "Cause we can settle that right now, on the cool."

"Not this time, my friend," the officer responded as he walked up and personally cuffed Rock. "We found a brick in the raw in your ride over there. As well as a firearm."

The officer turned Rock around and pointed to an officer who held up the evidence for Rock to see with his own eyes.

"Getting a little sloppy, aren't we?" The officer mocked as Rock frowned.

"Bullshit," Rock responded. "You know good and damn well I ain't that stupid to be ridin' around with that shit in my car. Y'all niggas trippin' for real."

"Maybe we are, but as of now, Jalen Johnson, you have the right to remain silent." The officer replied, smirking once again.

He continued to read Rock his rights before leading the drug kingpin over to a nearby squad car. Police officers continued to check the area, making sure Rock's most profitable corner was shut down.

Back at the motel, Sharice was in a room by herself, eyes still red from all the tears she had shed. She found out a couple of days earlier what happened to Jerome and hasn't been herself since then. The way they left each other weighed heavily on her, realizing she would never be able to make right with him. She wanted this to end. She wanted everything to do with Houston to end. His death was on her in her mind, and through all the stress she's been through, nothing else mattered to her at that moment. She wiped her eyes once more when there was a knock at her door. She quickly made sure she's presentable before walking over to the door and looking in the peephole. She unlocked the door to let Bull in.

"Hey. How you doin'?" He asked as Sharice closed the door behind him.

"I'm... I'm doin' how anyone would be doin', I guess," Sharice uttered. "What's up?"

"The police have Rock in custody," Bull answered

much to Sharice's delight. "He's being booked as we speak."

"What about the other one? His homebody?" Sharice inquired.

"Nothin' on him yet. It's like he hit the mattresses. If he shows his face, we're on it," Bull responded, letting Sharice down.

"Can't believe this shit!" she exclaimed. "I want that nigga! He doesn't get to get off. And let me find out he had somethin' to do with Jerome! I'll kill that nigga myself!"

Bull walked over to comfort Sharice, but she rejected him as she backed away.

"I wanna be the first on that nigga's visiting log," Sharice responded. "Get me on that list as soon as you can. It's time me and ol' boy have one last talk."

"I'll handle it," Bull responded with concern in his eyes. "Look, Reese, I wouldn't be your friend if I didn't tell you that maybe you need to get some rest. With Rock locked up and his corners gettin' shut down one by one by the cops, we can clean this up for you. You don't need to really be involved in this."

"Fuck rest!" Sharice responded with anger in her eyes. "Until I find that other nigga, there won't be any rest! Get me on that visiting list! Now!"

Bull nodded his head as he saw the fire in Sharice's eyes. She's no longer herself as hurt and pain have taken over. He walked out of the room, allowing Sharice to mourn a little more. After he was gone, she started crying uncontrollably once more as she fell onto her bed, heartbroken and full of regret. She would give anything to have one last touch, to breathe in his essence, to run her fingers through his beard. She hasn't felt a pain this bad since losing Lavina months back. The usually strong-willed Sharice was at her weakest point. She may be winning the war on the streets, but she's lost the war in her heart.

Later that evening, Police Commissioner Rollins was looking over some paperwork on his desk when his assistant knocked on his door to announce Sharice's arrival. He nodded his head as Sharice made her way into the office.

"Sharice, nice to see you again," Rollins responded, offering her a seat. "Is there anything I can get you?"

"No, I'm good," Sharice replied, not looking her normal confident self. "You wanted to see me?"

"Yeah, I did. I got word that you were trying to get on Rock's visiting list. Are you sure that's wise?" Rollins asked. "Let us handle it from here on out. I don't want a simple visit to lead to something more violent."

"I promise you, it will be cordial," Sharice responded with a forced smile. "Is that why you called me here?"

Rollins leaned back in his chair, with a smile and his hands crossing his belly.

"Well, since Rock is almost out of commission, I was wondering what the plan was," he said. "Let's face it, any decent lawyer is going to beat these trumped-up charges. The last thing I need is a drug war going on in my streets."

"Relax. I got this," Sharice responded. "Part of the reason I want to see him is to settle things before his lawyer gets him out. This will all be over temporarily."

Rollins chuckled as he pondered for a moment.

"I'm not understanding why you wanted me to arrest

him if you're going to go and settle things with him," Rollins said. "I mean, couldn't you have done that on the streets?"

Sharice smiled as she went into her purse, pulled out an envelope full of cash, and handed it to Rollins.

"People seem to listen better when they're behind bars," she responded. "Just a little taste for takin' care of him for me."

Rollins counted the cash, impressed with the amount.

"Your outfit pays well," he said before placing the envelope in his desk drawer. "A little too well if you ask me."

"Are you complaining?" Sharice asked.

"No, but since you're the new power in town, I guess it's time to officially talk about what you're going to do for me," Rollins responded with a slick grin.

"Do for you?" A confused Sharice responded. "What? Is money not enough?"

"Oh, money is just the beginning," the commissioner replied. "It's hard to keep my seat without a major bust or two, especially during an election year. I have to remain in favor for whatever mayor that's in office. I have to keep the bosses happy, as I'm sure you may know."

Sharice nodded her head.

"I'll make sure something is worked out," she responded.

"Good. Also, I deal with you, and you alone," Rollins pointed out. "I don't need any of your lackeys in my office. You seem to carry yourself well, and to be honest, are appealing to the eyes. No need for anyone else to do business with me."

"Well, that's gonna be a problem," Sharice replied. "I'm just here for set up. After all that's done, I'm outta here. This isn't my city."

"Well, you're right, that is a problem," Rollins said with a smile. "A *you* problem. If you and your organization want to do business, I do it through you, or I don't do it at all."

Sharice was silent, considering her options. This was never part of the plan. Rico was supposed to take it off her hands and run things after she dealt with Rock and his crew. Knowing that Rollins wasn't going to change his mind, she gave in to his request.

"Fine," she said with a hint of attitude. "Well, that better be all, 'cause now you costin' me money and time."

"Just keep your outfit in line, and we won't have any problems," Rollins responded as Sharice got up.

He noticed Sharice wasn't looking her best.

"Hey, you okay?" He asked.

"Well, after the shakedown you just pulled, you'll excuse me if I don't meet you with a smile," Sharice responded. "That's not the sort of fucking I'm used to. If you'll excuse me."

Sharice made her way out of the office and eventually out of the building. She met Bull in the parking lot and got into their vehicle with a scowl on her face. Bull noticed she was in a mood as he started the car.

"I take it that went well," a sarcastic Bull said.

"Son of a bitch!" Sharice yelled. "This asshole wants me to be his connect out here! Now I gotta spend my time flyin' back and forth to this shithole! Can't believe this shit!"

"May not have to," Bull pointed out to a confused

Sharice. "You may become a native yourself."

"Huh? What are you talkin' about?" Sharice asked.

"You're about to become boss," Bull reminded her. "New Orleans already has a boss. Wouldn't make any sense to have two bosses in the same city. A boss needs an area to call their own. You can't really run shit with Money lookin' over your shoulder, can you?"

Sharice was speechless because she never thought about that. Becoming a boss would require her to work away from home. Since she's a known face in Houston at this point, it would only make sense for her to be the one running things. She was taken aback by Bull's words and didn't know what to say.

"I… I never thought of that," she quietly replied.

"I don't see how you didn't," Bull said. "I mean, it was obvious to me."

"Fuck! I don't wanna leave New Orleans," she spat out. "The fuck I know about Houston?"

"I don't know, but you should have considered that before becoming boss," Bull responded as he slowly pulled out of the parking lot.

"Just bring me to lock up," Sharice fired back with an attitude. "I'll figure that shit out later. First things first."

Back in New Orleans, at Michelle's apartment, James and Michelle were having an intense sex session in her bed as he grinded on her like a wild animal. Michelle tried to fight off the pleasure as best she could, but she was fighting a losing battle as his manhood had her moist and ready to explode. Realizing she was at her weakest point, James decided to take advantage of his dominance.

"Say it!" He commanded as he continued to grind on her. "Tell me what I wanna hear!"

Michelle shook her head no, but she couldn't help herself as each thrust drove her wilder than the last. After a few moments of holding out, Michelle finally gave in, giving James what he wanted the most.

"You're the man! You're the man! You're the man! Fuck!" Michelle screamed out in mid-orgasm.

James continued to grind on her well after her state of bliss while a helpless Michelle could do nothing but take what's being dealt to her. Her words were no longer making sense as she was hit with a quick second orgasm that caught her off guard, causing her to scream out James' name. After several more pumps, James himself moaned as he finally hit his peak. An exhausted James collapsed on top of his undercover lover as both of them laughed, trying to catch their breath.

"You're such an asshole," a giggling Michelle responded as James rolled over to the side of her.

He grabbed his cigarettes and lit one up. After a couple of puffs, he handed the cigarette to Michelle, who took a couple of puffs as well.

"You see, this that shit you be missin' with that square nigga," James said. "Where his ass at anyway?"

"Out of town on business," Michelle responded before passing the cigarette back to James. "You think I'd have your black ass at my spot if he was around?"

"Whatever. You can't tell me you wouldn't wanna do this with a real nigga every day," James boasts.

Michelle didn't respond, which surprised her lover.

"What? No comeback? No 'Fuck you, nigga' or shit like that for talkin' about your boo thang," James said with a chuckle.

Michelle took a deep breath. She had been thinking about her and Theo's relationship a lot herself.

"To be truthful, he's been actin' kinda funny lately," she responded.

"I'll ask you again, why don't you just leave that nigga? It's clear that this shit ain't for y'all," James pointed out.

Michelle was still conflicted with her feelings for Theo as she looked at James. Something doesn't feel right. Her bed was only shared between her and Theo, and it felt wrong to have sex with another man in it. She quickly jumped out of bed and began getting dressed, confusing James.

"Yo, what the fuck you doing'?" He asked.

"This was a mistake. I shouldn't have hooked up with you here," she said. "Come on, let's get outta here."

"You said the nigga was outta town, right?" James confirms. "Then why you trippin'?"

"Because some shit just ain't right, you dig?" Michelle responded as she put on one of her shoes. "Come on, nigga.

Get your ass up!"

Michelle looked around for her other shoe but was unable to locate it.

"Hey, you seen my other shoe?" She asked as she looked around.

"You mean this shoe?" A voice said as the bedroom door flew open.

Michelle and James were stunned when they saw Theo holding Michelle's shoe in one hand, and a gun pointed their way in his other hand. He tossed the shoe towards her as a panicked Michelle tried to explain what's going on.

"Theo, what the fuck are you doin' here?!" She said, trying to remain calm. "What are you doing? Lower that gun! Have you lost your mind?! We... we can discuss this."

"Discuss this? What in God's name could you say to explain all of this?!" Theo replied as he became aggressive, scaring both James and Michelle. "How the fuck could you do this to me?!"

"Theo, my god, I'm so sorry," Michelle responded as she backed away towards the bed. "I didn't want you to find out like this! I'm sorry!"

Theo chuckled as he took a seat at the computer chair right across from the bed, making sure he kept the gun pointing at the two.

"You know, I've been wondering how I was going to handle this when I finally confronted you and your side nigga there," Theo said, looking at James. "Turns out, you've been lying more than just about this, haven't you?"

"Theo, I don't know what you're talkin' about," Michelle responded. "Look, if you would just lower the gun, we could-"

"Don't treat me like I'm a fucking moron!" Theo yelled, making Michelle and James nervous. "Don't give me that you're innocent shit! I know all about your secret life! Running the streets being a gangster! I know all about it! The drugs! The murders! I'm sick of all your lying!"

Michelle was stunned that Theo knew the truth about her. She glanced over towards James, not knowing what to say next. Theo chuckled once more cause he could tell she was speechless.

"Yeah, I know everything!" He exclaimed. "All the

bullshit you were feeding me! Our entire relationship is built off a lie!"

"Okay, so what?" Michelle fired back. "You know everything about me! What does that have to do with this, huh? What do you want from me? I'm sorry, okay? It's not something you tell a nigga on the first date and shit."

Theo frowned as heartache started to take over.

"I... I loved you," Theo responded, weakening his stance for a moment. "Did you ever really care about me at all?"

"Of course I did," Michelle responded as tears started to flow down her face. "I've always loved you. I made a mistake, I'll admit that. I'm so fuckin' sorry! Please... just lower the gun. We can talk this out."

The gun started shaking in Theo's hand as his emotions started to catch up with him.

"I... I actually considered making you my wife, you know," Theo said, stunning Michelle.

"No, I... I didn't know you felt that way," she replied.

"I did. Until I heard about your secret life," Theo said, embracing his anger once again. "I maybe could have lived with it. Maybe. That was until I found out about you and this asshole! I'm looking like a fucking joke while you and him are out fucking around town!"

"Aye, look, this shit is gettin' a little wild. Maybe I should get dressed and leave y'all to talk this shit out," James said before reaching for his pants.

Theo stopped his advances, cocking the hammer back on his gun.

"Stay your fucking ass right where you are!" Theo exclaims, freezing James in place.

"Look, Theo, chill, okay?" Michelle said, trying to get the attention back on her. "Look, put that gun away. We can work this out. I promise you, no more lies."

Theo looked at Michelle and could see the genuine look of interest in her eyes. He thought back to when they first started dating and how he fell in love with her from the very beginning. He slowly started to lower his gun as Michelle breathed a sigh of relief. James was relieved as well as he reached for his pants once more, startling Theo.

"I told you not to fucking move," Theo yelled, pointing the gun towards James once again.

The gun accidentally went off with the bullet striking James, shocking Michelle and scaring Theo.

"Theo! What did you do?!" She exclaimed as she quickly jumped on the bed, checking out her friend. "My god! James! Talk to me, James!"

"I... I... I didn't mean to shoot him," a startled Theo responded before dropping the gun. "The gun... it... I didn't mean to shoot him."

Michelle checked James' pulse and was relieved that he's still alive.

"Shit, he's still breathing," she said before jumping out of her bed and quickly picking up the gun Theo had discarded seconds ago.

She handed the gun back to Theo, who was confused.

"What? What are you doing?" He asked.

"You need to get the fuck outta here now!" Michelle commanded.

"I don't understand. He needs help. We need to take him to a hospital now!" Theo responded.

"They have ambulances for that. If he dies, you could catch a manslaughter case if you're still here," Michelle responded before running over to the nightstand and locating her cell phone.

"Manslaughter?" A scared Theo replied. "But... but it was an accident!"

"That's why it's called manslaughter and not murder!" Michelle explained as she frantically looked around the room. "Hopefully, the ambulance can keep him breathin', but you gotta get out of here! Hurry the fuck up!"

Theo nervously nodded his head as Michelle began to dial on her phone.

"Wait! Theo!" she yelled, running out of the room to track him down before he left her apartment.

"Yes," he said, running back over to her.

"Kick open the door before you leave!" She said. "We need to make it look like forced entry. I'll wait for that before calling. Please hurry!"

Theo nodded as Michelle ran back into her bedroom and approached James. She waited until she heard the door kicked open before dialing nine-one-one on her phone.

"Stay with me, boo. Don't you die on me," she uttered to herself, watching James fade.

After several moments, the operator picked up as a panicked Michelle explained to them that James had been shot, and requested an ambulance to her location.

Rock was sitting at a visitor table curious to see who had the authority to visit him at such a late time frame. The once-powerful drug lord had been reduced to a common thug wearing state-issued prison wear. He looked up and chuckled as he noticed Sharice being led to him. He admired the business skirt outfit she's known for as she took a seat across from the gangster.

"Only you would have this type of power," Rock said. "I mean, no way you get in the door wearin' that skimpy shit unless you had some sort of pull."

"What can I tell you? Money makes the world go round," Sharice responded as she got comfortable.

While Sharice was carrying herself well, Rock immediately noticed she's not her normal confident self.

"Uh oh. I see red eyes," Rock pointed out, smirking. "Tell me you're not takin' business personal. I had a lot of respect for you throughout this whole thing. You were cool and calculating sorta like me. I missed my mark, sure, but I never took anything personal. Even though y'all got me locked up in this joint."

"I'm not here for conversation," Sharice responded. "I'm here to bail you out."

"Bail me out? The fuck you talkin' 'bout?" Rock asked. "I don't need you to bail shit. I got my people on that, even though y'all makin' it hard out there."

"I'm not talkin' about bailing you out of lock-up. I'm talkin' about bailing you out of this situation," Sharice clarified. "You see, no matter how you try and slice it, it's over for you. You've lost. All you can hope to do is to survive now. I'm here to renegotiate the terms of the settlement."

Rock laughed as Sharice remained unfazed with his reaction.

"I swear, y'all Faction niggas are some bold muthafuckas," Rock responded. "This is my city. Y'all niggas can't touch me. In here, out there, it doesn't matter. I run shit. I took care of Houston, so I'll always be the man out here. So you may wanna rethink these threats you tryin' to spit my way."

"Your city? You really are delusional, aren't you?" Sharice responded, managing a smile for the first time. "While you've been in here tryin' to stay relevant, my people have been out there working. The police have cleaned all your corners. The niggas who was runnin' those spots made a deal to work with us now. The Fifth Ward is mine. All of it."

The smile on Rock's face slowly faded, hearing that all he had worked for had been torn away from him in less than a day.

"The Third Ward is mine too," Sharice pointed out. "The nigga Paul who runs shit out there, was a little easier to convince than you were. He's gonna make more money than he ever did because he didn't act like a God and shit when we approached him."

Rock sighed as he shook his head.

"Fuckin' pussy ass nigga," he uttered, referring to his old Third Ward rival.

"Whatever he is, he's a part of the crew now," Sharice said as she crossed her legs and leaned back in her chair.

"So you see, Rock, you're no more than just another nigga in jail right now. The price I can put on your head will make sure you never see the daylight again. That is unless we can come to terms."

"Terms? What the fuck else could you possibly want?" Rock responded before realizing what Sharice was looking for. "Oh, I see. You lookin' to settle with Troy. Can't let that shit go, can you?"

"Like you said, it's only business," Sharice responded, smirking. "Here's the deal, give up your boy, and you can fight the charges without any interference from us. I'm sure your lawyer could beat this weak ass shit regardless. As long as you stay outta the game, as far as I'm concerned, you're allowed to live your life however you want."

Rock was silent as Sharice leaned forward to give him his second option.

"Now, you could tell me to go fuck myself, and it's well within your rights to do so," Sharice continued, smiling. "But, if you choose that route, I promise you that you won't make it to your bail hearing. We will eventually find this nigga anyway, so why die for some shit that's gonna happen regardless?"

"So I give up my nigga, and you'll just let me roam free, is that it?" Rock responded with a smile. "After what I heard you did to Double R, I'm supposed to be let go? Somehow I don't believe that shit."

"I guess you've made your choice then," Sharice responded, getting up from her chair. "Well, can't say I didn't give you a chance. And for the record, your boy Double R got exactly what he deserved. That sick son of a bitch came there with thoughts on his mind other than killin' me. In the end, I made sure he blew his load one last time. Maybe you don't get that final courtesy."

Sharice was about to walk off as a conflicted Rock quickly considered his options.

"Dallas," he said before she had a chance to alert the guards. "The nigga is out there in Dallas."

Sharice smiled as she made her way back over towards her rival.

"Dallas, you say?" She said to confirm. "Where in Dallas?"

"He got some people that stay out in Oak Cliff. He was layin' low until the heat dies down," Rock explained. "I'm sure you well-connected niggas can figure it out from there."

Sharice nodded her head, pleased that Rock finally came to terms with her.

"See, that's the thing about you niggas I'll never understand," Sharice said. "Loyalty only goes so far. That whole ride or die shit was just for the rappers and movies. Y'all will sell each other out at the drop of a hat."

"Like you wouldn't do it if you were in my position," Rock fired back. "Like you said, y'all gonna catch up to him with or without my help. Either way, he's dead."

Sharice chuckled to herself before responding.

"True. Either way, that nigga's gone," she said. "But it didn't have to be you to do it. And for the record, I have been in your position behind mine a few times. Each time, I never gave her up. That's a real ride or die right there. Not a fuckin' rap song."

Sharice looked over Rock one last time before alerting the guard that she's ready to leave. The guard walked over and escorted her out, leaving Rock with mixed feelings about what he just did to one of his oldest friends.

Sharice made it back to the parking lot where Bull was waiting in the car. He had a look of concern on his face as a satisfied Sharice hopped into the passenger side.

"Fuckin' Dallas," she said. "Get some people on it. Apparently, he's hidin' out in some hood known as Oak Cliff."

"Sure, I'll take care of it, but we have a problem," Bull said as he started the car. "Your phone was ringin', and normally I don't answer, but Michelle kept callin'. It's James. He's been shot."

"Shot?! Shot by who?!" A concerned Sharice asked.

Bull hesitated for a moment before explaining the situation of the love triangle. She grabbed her head, frustrated before ordering Bull to pull off.

About a half-hour later, Sharice was at a payphone on the line with Michelle, who was pleading with Sharice.

"Reese, please. I love him," she said. "I know he fucked up. It was an accident. James is gonna make it, according to doctors. There's no need to go this route. Please don't make me do this."

"You know the rules. He hit one of ours, he has to go," Sharice responded. "Besides, if the police find out it's him, how long do you think it'll take before he rats you out?"

"I'll make sure he keeps his mouth shut, I promise," Michelle pleaded.

Sharice thought for a moment when she glanced over and noticed Bull in the car waiting for her.

"Michelle, it's either him or you. I don't care which one, but you need to make up your mind," a ruthless Sharice responded. "I'm gonna send Bull back home to handle it. I don't want you to be involved. I'm not goin' that route again. He'll be in touch."

Sharice hung up the line and walked over to the driver's side of the car, causing Bull to lower the window.

"I'm sending you back home," she said. "I need you to take care of Michelle's problem. I don't want her to have to go through what you did."

Bull slowly nodded his head, remembering how it felt when Sharice gave the order to him to take out Ritchie. He knew all too well how that can hurt someone emotionally.

"I'll get it done," Bull responded. "I just got off the line with some connections in Dallas. It shouldn't be too long."

Sharice nodded her head and sighed because it had been a long day for her. She was still emotionally drained with everything that's happened, but she wouldn't allow herself rest until she gets her revenge on Troy.

The next day, Michelle quickly pulled up to Theo's apartment complex and looked around the area before hopping out of the car, hurrying to his apartment. She used her key to get in his front door and was stunned to see Theo still packing his things in his bedroom.

"What the fuck, Theo?" She asked. "I told you to be ready! Why are you still packing?"

"It's not like I've done this before," he fired back. "I've never received a call in the middle of the morning telling me to pack my life away in like a half-hour!"

"Don't you understand?! They are coming for us!" Michelle exclaimed. "They could be here in any minute. Just take what you can, so we can get the fuck outta here!"

"I can't believe you got involved with these people," Theo responded as he quickly zipped up his bag and looked around. "Okay, what am I missing?"

"It doesn't matter! We'll buy new shit!" Michelle exclaimed. "Come on, let's go, let's go!"

Theo nodded his head as he and Michelle quickly made it out of his apartment and down to the first level. He was heading to his car when Michelle stopped him.

"No! We're not taking your car," she said. "They probably already got that one marked. That black car over there! I got it clean, so they can't track us!"

Theo nodded and was about to run over when he noticed how distraught Michelle was. He slowly walked over to her and kissed her, catching her off guard.

"What… what was that for?" Michelle asked.

"You're risking your neck for me. I know this is hard for you, and I wanted to show you I appreciate everything you're doing," he said, leaving Michelle speechless. "I know we have a lot to talk about wherever we end up, but I'm willing to listen if you're willing to open up."

His act of genuine love touched Michelle. She was

about to say something to confirm her feelings for him but remembered that they are on borrowed time.

"Look, we'll do what we need once we get where we're goin'," she said before checking her pockets. "Fuck me! I left the keys upstairs. Go pop the trunk and put your shit in there, I'll be back."

Theo nodded his head before he quickly ran over to the car and got in the driver's side, looking to pop the trunk. Before he was able to locate the button, Bull surprised him from the back seat and wrapped a wire around his neck, strangling him. Michelle glanced back at the car, noticed what's going on, and ran back over. She ran over to the driver's side and watched as Theo gasped, calling out to her as best he could. Michelle was crying as Theo reached out to her before his body went completely limp. After several moments of making sure Theo was dead, Bull finally released his hold on the wire and exited the vehicle. He walked over to a tear-filled Michelle, who looked on in grief at her old lover.

"It's over," Bull said to her, not getting a response. "The car's clean, right?"

Michelle didn't hear Bull as she continued to focus on her fallen boyfriend.

"Michelle. Michelle!" Bull said once again, trying to get her attention. "The car is clean, right?!"

"The fuckin' car is clean!" She snapped back. "I know what the fuck I'm doin'! Now get the fuck outta my face!"

Bull backed away, knowing that she was hurting right now. He headed back to the car and moved Theo's body to the passenger's side before hopping into the driver's seat, pulling off. A distraught Michelle watched as Bull pulled out of the complex, heartbroken to have lost the man she loved.

Later that night, in Club Exotica, Connie was in Sharice's office with her feet on her friend's desk living the life like a boss once again, as she smoked a cigar feeling herself. She was caught off guard as Money Mike entered the office. She quickly straightened herself out as he approached her with a big smile on his face.

"Ms. Constance. It's been a minute, for real," he said before taking a seat across from her. "How's life been treating you?"

"I'm… I'm cool," Connie responded with curiosity. "So, what's up? What did I do this time?"

"Girl, don't trip. I'm not here for you," Money responded with a chuckle. "I'm here for your boss. Where she at?"

"She still in Houston," Connie answered, confusing the Faction boss.

"In Houston? Thought I heard her and Bull were back already," Money replied. "In fact, somebody saw that nigga earlier today."

"Oh, yeah, Bull is back. He had to do some shit earlier today," Connie explained. "I think he's gonna head back to Houston tomorrow morning or somethin'. Why? You need somethin'? I can take care of anythin' you want, for real."

Money was disappointed as he stood up from his chair.

"Nah, baby. I need the brainchild, not just the muscle," he responded, offending Connie.

"Whoa, hold up a minute," Connie said as she stood up from behind her chair. "I got skills too. Sharice ain't the only bitch up in here that can get shit done. Tell me what you need, and I got you."

Connie was tired of being known only as a muscle. She was ready to show the bosses that she was just as capable as Sharice was with strategy. Money smiled as he approached Sharice's number one soldier.

"Really?" Money said with a slick grin. "Look, I know you have skills with the way you took out that witness for John. I already know that shit, but we all know Sharice was the mastermind behind that. That's the shit I need right now."

Connie frowned. She was finished taking a back seat to her friend.

"Look, y'all niggas got it twisted," Connie replied. "Sharice ain't have nothin' to do with that shit. It was all me. I planned it out and took him out. Sharice took the credit 'cause she knew y'all never liked me. Said we would move up together and shit. So everything you thought you knew about that was bullshit. I love my girl, don't get me wrong, but it's time you trust me with some shit. If I can pull that off, just imagine what I can do for you, ya heard me."

Money chuckled as he thought for a moment. He didn't come to the club to get Connie on tape, but this worked out better than he had hoped. After a few moments, he nodded his head with approval.

"Alright, baby girl. I see you," he responded. "Let me think on it, and I'll holla back at you."

"For sure," Connie responded as the two dapped each other.

Money made his way out of the office as a satisfied Connie took her seat back behind the desk once more, kicking her feet up. After several moments, her cell phone rang, which she quickly answered.

"Yeah, what's up?" She asked as she received word from Sharice to catch a plane out to Dallas. "Dallas? What the fuck is out in Dallas?"

She continued her conversation as Sharice filled her in on the day's events.

A day later, Connie was in Dallas riding passenger in a car heading down the freeway. She looked a little anxious, not knowing where she was being taken, and not knowing what waited for her. The car pulled up to an abandoned gas station where Sharice and a few other crew members were waiting for her arrival. Connie hopped out of the vehicle and walked up to Sharice, who greeted her with a quick hug.

"Hey, girl. Is it really him?" Connie asked, looking around excited.

"Yeah, it's him," Sharice confirmed as they headed towards the store entry of the gas station. "I had to rough him up a bit for some shit I needed, but he's all yours. Sorry about the other one too, but I made sure he went out very painful. I'm sure the Feds are gonna try to pull me for it, but they don't have shit on me."

Connie looked at her friend and could tell she's stressed.

"You alright?" She asked Sharice.

"Yeah, I'm good. Just ready to get back to my own house," Sharice admitted. "I have one more thing I need to take care of, then I'm back home."

Before they entered the shop, Sharice stopped Connie

before she walked in.

"Hey, before you go, I'm gonna let you know that what you're about to do, you're gonna have to live with," Sharice warned her friend. "I haven't been able to sleep since I did what I did to the other nigga. Looking in the mirror, it… it hurts."

Connie nodded her head. She could tell the emotional toll this whole Houston trip had taken.

"I've done a lot of shit, Reese," she replied. "What's one more thing, you know."

Sharice sighed but realized that if anyone was built to handle it, it was Connie.

"How's James?" She asked, trying to change the subject. "Any news?"

"Yeah, I saw him before I left," Connie responded somberly. "He gonna live and shit, but they don't know if he's gonna walk again. Might as well have killed him if you ask me. I wouldn't wanna live like that."

Sharice was stunned hearing the news about her crew member.

"Fuck me," she responded. "What about Chelle?

How's she doing?"

"You know me and her ain't never got along, but I'm gonna be real, she's takin' this shit hard too," Connie answered. "She's feelin' that shit losin' her boo, but she's also hurt over James too. She's probably gonna need a couple of days."

Sharice nodded her head, knowing that she might be without Michelle just as she was without Bull after the Ritchie hit. Connie walked into the shop and was excited to see Troy butt naked and tied up on a chair surrounded by a few crew members. He had been beaten, but he was still breathing, which was all that concerned Connie. He looked up and noticed her walking in.

"My nigga," a cryptic Connie said as she approached him. "Hope my folks been treatin' you right cause we got a long night ahead of us tonight."

Sharice looked on with concern and watched until the door closed completely. She lowered her head before walking to the car Connie arrived in. She looked at the driver and motioned him to pull off, leaving Connie alone to take her revenge.

In a local New Orleans hospital the next morning, Michelle walked into James' room and gently knocked on the door. James looked at her but didn't respond. He was struggling to accept his new life. He had been told that he'll never walk again and had been contemplating suicide. She slowly made her way in, scared to make eye contact.

"Hey," she said before taking a seat next to him. "How are you?"

"How am I? How the fuck do you think I am?" James responded. "I'm in this bitch and not gonna be able to walk again! How would you feel in this position?"

Michelle teared up as her guilt overwhelmed her. She tried to comfort James by grasping his hand but was rejected by her former lover.

"Whatever you need, James. Whatever I can do, please, just let me know," Michelle said. "This is fucked up, and I know you're pissed. I'm sorry, James. I'm so so sorry."

Michelle's words didn't bring James any comfort as he looked away from her.

"I was a professional thief, and I was fuckin' good at it," James said. "Remember the Hibernia job back in '07?

Niggas said nobody can rob them niggas and live to talk about it. I did though. Took them for more money than they ever lost before. It was how I made a name for myself. Fuckin' Feds still lookin' for who robbed that bitch to this day. Now, look at me. Can't rob a five-year-old in a wheelchair. I'm fuckin' done, Chelle. I'm done."

Michelle wiped her face, trying to control her emotions as best she could as James looked back towards her with several tears in his eyes as well.

"That nigga should have just killed me," he said, struggling to hold it together. "He should have just fuckin' killed me."

Michelle leaned over and hugged James, who was reluctant to embrace her at first, but as his emotions hit him, he hugged her back and began sobbing. The two held on to each other tightly, letting everything out with an uncertain future facing them.

Back in lock up in Houston, it was lights out as everyone was in their bunks asleep. Rock was in his bunk, trying to get comfortable when he was suddenly gagged, taken from his bed, and brought over to the corner of the holding area. Seven inmates all surrounded Rock, who was finally able to remove the gag from his mouth. He looked around at his attackers and noticed that they all have shivs in their hands. He chuckled as he slowly stood up and faced his attackers.

"Tell shorty it was never personal. I always had love for her," Rock said, realizing the end was coming.

"Actually, she told me to give you a message," one of the inmates responded. "She said this ain't business. It's fuckin' personal."

Rock nodded his head as he put his hands up, prepping to defend himself from his attackers. He was attacked from all sides, with each inmate getting a piece of the former drug lord. The attack didn't last long. He was cut up pretty badly. The final cut came from an inmate to Rock's neck who fell to the ground and bled out. The inmates all scattered back to their bunks to avoid discovery while Rock spent his final moments in life choking on his own blood.

Aisha walked into her apartment back in Houston, talking on the phone about Rock being locked up to one of her friends upset about how everything that had gone down the last few days. After a few more moments of conversation, she hung up the line and walked into her kitchen, looking for something to eat. Much to her displeasure, she closed the fridge and was about to head over to a cabinet when she was startled by a figure standing just outside of her kitchen, pointing a gun at her. The figure was Sharice, who was full of rage looking at a terrified Aisha.

"You know who I am?" Sharice asked as she slowly approached her soon to be victim.

Aisha nodded her head, putting her hands up, backing away from Sharice.

"Good, that saves us a lot of time," Sharice responded. "So, check it out, I spoke to your boy Troy, and he had a lot to say about how a friend of mine went down. He said you were there, and that it was you that pulled the trigger."

"That nigga lyin', for real," a nervous Aisha replied. "He's the one that did it! You gotta believe me!"

369

"You know, I might have believed you at first. It wasn't until I heard the police found the broken heel of a shoe in the area, one which Troy said you broke when firing the gun," Sharice pointed out. "When I heard about that, the story seemed to add up then. You killed Jerome. You took him away from me. I'll never be able to make up with him. We left on bad terms, and because of you, I don't have the option of making things right. Did you talk to your boo today? Did you tell Rock you loved him?"

Sharice was getting emotional as Aisha nervously nodded her head.

"It must be nice," she continued. "It must be nice to tell the man you love that you love him one last time."

"Please, I was only doin' what they told me to do," Aisha pleaded. "Please don't shoot me."

Sharice chuckled as she wiped the tears from her face.

"Shoot you? I'm not gonna shoot you," she said as she unloaded the clip and popped the one from the chamber. "What I am gonna do is beat your muthafuckin' ass!"

She tossed the gun on a nearby dining room table and kicked off her heels before rushing Aisha slamming her into the refrigerator. Aisha was overmatched as she tried her best to fight off Sharice, but she was eating every punch thrown her way. One blow sent Aisha to her knees as she struggled to breathe. Sharice grabbed her by her hair, dragged her from the kitchen, and tossed her into the dining room table, ripping out her hair extensions in the process. A bloodied Aisha tried to crawl away from her attacker, but Sharice stomped her on her back and repeatedly kicked her. The rage in Sharice's eyes drove her hatred as she kicked Aisha until her foot was sore. She was almost out of breath as she looked down at her fallen foe. She flipped Aisha on her back, mounted her, and started to choke her. Aisha tried to kick herself free, but Sharice was in total control as tears began to stream down her face. Aisha was gasping for air, trying to break the hold, but eventually, she lost the battle as well as her life. Sharice gritted her teeth as all her hate and anger was taken out on Aisha well after she was dead. Sharice snapped back once she noticed Aisha was no longer breathing and slowly stood from her fallen victim. She looked down at the damage she had done, but unlike with Double R, she relished in it. She had taken Jerome's life, and deserved to die in Sharice's eyes. After she calmed down, she pulled out her cell phone and made a call.

"Yeah, it's me," she said. "You can come up. Gonna need this place cleaned, and the body removed."

Sharice hung up the phone as she slipped back on her heels. She looked for her gun, clip, and bullet that had fallen to the floor during the tussle. After she's collected her things, there was a knock on the door. Sharice took a peek and opened the door for a crew member, who assessed the damage before beginning the cleanup process.

The next morning, Sharice made her way back into her office that she had missed so much. She breathed a sigh of relief as she dropped her bags on the floor and headed towards her desk. She took her familiar seat and sighed, trying her best to forget her trip. Before she could get comfortable, there was a knock on the door. Tracy, noticing her friend was home, was ecstatic until she noticed the condition she was in.

"Jesus, Sharice," she said as she approached her. "Are

you okay? You look like you haven't slept in days."

"Hard to sleep when shit weighs heavy on you," Sharice responded. "What are you doing here anyway?"

"Checking the bar so I can head to the store and do a liquor pick up," Tracy answered.

"Why are you doing it? Isn't the shit delivered?" Sharice asked, getting comfortable in her chair.

"Yeah, but the truck got in an accident, and they said they may not make it today. I figured I'd better not chance it," Tracy answered as she took a seat across from her longtime friend. "I heard some of what's been going on. Is it true that Jerome was shot?"

Sharice sighed, somberly nodding her head.

"Oh my god. Sharice, I'm so sorry," Tracy covering her mouth with sadness. "Are you okay?"

Although Sharice nodded her head, signifying that she's fine, Tracy could tell she was still struggling emotionally with the loss.

"You wanna talk about it?" Tracy asked.

"Not particularly," Sharice replied. "It's just... I don't know, I guess I never saw it ending up like this, you know."

"Like what?"

Sharice was quiet for a few moments. She didn't want to get into too many details about what happened. She took a deep breath, still fighting back her emotions.

"All my time in this thing, I've been fighting to achieve one goal," she started. "It was the only thing motivating me in life. I did what I needed to do to get where I wanted to be, but the cost... lookin' back at it now, the cost was too high. It's not worth it. Not at all."

Tracy nodded her head, understanding what Sharice was hinting at. Sharice wiped the few tears that trickle down her face just as Connie walked into the room. She had a smile on her face until she noticed her friend's mood.

"Hey, my bad. I didn't mean to interrupt anything," Connie said.

"No, you're good. Come on in," Sharice responded as she waved her in.

Tracy walked over and hugged Sharice hoping to comfort her slightly before making her way out of the office, closing the door behind her. Connie took a seat across from Sharice, realizing her friend was still in mourning.

"Hey, Reese. I see you're still heavy with it," Connie said, referring to Jerome's loss. "I know you're gonna carry it for a while, and whatever you need me to do, I got you."

Sharice forced a smile on her face as she nodded her head.

"So, how was Dallas?" She asked, changing the subject. "Did you get what you needed?"

Connie sighed before responding.

"Truth be told, you were right," Connie answered. "I mean, while I was fuckin' this nigga up, all the fuckin' anger I had was right there. I wanted that nigga to feel everything I felt. When I was done though, I thought I'd feel satisfied, but I didn't. Killin' this nigga didn't do shit for me. I don't think I felt like a monster like you was sayin', but it left me feelin', I don't know, all empty and shit."

Sharice nodded her head, knowing all too well how emotionally unfulfilling she felt after she tormented Double R.

"What about you?" Connie responded, smirking. "I heard you beat a bitch's ass up in Houston. Fucked her up real nice."

Sharice chuckled to herself, reminiscing about the beat down she put on Aisha.

"That shit… that was personal," Sharice admitted. "It was sloppy though. Between that shit, and the hotel, Feds might have my DNA on all kinds of shit. It's what happens when you let emotions get in the way of things. I be fussin' at your ass about it all the time, and here I am doing the same thing."

"You'll be alright," Connie responded as she relaxed. "From what I hear, that hotel room was burned the fuck up. Seriously doubt any evidence is up in that bitch. As for the other thing, I heard you used a cleanin' crew, and they are very skilled when it comes to cleanin' shit up. Don't stress."

Sharice nodded her head but still was concerned about what she may have left behind in her anger.

"Anyway, did they officially baptize you as boss yet?" Connie asked with a smile. "You movin' on up like The

Jefferson's and shit. Now that you're movin' on to bigger and better things, who's gonna be runnin' this here?"

Sharice shrugged before breaking news to her friend.

"On the real, Connie, I don't know," she answered. "If they keep their word and make me the boss, I'm probably not gonna be in N.O. anymore. There's already a boss here. More than likely, I'm headin' to Houston."

Connie was stunned as she tried to gather her thoughts.

"Wow... I... I didn't think of that shit at all," Connie responded. "Is that what they said?"

"Nah. I'm just speculating at this point," Sharice responded before sighing. "Either way, if you stay here, you know Mike gonna be on your ass. So you gonna have to figure out what you're gonna do."

Connie hesitated for a moment, not wanting to break the bad news to her friend about not coming with her. They've have been together since high school, and while Sharice did help her move up in the ranks, she felt it was her time to finally make a name for herself without being in her friend's shadow.

"I'm not goin' to Houston," Connie responded,

shocking her friend.

"Are you serious?" Sharice asked. "You do know Mike wanted you dead like five times, right?"

"I had a conversation with him the other day," Connie pointed out. "Before I left out to Dallas, we sat down, had a few words, and worked out a few things. He was thinkin' on giving me a few extra responsibilities and shit."

"Oh," Sharice responded, feeling a little disappointed. "Well, that's good, I guess."

Connie could tell her news didn't excite her friend as it did her.

"Look, Reese, we've been through a lot together. I know we've had our issues, but in the end, you handled your business like a boss. I appreciate everything you've done for me, for real. I just… I can't be the bitch I wanna be if I'm always in your shadow, ya dig? You did what you set out to do. You became boss. Now it's my time to do what I need to do."

Sharice sighed and nodded her head with understanding. Leaving Connie behind would be a lot less stress on her, but whatever Connie was, she still was a friend, even after the Lavina murder. Taking on Houston alone was a little daunting, but Sharice knew that she had been ready for this for quite some time. Sharice was about to respond to her friend when a buzzer sound in the office caught their attention. Sharice quickly pulled out her phone and checked her security app, which showed law enforcement entering into the building. Connie walked around the desk and looked over her friend's shoulder, surprised to see agents making their way into club.

"The fuck?! What are the cops doin' here?" Connie asked.

Sharice recognized Agent Daniels and chuckled before tossing her phone on her desk.

"Not cops. Feds," she corrects as she prepared herself mentally to be arrested. "Look, get the lawyer on the phone as soon as they take me. These Feds like to make you wait and shit hopin' you'll break. Reach out to Mike and let him know what's goin' on too. I want you and Chelle to work together while I'm down. You may not know it, but y'all two bitches need each other, for real."

Connie nodded her head as Sharice rose from her chair.

"I got you, Reese, for real," Connie said with reassurance.

Sharice sighed before sharing a hug with her longtime friend, knowing this could be the last time they see each other. After embracing for several moments, Sharice let go of her friend, ready to accept her fate.

Daniels and Davis walked into the office and approached both women. Daniels and Sharice shared a look with each other as Sharice waited their orders.

"Constance Shaw, you are under arrest," he said, turning his attention towards Connie, stunning her. "You're being charged for the murder of a federal witness."

"Say what?" A confused Connie responded as Davis turned her around, cuffing her before searching her.

Davis read Connie her Miranda Rights as he led her towards the exit. Connie took one last glimpse at Sharice, who was just as confused as she was. After they've gone, Daniels turned his attention back towards Sharice and could see the uncertainty in her eyes. He reveled in it for a moment before backing down.

"Seems like you made it out unscathed once again," Daniels said, which relieved Sharice. "But don't get too comfortable. I know about your Houston visit. I'm sure after I work back a few things that I'll be leading you out in cuffs as well."

Sharice put on a confident face with a sly smirk before nodding her head. After a brief stare down, Daniels made his way out of the office as well. Sharice breathed a sigh of relief as she was taken aback about what she just witnessed. Several moments had gone by when Tracy rushed back into the office, looking for answers.

"What the fuck just happened?" She asked.

Sharice was speechless as she took a seat back behind her desk. While she was concerned about Connie being taken into custody, a great weight was lifted, knowing she wasn't the one they were looking for. After gathering her thoughts, she went into her phone and looked up her lawyer's number, and called hoping to help her friend out of her situation.

A couple of nights later, at the Ritz-Carlton hotel in the

uptown area of New Orleans, a lavish suite had been rented out by John to celebrate Sharice's ascension to boss in the organization. John and Rico were there along with several associates conversing with each other, waiting for the guest of honor to arrive. All the men in attendance were dressed to impress in their thousand-dollar suits, as was expected to with an event like this. The room door opened, and Sharice caught everybody's eyes as soon as she stepped in. She was wearing a split leg gown with her hair pinned up and her back out as if she was royalty. She was trailed by both Bull and Michelle, who were equally dressed to impress. She smiled and greeted several associates. Her face was made up to perfection that lit up whenever she addressed someone. She made it over to John and Rico and kissed both of them on the cheek as they checked her out.

"All you're missin' is the crown, hun," John joked. "My goodness, you are a sight to see."

"She sure is," Rico chimed in. "I can't thank you enough for what you did for me. I can't tell you how much this is gonna help in my absence."

"In your absence?" A curious Sharice asked. "Where are you goin'?"

"We'll talk about it after. Right now, let's get things started," John responded as he led Sharice to her seat.

The main table, consisting of John, Rico, and Sharice was front and center facing the other two tables, which the other associates all occupied. Sharice was in the middle as John tapped his glass to get everyone's attention. A smile grew on his face as the chatter simmered down. Sharice looked around and noticed that Money Mike was not only missing, but there was no place set for him at the main table.

"Today, we're here to celebrate somethin' that is unheard of in this thing of ours," John said, smirking. "In all my years of doin' this thing, I never thought I'd see the day that a woman would hold the title of boss. As shocked as some of you are, are we that surprised? Most of you have been following a woman boss for years. You call her wife."

Laughter erupted over the lame joke as Sharice snickered herself before John continued.

"In all seriousness, I can't think of a better person, man

383

or woman, who deserved this honor," John continued. "She has done more for this Faction than anyone else I can think of, and it's my pleasure to introduce the newest Faction boss. Please raise your glass, and join me in toasting Sharice! Salute!"

The group all raised their glasses and chant 'salute' before sipping their wine in celebration. Sharice raised her glass as well smirking, looking towards Bull and Michelle. She nodded her head with appreciation towards them before taking a sip of her drink.

"Now, I know why most of you are really here. The food," John joked as several waiters entered into the room with trays of food. "Enjoy."

He took a seat next to Sharice, who was impressed with the meal selection offered. Before she can say anything, Rico rose from his chair and bid her farewell.

"Sharice, thank you once again. I may have had my doubts on you, but John was right, as he normally is," Rico said before kissing her hand. "I'm sorry I'm unable to stay. John will fill you in on the details."

A confused Sharice watched as Rico, and several of his

men quickly exited the suite. She looked towards John, who waved her off.

"Don't worry about it. We'll talk," he said, trying to calm her.

"What's he talkin' about? What's goin' on?" Sharice asked.

John could tell that Sharice wasn't going to let this go. He sighed and motioned for her to meet him out on the balcony. Both he and Sharice made their way outside and looked down towards the city street. John took out a cigar and lit it up as an impatient Sharice waited for an explanation.

"Well?" She said, waiting for John to talk.

"Rico's goin' away for a while," John answered, stunning Sharice. "The Feds are looking to indict him. One thing about the Feds is they have a ninety-five percent prosecution rate. If they come for you, it's almost certain they're gonna win."

Sharice was blown away with the revelation as she looked at John, waiting for more information.

"Look, I didn't want this to ruin your night. I was

gonna let you know once we were done here," John continued. "Mike is a rat. He's been spillin' his guts to the Feds for a while now. It's the reason that Rico has to go into hidin'. I told him he shouldn't risk comin' here, but he said he owed you that much. That new Houston money is gonna tide him over since the Feds don't know the inner workings of that operation yet."

Sharice was still speechless as she tried to process what she's just heard. Money being a rat was problematic, to say the least, for her and her crew. She kept him out of the scene as much as she could, but he still was the boss. There were a lot of things he could have manufactured on her.

"Rico's nephew, Pele, will be running things in his absence. He's a young up and comer, but I think he'll fit in well," John said. "Also, that thing you have with your girl, Connie. You can thank Mike for that too. You're the boss now. It's your shop to run. If the Feds haven't picked you up yet, it's because they don't have anything on you. Still, just to be safe, I'd start cleaning up soon as we're done here."

"How... how do you know all this?" Sharice asked,

still trying to put everything together. "I mean, about Mike being a snitch."

John took a few puffs of his cigar before responding.

"We have a guy on the inside," he revealed. "Any time indictments are coming, they give us a heads up. Normally, they are pretty good at givin' us rats in advance, but the Feds kept a tight lid on this one. This guy on the inside, it's for your ears only. You're a boss now, so intel like this is gonna come your way."

"But does Mike know about the inside guy?" Sharice asked. "I mean, I'd think that would be the first thing he'd snitch on."

John chuckled as he took another puff of his cigar.

"Only I know about it," John admitted. "Well, Rico knows now. Had to tell him. And now you know. I always kept this one in my pocket just in case, but Rico is a dear friend. I couldn't let him go down like that. Not now."

John looked over and could tell Sharice was in a state of disbelief.

"Connie," she uttered, realizing how Money screwed her friend. "She told me she sat down with Mike not too long ago and had a chat with that asshole. Christ, the rat bastard was probably wired then! I can't believe this fuckin' shit!"

"Calm down," John warned. "You think this is the first time we've had to deal with shit like this? It's part of the game, Sharice. There's always gonna be rats in this thing. Separate yourself from everyone, no matter how connected you are with them. It'll be the only thing that saves you from being a guest of the government. There's no room for friends at the top level. Learn that, and you'll last."

Hearing John's words had Sharice second-guessing herself once more, wondering if this is what she wanted. It seems things were falling apart all around her. John patted her on the shoulder to comfort her as best he could.

"Welcome to the top level," he said before putting out his cigar and heading back into the party.

Sharice turned around and peeked into the suite through the glass. She watched as everyone was laughing and filling their faces, not knowing half of what's going on right now. She looked over to Michelle and Bull, who were also taking in the atmosphere. Michelle was giggling until she and Sharice made eye contact. Sensing something was going on, Michelle excused herself from the table and made her way out onto the balcony with Sharice.

"Hey, boss. You alright?" She asked.

"I... I don't know," Sharice responded, trying to put things together. "I... well, I don't know. You seem to be enjoyin' yourself. Don't mind me."

"Is that what you see?" Michelle asked as she walked over to the edge of the balcony. "It's all a defense mechanism. Honestly, I could take a header off this fuckin' balcony the way I feel. All the laughing and joking is making sure they don't see the tears in my eyes."

Sharice nodded as she joined Michelle over by the edge of the balcony. She looked down towards the street and the ongoing traffic below.

"I told you that you didn't need to come here," Sharice said. "I know it's difficult what you been through, and I didn't wanna force you to this."

"Boss, I look at it this way. What else am I gonna do right now?" Michelle responded. "Sit at home and cry about it? I've done all the crying I need to. Only way to get over this shit is to jump on the saddle and move forward. I'll be there for James when he gets out. If he wants me, that is. It's the least I can do. Other than that, what else is there for me? What else can I do? I'm here with you 'til the end. With Connie locked up, you're gonna need someone who has your back. I'm here for whatever."

Sharice smiled genuinely for the time, appreciative of the support she was receiving.

"A lot of shit has changed," Sharice admitted. "Never thought I'd live to see this. Now that I have it, it's like was it worth it, you know."

Michelle walked over to the balcony entrance and peered through the glass on the doors.

"Come check this out real quick," she said.

Sharice made her way over and peered into the glass as well.

"Tell me what you see," Michelle continued as both women looked at the associates who attended the dinner.

"Bunch of niggas eatin' and drinkin' for free," Sharice pointed out, causing Michelle to giggle.

"Well, yeah, that too, but there's something else I see,"

she responded as she looked around. "I see a room full of ballers and gangstas that all answer to you now. Here we are with some of the biggest guys in the game, and they all are beneath your feet right now. Well, except for John, but I'm sure you can even handle him."

Sharice continued to look around the floor and realized for the first time that she was, in fact, the boss. She slowly nodded her head as she turned to her friend, smirking.

"It does feel nice being the head bitch in charge," Sharice admitted. "I guess I'm strugglin' to enjoy it after… well after Jerome's death, it's kinda hard."

"True. I get that. The thing is Jerome wanted this for you so bad. He wouldn't want you to sit here and mope on his behalf," Michelle responded, turning to her friend. "He followed you because he believed like we all did that you was the best one to lead us. John, Rico, and Mike, they cool and all, but it's an old regime that needed new blood. He believed in you, and although it's tragic and he'll most certainly be missed, this is what he wanted for you."

Michelle's mood changed for a moment as she walked back over to the edge of the balcony, followed by Sharice.

"I'm gonna be real with you, I thought about runnin'," she admitted. "When you gave the order for Theo, I thought about leavin' with him. I... I think I actually loved him, and it hurt when I couldn't save him. The only reason I didn't is that I love our thing more than anything. I remember a while back after that Dre bullshit, I said somethin' about how you gotta have somethin' else in this game, and that there has to be more than that. Truth be told, you were right. This game isn't meant for couples. At least not for us. Women don't have the luxury, and my fuck up cost James his legs."

An emotional Michelle tried to hide her face as Sharice walked over and comforted her.

"It's funny, 'cause I remember that conversation, and to be honest, I think you were the one who was right," Sharice responded, surprising Michelle. "I didn't see it until it was too late, but Rome was my heart. He made all the stress worth it, you know. I wish I could have told him that, but me and my closed-off personality had trouble with expressing my feelings and shit."

Michelle nodded her head as Sharice peeked down at

the street once more.

"Maybe one day I'll find someone who can make me feel the way Rome did," she said. "Maybe I won't take that person for granted. Don't give up hope, Chelle. These niggas drive us insane, but they are worth it. If not only just to remind us how it feels to be human."

Michelle chuckled as she wiped a few tears from her face.

"Look at us. The exact opposite of who we were that night," she said.

"Time changes all," Sharice pointed out before looking back towards the suite. "I guess I better get back in there. They are celebratin' me. The least I can do is enjoy the party. Enjoy the night, Chelle, 'cause we got a whole lot of shit to do come tomorrow."

"Yeah? What's goin' on?" Michelle inquired as Sharice gently grabbed her by her arm.

"Change, my sister. Change," she responded, smirking as she led her back into the suite.

Sharice made her way back towards her seat as John shared a look with her. She smiled, reassuring him that things are alright. Michelle took her seat next to Bull, who was interacting with several associates around him. The two friends shared a look as Sharice smiled back at her friend. Feeling like the boss for the first time, Sharice crossed her legs and leaned to the side of the chair. It was her time, and although it cost her a lot, she would make sure not to take anything for granted. The empress was finally here, and the throne was finally hers.

Check out more great Eric Nigma readings at:

www.enigmakidd.com

To submit a manuscript to be
considered, email us at
submissions@majorkeypublishing.com

Be sure to <u>LIKE</u> our Major Key
Publishing page on Facebook!